THE
CONCIERGE

CWC Collaborative Fiction Novel

Written by 19 International Authors

ISBN: 0986315915
ISBN-13: 978-0-9863159-1-6

PILOT PROJECT - THE CONCIERGE

As this is CWC's pilot project, all profits from the sales of this book will be donated to the charity IBBY. This is a wonderful organization, dedicated to providing children from all over the world access to books.

We will be donating to the specific project called the **IBBY Fund for Children in Crisis,** which provides support for children whose lives have been disrupted through war, civil disorder, or natural disaster. The two main activities that will be supported by the Fund are the therapeutic use of books and storytelling in the form of Bibliotherapy, and the creation or replacement of selected book collections appropriate to each situation.

Please see further details about this charity by accessing their website: **www.ibby.org**

ABOUT CWC

Collaborative Writing Challenge is aptly named to describe what we do. We bring aspiring writers together from all over the world to collaborate on a full-length fiction novel. We accept writers of all ages with varying degrees of experience, as we believe everyone has something to offer.

Each chapter is written by two or three different writers, and each week one is selected to form part of the ongoing novel. The experience is challenging and unique, as the writers never meet or discuss their visions for the story.

The book is guided by a story coordinator, who checks names, facts, and integrity, and who works with each chapter writer to get the best results. With ongoing help from backup writers and editors, the story has been kissed by many hands who have yet to read the completed novel.

For more information, please visit:
www.collaborativewritingchallenge.com

DEDICATION

This book is dedicated to all the writers who dared to get involved in an ambitious collaboration, with nothing more than an emailed invitation from a total stranger. They made this project successful and most importantly fun! Special thanks goes to all the volunteer editors and back up writers, to whom I am forever indebted. I of course have to mention my wonderful husband David and beautiful daughter Olivia, who watched me slave over my laptop to make this happen, and encouraged me every step of the way.

Laura Callender - CWC Founder

THE WRITERS

We had submissions from twenty six writers, nineteen of which had chapters selected for The Concierge.

Rather than fill these pages with details about our authors, all their pictures and bios can be found on the CWC Website. Please do stop by and learn more about our talented contributing authors. Some have very little writing experience, and some have reels of accomplishments under their belts. I think you would be hard-pressed to identify their individual chapters, and it's just possible that your favorite chapter could have been written by a fresh-faced, up-and-coming writer. There are certainly a few names that I will be looking out for in the future.

With this project it is inevitable that some writers will have their chapters rejected. We had some incredible submissions that we just couldn't use. These chapters were integral to shaping the story, as the variety in chapters gave me the chance to find the best fit. These writers are as much part of the team work that brought this project to completion. **Courtney Hulbert, Sarah Clachan** and **Cristel Benitez,** and those who go unnamed: Thank you for your wonderful contributions!

ACKNOWLEDGMENTS

This project has brought together so many talented people. Our cover photo was taken by **Timothy Neesam**, who captured a great shot of the Langham Hotel in Boston, USA. You can see more of his photography at GumshoePhotos.com.

I was delighted to receive offers from volunteer editors who wanted to help make this project a success. A special mention goes to one of our writers **Mandi Millen**, who not only edited eight chapters of the story, but was always on hand for guidance and advice along the way. **Sharon Flood** kindly edited a whopping thirteen chapters for us, and was always available at a moment's notice. **Bob Fisher** kindly edited five chapters for us, and **Kat Hutson** offered us her editing skills for nine chapters, and has been appointed one of CWC's Story Coordinators. **Rochelle Vaisanen, Tiffany Rias** and **Mary Restino** all did some editing along the way. Lastly, one of our contributing authors **Elaine Carnegie** offered to do a final full edit to ensure the story was consistent. Elaine has a sharp eye and was delighted to offer her help, for which I am very grateful. My biggest thanks must go to **all of our writers** who agreed to participate in this project after nothing more than an invitation email. There was no website to refer to at that early stage, and many doubted if we could actually keep the project on track. But we did, and it's thanks to you *all*.

Thank You!

A NOTE FROM THE STORY COORDINATOR

Guiding this story to completion has been hugely rewarding. Not only have I developed my own skills as a writer, but I have come to respect and appreciate everyone's individuality. Despite the variation in ages, occupations, experience, and locations of our writers, everyone still managed to find the voice of the characters. Keeping the story consistent was not as hard as I anticipated.

There were of course many challenges. We had weeks when no one submitted, and I called for backup writers to produce a chapter in under forty-eight hours. Some of the best chapters were written at these times. There were also two weeks when I just couldn't choose between two chapters, as the writers had picked up different aspects of the story. I decided to run both chapters consecutively, and they worked perfectly with very little editing.

Once we reached chapter ten, I saw a great opportunity to introduce some flash chapters. These were written in third person about each significant character. This added a lovely flow to the story and great insight into certain scenarios. That is hard to achieve when the core of the story is written in first person and centered around one character. Every chapter received a minor touch up. As the coordinator is the only person to read every full chapter, I had an insight into the story that no one else did. Changes were always received well by the writers, and the chapters went on to get edited by volunteers three more times before the book was completed.

I would say the most challenging aspect of coordinating this story was being unable to write the next chapter myself. I always imagined what would happen next, and I can honestly say that it never worked out that way. It was very humbling to accept the fact that I didn't guide or control the content of the story, but that I simply had to make the writers' visions work within the context of what had been previously written.

I wrote over 12,000 words in Chapter Summaries, which the writers used as a quick reference guide to previous chapters, and I sent over 1,000 emails throughout the duration of the project . At the end of the book I have included the three final chapter submissions that were not selected. As you will see, the standard of submissions was very high, and the slight variations in each chapter are entirely plausible even at this late stage of the story. I hope you enjoy reading this book as much as I have enjoyed bringing the story to life.

Laura Callender -
CWC Founder & Story Coordinator of The Concierge

CONTENTS

Alternate Endings:

End Note:

CHAPTER 1

I returned key number 427 to its designated silver-plated hook, and smiled knowingly as the guests picked up their bags to leave. They had been staying in that room on and off now for over two years, always requesting it far in advance of the dates they actually wanted, just to secure its availability. Truth is, it always would be. The hotel manager doted on Mr. and Mrs. Devlin and would do all that he could to ensure they remained loyal customers. As long as the Devlin's continued to stay, the hotel wouldn't have a problem maintaining their already healthy profits. It seemed unfair that I was paid minimum wage to check in these pampered socialites, knowing full well the extortionate rates they pay to stay here.

I had been welcoming them for over six months now, yet they still seemed to look at me through glass eyes. As the Concierge, I always had more interaction with the guests than reception did, but still they did not know me. I was nothing to them. As functional as a door handle, I was constantly being pushed to and fro to get them where they were going. They barely noticed anyone else, they were so wrapped up in their own lives. I can't recall them even once looking straight into my brown eyes brimming with sorrow. They never noticed my admiration for them, nor my status-less efforts to please.

They glided with grace out of the hotel doors, followed by the gazes of all those in the lobby, much as a celebrity would attract looks of curiosity and envy. It was normal for the Devlins, they were accustomed to it.

The doorman reached for the heavy maple oak doors, sparkling with Swarovski crystal. Rainbows of broken light danced around the lobby as he heaved them outwards, giving the Devlins a clear path back to their plush suburban life. I watched, lost in thoughts of what it must be like to live in such comfort. I imagined their home set on impressive grounds that offered spectacular views of rolling hills and melodic birdsong. I could almost smell the crisp fresh air, reminiscent of the most luxurious laundry detergent. How could they just spend weekends there, returning to the smog-filled city Monday to Friday? I never understood why regular guests like the Devlins didn't simply buy a second home in the city rather than fritter away millions on a hotel suite. The question haunted me, washing unsettling waves of curiosity across my mind. I wanted to delve further, to discover if there was more to life behind the façade. But I knew it was none of my business. My position at the hotel was clear, and I needed this job.

Friday had come around quickly. I was fortunate to have weekends off, which was unusual with this job. I savored those free weekends, knowing they could be taken from me at any time.

Before heading home at around six on Friday evenings, I often sat up in the staff cafeteria, hoping for the odd leftover toasted sandwich occasionally offered to famished-looking staff.

The kind-eyed, old canteen lady began to wind down her shift. It didn't look like there would be any free food today, so I sat glumly stirring my weak milk-stained coffee. I wondered why I continued to put a dollar into the hot drink machine, even though I hated the taste and failed to get any comfort from the drink it offered. In truth, it had become routine. Not just on Friday evenings but every day. That bad coffee had become one of my daily habits that helped the clock hands turn faster around the cheap watch on my wrist.

I never quite understood how I got this job. I am, of course, more than capable of checking in guests, but I don't walk around with a plum in my mouth and I don't embrace the designer culture. There was nothing about me that declared I performed the job for fun and fulfillment instead the money. I *did* need the money, but then so did most of the hotel employees. It was ironically amusing to watch those staff who embraced that arrogant attitude, knowing full well they had bills to pay when they got home just like the rest of us.

With such musings of misery and resignation dancing in my head and no real plans for the weekend, I got up and headed off home, another week under my belt.

***

I grew up in Queensbridge Houses, North America's largest communal housing project, whose residents were commonly referred to as 'city rats'. That never really bothered me. I always kept to myself, earning the nickname 'mute', which I found much kinder and manageable. I never wanted anyone to know my business and I was careful to ensure that nobody knew where I worked. You couldn't trust anyone around here, especially if they thought you had something.

I went through my daily rigmarole of scurrying off to McDonald's around the corner from the hotel, tidying myself up, changing my clothes and preparing for work. The store's deputy manager had always found me intriguing. I could tell by his blatant admiration. It seemed a joy to his day when I stepped through the doors and gave him my cutest grateful-yet-innocent smile. That would make him melt, which was hugely convenient. Not like at KFC, where the Manager forced me to change my routine after he politely asked me out for a drink, and I politely refused. From then on, the toilets were conveniently locked.

I never liked KFC anyway.

I dreaded the day when Jim, with his four shiny 'McStars', would actually approach me. He wore that name badge proudly, like an officer's insignia, paired with his goofy red hat. Maybe he never would ask me out, but if he did I might not mind so much....

I surprised myself wondering if he was a good kisser. It was the first time the thought had entered my head, and I laughed as I imagined the party in Jim's pants if he could read my mind for the slightest hint that I toyed with the idea. He definitely wasn't the most unattractive guy in the world, quite the opposite. Funny how most women wouldn't go for a guy who worked in a fast food joint, even if he was handsome. I found Jim strangely attractive, and knew that thoughts of possibly hooking up with him would linger in my mind during the coming weekend. It had been a long, long time since I had let a man into my bed, and my body was calling out for some attention.

***

The weekend went by so fast, and the week ahead was shaping up to be slightly odd. Everything I was accustomed to seemed different. The trees were turning to that beautiful auburn colour as autumn eased its way in. The park benches I walked past every day sported a fresh coat of green paint. To another set of eyes, they might look the same, but I picked up on the subtle shade change. It made me wonder if it was either an error that would go unnoticed in the grand scheme of things, or the result of a conscious effort to brighten up the area as the season changed. I walked past the phone booth and slowed, watching a young European-looking guy with strong arms squeegee the inside of the booth clean. I didn't actually know that someone was responsible for cleaning phone booths. *Why had I never noticed that?*

My reverie was broken by the chiming of a wall clock as it struck the hour. 7am? That was wrong - it was clearly 8am. "Shit," I exclaimed, surprising the guy in the booth. I smiled a coy apology then hurried towards the hotel.

"You're a bit early today." Joy giggled at me as I hung my jacket on the coat stand.

"I just realized that I forgot to change the clocks last night. What an idiot, huh?"

"Don't worry, Clarissa. It happens to the best of us," Joy proclaimed Joy-fully. She certainly lived up to the proud name her mother had given her. I often wondered what my mother would have called me had she actually wanted a daughter.

As I started to arrange my paperwork for the day, the doors flew open and in strode Mr. and Mrs. Devlin. They were an hour earlier than their usual check-in time, which was bizarre considering I shouldn't have even been there. Then I noticed it. A stylish shimmering metal suitcase handcuffed to Mr. Devlin's wrist. It was brand new and larger than the normal one he usually brought in without attention. No such discretion today. It looked somehow weighty and fierce, commanding inquisitive gazes from everyone else nearby.

I stood tall and poised, ready to greet our guests and help with their check-in, but was sharply cut off at the last moment by Mr. Watts. We rarely saw the grandson of Lord Watts II; founder of the Watts Regency, now one of the most prestigious and abiding hotels close to the heart of Manhattan's wealthy. Sweeping me aside, he effusively greeted the Devlins like old friends, quickly marching them off away from the prying eyes in the lobby.

Joy and I exchanged bewildered glances. We saw a lot from our front row seat at the concierge desk, but were never privy to the meaning behind what we saw.

There was a very clearly-defined hierarchy among hotel staff. Everyone knew their place. I was disappointed when I found out that even the cleaners ranked higher than the Concierge on the need-to-know gossip scale. After all, one of the perks of a low-paid hotel job was access to the delicious, juicy scandals played out inside the rooms. Gossip was the life and soul of this place. Without it, the industry would die. No one would put up with all the stress, unsocial hours and poor pay. It was certainly part of why I had done all I could to get this job, but it wasn't the only reason.

CHAPTER 2

My fingers picked unconsciously at the edge of the thick, sticky band-aid on my palm. A remnant of the night before, when I had clumsily cut myself picking up large pieces of broken glass off the floor. I had returned home, determined to change every single clock in the house. That wasn't difficult, considering there were only three including my alarm clock, but the one in the kitchen proved to be tricky. As I was removing it from the wall, my elbow touched a cheap, dusty glass vase on the adjacent shelf. I had felt the light contact, but made no effort to save it from the crashing fall. It had happened too quickly.

"Daydreaming again?" Joy nudged me playfully out of my memories, bringing me back to the present.

"A girl can always dream, right?" I raised my hands in defense. It had been a surprisingly slow Tuesday morning, nobody around to interrupt our own entertainment of short jokes and casual banter.

"Hey, what happened to your hand?" Joy flinched, as if a glass shard had just driven through her own hand.

"Just a small cut."

"Does it hurt?"

"It's nothing, really. I was…"

My story was interrupted by the hurried steps of a man who appeared through the large elevator a few feet away. His forehead was covered in a thin layer of sweat. His eyebrows pressed tightly together in a fearsome arc, while his clenched mouth revealed tension almost equal to that of his clenched fists. A copy of The Times was tightly locked in his armpit. The man was heading straight towards us. For a frightening moment I thought my days at the hotel were over, because that man was Mr. Watts.

For the first time in my six months at the Regency, Mr. Watts asked, or rather ordered, me to inform him of Mr. and Mrs. Devlin's arrival that afternoon. The urgency in his voice made those in the lobby turn to look at him, despite his effort to keep the matter between us.

He told me that I was not to waste a second on anything other than to pick up the phone from the desk and call him the very moment the Devlins crossed those heavy hotel doors. It was imperative that I did as I was told. My job depended on it. Mr. Watts' forefinger jumped from the heavy door to our desk phone in between sentences. I mostly nodded and tried to assure him that I understood. There was no way the Devlins would come in without my employer being the first to know. Joy appeared to be excluded from that duty.

We watched Mr. Watts walk away and he seemed more concerned than he had been when he first approached us.

"It is imperative," Joy whispered in a failed, perhaps on purpose, effort to imitate him, then giggled as she returned to sorting the spare keys. It was that moment that I realized I had been holding my breath throughout his speech. Not wanting my

20

colleague to notice, I exhaled as quietly as possible.

A short while later I resumed my story, explaining to Joy that my only concern about my cut was how visible the band-aid was. I didn't want any of the guests to notice it, and I thankfully had the insight to keep my hands hidden in Mr. Watts' presence. It didn't look professional. After a few Joy-full remarks, she suggested I look for a pair of old bellhop gloves in the small staff storeroom. They kept all kinds of things there. I followed her advice only after having made sure, by making her swear, promise, and repeat after me, that she would contact me right away at the mere glimpse of the Devlins entering the hotel.

Several hours later, wearing a pair of simple yet matching gloves I had found tossed over a storage box, I wondered whether I had missed the Devlins after all. There had been no sign of them. Joy had knocked on their door a number of times to make sure, and I often turned to look at their unclaimed key, as if thinking about them would make them magically appear before me. But key 427 remained abandoned on its hook until the end of my shift.

They were only supposed to be away for a few hours. I hoped that their unexplained change of plans would not cost me my job. After a few deep breaths and several quick glances at my watch, I decided it was time to call Mr. Watts. Talking to him was a lot easier than I thought it would be. He accepted, sounding a million times calmer than the last time we had spoken, that the Devlins has not returned since their last check-in earlier that morning. I hung up the phone, relieved.

***

Our missing guests had consumed my mind so intensely that I reached McDonald's without realizing it. Suddenly, I found myself fueled by the need to see a familiar face in the crowded restaurant. My eyes sought out Jim, only to fall upon hungry strangers. Even the regular employees didn't look the same. On my way to the toilets I stopped to observe a sluggish cleaner in light blue gloves, presumably near retirement age with a flushed face. He was picking up a crushed, half-eaten burger from the floor before slam-dunking it into a plastic trash bag. I turned my head away, coming face to face with a one of those new McDonalds' posters that depicted a teenager, mouth stuffed with fries, and two giant double-decker burgers with photoshopped oozing cheese flying in opposite directions over his head. He was loving it.

I walked out of McDonald's with the gloves I had been wearing all day still in my hands. They were purple and worn out, with Lord Watts' age-faded gold crest embroidered under stains that I would deal with later at home. With a thumb tracing the delicate crest and my head lowered toward them, I tried to imagine what they might have looked like decades ago. I wondered about the history of all those who had worn them before me.

"Shame I didn't catch you while you still had them on. I bet they look good on you." Jim's voice startled me, and I dropped a glove. He immediately recovered it, dusting it with his fingers, then offered it to me with both hands and a smile of which I never thought he was capable. His attention to an old glove impressed me, and I wondered if his dates received equal care. I couldn't think of anything to say.

"Have a nice evening," he said. He gave a small, departing nod, the smile never fading from his face. When I finally opened my mouth to speak it was too late for him to hear me. He was already gone. Frustrated, I shoved the cursed pair of gloves in my handbag and headed home.

***

Autumn slowly descended upon New York, the pale blue

sky above me minutes away from fading to the dark of night. The neighbourhood lamp posts were already lit, a small group of kids taking advantage of the yellow light with a game of basketball on a nearby court. Not very far from them another teenager attempted to train his Pit Bull mix to attack, waving his lifted arm and calling after the dog with no apparent immediate success. I greeted the boy's mother Suzan as I passed them, who sat smoking on the grass.

I didn't know if I was coming down with something or if the cooling breeze was to blame, but on the way to my building sudden fatigue washed over me. My shoulders felt stone-heavy, invisible nails pricked my feet in my shoes, and the memory of the sandwich I had been lucky enough to eat at the staff cafeteria sparked waves of indigestion. Simple actions such as lifting my arms or going through my bag for my keys required effort, and I realized I had to nip whatever it was in the bud. I was not going to let anything stop me from going to work the next day.

When Queensbridge first opened in 1939, the elevators only stopped on the first, third and fifth floors, the product of a tight construction budget. I lived in a sixth-floor apartment, a floor with no elevator access. So I took the elevator up to the fifth, then climbed the stairs to my apartment. Every single day.

I was on my second cup of instant chicken and vegetable soup when the there was a knock on the door. It was rare for a visitor at my door, let alone at night. I decided to let it ring for a while, hoping whoever it was would go away. Trouble in this building all too often enough began with a knock on the door. Not that long ago, a neighbor on the fifth floor had been attacked in the middle of the night by her ex boyfriend in her own apartment, and I remembered it quite distinctly now.

The knocking didn't stop.

I glanced through the peephole for a few seconds and

opened the door to Suzan on the other side. She lived with her son and their mutt dog in the apartment next door, and were generally quiet people who neither snooped nor caused any trouble.

It was one of those times when I felt relieved for having eventually changed my mind. Suzan had only visited to explain some minor public works scheduled in the area the next day, and that we were not going to have any access to water from as early as six am. She also thought I looked a little bit pale, but admitted her vision was not what it used to be. I thought it a bit strange that she would knock so incessantly just for this, but I supposed a mother's protectiveness sometimes extended to neighbors.

The conversation could have ended nicely right then, had I not been so tired and clumsy. In one effortless sweep, I knocked my handbag off the side unit by the door with my elbow. Next to my keys, cell phone, and a bunch of random things now scattered on the floor lay one of the hotel gloves. Suzan's gaze lingered on the glove, but I pretended not to notice. I bent down to replace my bag's contents with moderate haste, playfully blaming myself for being so awkward. I thanked her for her consideration and wished her goodnight.

***

As a child, I didn't always get along with my therapists. At times I thought that I was sent to those hourly sessions only to be reminded of how terrible my life was instead of actually being offered support. I didn't like any of them. One in particular was harder to fool than the others. I only remembered him as 'Theo the therapist'. He was tall, wore black-rimmed glasses that contrasted his striking paleness, with traces of a receding hairline and the prevailing scent of nutmeg.

A framed photo of Theo's family faced me in his office. I never understood why doctors faced their family photos toward their patients instead of themselves. His son seemed about my age, his little girl a bit younger. He and his wife stood behind their children, all of them smiling at the camera. A large, bronze-coloured dog sat proudly between them. Labrador? Golden Retriever? I was never good at dog breeds.

"We have a dog like this one too," I had said. "We call him Waffles. Mom lets me take him out for a walk when I'm done with my homework. He's too big for me, but my arms are stronger now that I play basketball. Dad's taught me how to shoot free throws without missing much. Dad was captain of the basketball team in high school…" I kept blabbing, but Theo wasn't taking his usual notes. I sat across him in my dirty grey sweat pants and worn out pink Hello Kitty hoodie.

"Is that so?" Theo interrupted, offering caramel candy from a bowl placed next to the framed photo. I shook my head. I liked caramel as much as I liked him. "And what does your Mom do?" he asked with a smirk. I frowned and stared angrily up at him. The large chair was made for adults, not children, and my dangling legs made me feel even smaller than I already was. "It's okay, Clarissa. You don't have to lie to me. I'm here for you."

This time I pursed my mouth and wiggled the arm of a Mike Wazowski wind-up toy, found in one of the few McDonald's Happy Meals that I ever got, that rested in my lap. I always hoped for a James P. Sullivan instead, but was never that lucky.

"Do you sleep well now?" Theo asked. I nodded, never taking my eyes off Mike.

Outside we could hear two boys playing with one of the year's last remaining pile of autumn leaves. When a woman called after them I turned my head to the window, and so did Theo. We watched all three of them laugh in the distance and get into a parked car a few feet away to disappear moments later.

Theo turned back to me, about to ask another one of his silly questions, but then decided against it. We were left looking at each other in the silence. The only sound in the room came from a shiny, clicking Newton's Cradle. I thought those only kept going in the movies.

Theo asked me if I liked basketball, swimming, or dogs. Then he asked me to write an essay about my imaginary parents that I was to bring over the next time I came. It didn't matter which version, whether it was the busy, athletic ones or the lazy and sloppy ones, as long as I'd write it down. When he took a glimpse of his watch I thought our time was up for the day, but I was wrong. He continued with more questions, such as what was it that made me happy, or brought me joy, or what my favourite color was. Once he finally ran out of questions, I returned to winding up my One-Eyed Mike, who waved at me loudly, blinking and showing me his sharp teeth.

"I hate cars. I don't ever want to learn to drive," I blurted, and placed a sitting Mike on the desk next to the family photo.

'Why is that, Clarissa?' Theo at least sounded concerned.

"Cars take people away," I whispered.

Theo told me that a very nice couple was about to adopt me. He had talked with them, he said, just like he and I were talking, like friends. He was certain that they were going to give me the family I had always wanted. They couldn't have a little girl like me of their own, they wanted an older child so they wouldn't have to drop the adoption bombshell later on. That made me an easier choice. Theo told me that they'd taken one look at my picture and they'd said 'This is the girl!' He reassured me that this time would be different, that these people were loving and kind, and everything was going to be all right again.

CHAPTER 3

I woke to a throbbing head. The layer of dampness against my warm skin was the first indication that I could no longer ignore the impending illness. I rose out of bed and headed straight to the kitchen, my hot and suddenly clammy body desperate for a chilled glass of water. I opened the fridge and took out the jug sitting alone in the door, a reminder that I really should buy more groceries. Gulping straight from the jug, razor blade pains slashed my throat as I swallowed. Each sip made me grimace, but I knew I was dehydrated.

I stared out of the kitchen window, leaning on the bench top to support my weakened frame. The changing autumn leaves on the trees below were battered by a morning breeze. "I can do this," I declared. "I can't let Mr. Watts down."

I flicked on the small retro kitchen radio and caught The Dana & Jayson breakfast show. It always provided me with a little motivation, with the quick quips and banter. I rubbed my eyes and daydreamed of a steaming cup of coffee with a warm, sweet cinnamon roll, wishing I could eat it in bed before rolling over to shut the world out for a day. I reluctantly made my way down the hall to the bathroom in a haze, shivering. It was colder than normal this morning.

Remembering that we had no water today, I did not relish the prospect of going unwashed until I got to work, I would have to form my own secret operation just to get to a vacant room. Just to satisfy my agitation, I turned on the shower faucet to check. There was water, but it trickled lightly to a stop.

"Fantastic. Just what I need." These things always happened at the worst times. I felt weak, wanted so badly to feel hot water soothing my aching muscles. A shower at work was now my best option. If I got caught, I knew what would happen. Marie had frequently done the same thing. It was easy for her as a maid, but even then she got caught. She had said she never had time at home with seven kids running around, but I heard Mr. Watts took no pity. It wasn't just about sticking to the rules. I think he looked down on her, despised the life of those without. Clearly he had been groomed that way, but that didn't make it right.

I made my way out of the building a little earlier than normal. The leaves from the park across the road soared through the air in the autumn breeze. Crisp and cold, it was my least favorite season by far. Autumn held nothing but the promise of impending cold and wet disruption, although the season was great at the hotel. Even with all his upper class prejudices, Mr. Watts said nothing about the kids running in, shouting 'trick or treat'. Joy told me that he saw how it charmed the guests, and made sure we had candy on every desk. I couldn't wait to see it for myself. I already put my name down to work on Halloween.

Departing 21st Street-Queens-bridge westbound, the train entered the 63rd Street tunnel, it's majestic high arch ceiling that covers both tracks was something that always surprised me. The

6:35 to Penn Station was unusually quiet that morning, so finding a seat was not a problem. I allowed myself a moment of time this morning to enjoy the ride to work, to watch people and imagine their lives. It was one of my favorite things to do.

The train stopped at Roosevelt Island and a very well-dressed woman stepped aboard, followed by what might have been her boyfriend. They were quietly bickering. She had vibrant red hair and porcelain skin, beautiful in her agitation. They sat across from me, and I tried to listen in without staring. I was secretly glad to never have had a spat on the subway, especially at the start of the day. I imagined how the rest of their day would pan out, and where those beautiful Louboutins would take the woman.

Looking down at my own worn, red pumps, I had to stop thinking about the woman's life. No, my life wasn't perfect, but I had done pretty well in finding gratitude in unlikely places. Getting lost in thoughts of what I didn't have had never helped me before. I remembered one of my childhood therapists telling me that I had incredible resolve for someone who had been through so much. I didn't really know what she meant then. But now, as my life had slowly improved, I could appreciate what she had seen in me then.

I left the subway, pushing myself through the haze of sick I actually felt, and turned the corner to McDonald's. I caught a glimpse of Jim just as he entered ahead of me. His shifts seemed to more frequently match the times I walked past the place. I considered testing that theory, maybe swap a few hours around, but I liked the hours I worked. Heaving the door open I was hit with a warm blast, burning my cheeks after the bite of cold. I unraveled the scarf wrapped tightly around my neck.

I went to the bathroom to change, and came out to see Jim in the distance, waiting next to a table with two cups of steaming coffee and a charming smile. I could have considered this an improvement. Maybe a date wasn't so far off. I realized I actually looked forward to the stolen glances, and to each smile that felt like it was served just for me. Every time I saw that smile, it brought up things I hadn't felt in a long time, some things I didn't entirely recognize. It was strange not to worry about Jim eventually asking me out. Then I decided that this time, if he asked, I would say yes.

A group of young girls plowed past me. I overheard one of them say. "O.M.G. He is delicious." I glanced at them, and followed their hungry gazes. "He looks a bit like that guy from Spider Man. But hunkier," added another. I smiled at their comparison. I hadn't thought of that myself, but they were right. Forcing myself to keep moving, I enjoyed thinking about Jim, I took a minute to watch him from behind the corner of the bathroom hallway. Seeing him made my stomach flutter, his short salt and pepper hair and neatly trimmed beard. His tall, 6ft 2 slender, muscular frame was quite imposing. He wasn't typically Jewish, or at least not how you may imagine a Jewish man. He was more rogue, leading me to wonder about his family. He was definitely over six feet, muscularly trim in a way that I thought may have intimidated other people. But he had a way of carrying himself not with threatening power, but a calm, gentle awareness that made me think he was used to being alone, that he could make his own way anywhere. Though we'd never gotten very close, I never smelled the stink of fry grease on him. He always managed to smell clean.

I finally reached him at the table and had to apologize. I didn't have the time to join him for a coffee. I thought it better not to add that I needed to squeeze in a shower before my shift started, and try to shake off the bug that threatened my health.

His smile faded, like he had just taken the wrong turn on

the highway and was trapped on a long, lonely road. He was obviously disappointed, and while I felt badly about it, I was surprised to find it pleased me. It was exactly what I needed to see, the way he looked at me. He really *did* want to spend more time with me.

"I'll see you later, then," he said, and his smile returned. He caught my eyes with his own, and I felt suddenly like he could see something inside me I didn't know was there. I walked to the door and turned to offer him an encouraging smile. I hoped with all my heart that this wasn't his last try.

Jim had said nothing about the way I looked, but I knew I definitely wasn't at my best. Joy, on the other hand, had no problem pointing it out.

"What a vision," she teased. I rolled my eyes in response. "And how come you're in early again?"

"Don't get mad at me, but I'm going to take a shower in one of the vacant rooms." Joy's skepticism fueled her frown. "Hey, my water was turned off this morning, and, well, look at me. If I ever needed a hot shower, it's today." Joy didn't even have to say she did not approve, but it's not like she was going to stop me. I needed a shower and this was my only option.

She mumbled and grabbed the key to room 426, handing it to me. "Here, this room is out of action, so you're less likely to get caught. Just pick up after yourself, please." She glanced sideways to make sure nobody was watching. "And don't let any of the maids see you, for the love of God." She inched in closer. "You know those girls can talk." Then her cheery grin returned, and she went back to work.

I rolled the key discreetly around the palm of my hand. In the six months I had been there, I had never noticed which rooms weren't frequently used. That was definitely a mistake. If this morning ever repeated itself, and I had to do this again, I didn't

31

want Joy to know about it so I would need to be better prepared. If my foggy head cleared at all, I would check the occupancy of other rooms on that floor and make a backup plan for the future. But for now, my mission was assigned, and time was against me.

I returned to the reception desk a minute before 8am. The usual morning freshening up of the lobby was in full action. The day-old flowers were changed, the floor was buffed to a shine, and the receptionists were frantically getting their paperwork in order for the rush of the 10 o'clock check out.

As we looked over the list of tasks for the day, I felt like I was being watched. The strong scent of Old Spice almost made me choke as somebody approached. Joy must have caught it too, because we glanced at each other with questioning frowns before turning around. Standing tall, with the day's issue of the Times locked tightly under his right arm, stood Mr. Watts.

"They still haven't returned," he said without hesitation, the creases in his brow causing the rim of sweat to ripple down his face. "Your duties, as instructed yesterday, are to resume. Are we clear?" His voice was flat and monotone, which I'd come to learn meant things were serious.

He walked away, and I let out my breath. *I have to learn to relax around him*, I lectured myself. The pounding in my head was only intensified with now anticipating the Devlin's arrival. I was suddenly light-headed and grabbed the corner of the desk. "I can do this," I whispered.

Joy glanced over at me with a frown, then pressed her lips together. "I'm going to check the luggage room to see if anything needs delivering." I nodded and took a few deep breaths.

As I composed myself, someone else approached the desk. "Key 427," she whispered. I looked up but couldn't meet her gaze. She was glancing in all directions, searching for someone or something that I couldn't see. "I'm sorry, ma'am, but that room is currently occupied..." Then I realized that it was Mrs. Devlin standing before me. Her usual silk shirts and patent leather heels were replaced by sweats and joggers. Not once had I ever seen Mrs. Devlin dressed this way. I wasn't even sure if she *did* exercise. She had pulled her bobbed hair back into a tight ponytail, covered by a baseball hat drawn low on her face.

"Key, please." The politeness of the words was delivered through gritted teeth. Without hesitation I handed her the key.

"Do you need..." Before I could offer assistance she scurried past the reception desk and stood in front of the elevator. She impatiently stabbed at the button, sneaking glances around her. When an elevator opened, she almost threw herself inside it and punched the buttons until the doors closed.

I picked up the phone to call Mr. Watts, then thought that maybe it was best to deliver the news in person. I looked sideways to see if anyone had noted the exchange. There were no other guests, and the other employees seemed preoccupied in their own roles. I set the phone down and approached the elevators.

Mr. Watts' office, along with his private meeting rooms, took up the entire second floor. I had only been to the second floor a handful of times, and I didn't know if I had the energy for this. There was a good chance that he would notice I was sick and question why I was there. But I had no other choice. I had to deliver the news that Mrs. Devlin had arrived, alone, and not presented in her usual manner. It was my job.

I stepped into the elevator and pressed button two, leaning against the wall for support. I would need all the energy I could muster. I imagined that Mrs. Devlin looked on the outside exactly how I felt.

CHAPTER 4

My heartbeat rose with the elevator. Was it the illness desperate to ruin my day, or the bizarre thing I'd just seen? I took a moment to steel myself for the upcoming confrontation. Resting my head against the cool metal side of the elevator alleviated the throbbing somewhat, but did nothing to reduce the anxiety. I moaned that it was all too short a trip to the second floor as the chime sounded and the doors slid open. As I stepped out and looked around I was instantly reminded of my other trips to this floor. The place was no less strange this time. It was easy to forget this floor was in a hotel. Open rooms sat next to open offices, across from closed doors and closed offices with large glass panels like board rooms. The corridor stretched both ways but Mr. Watts' office was at the end on the right.

I walked along the corridor, more surprised by the quiet, deserted space than the design of the second floor. Mr. Watts was the only one ever here. Innocent or not, something about this level always made me feel uneasy. That discomfort did not mix well with my rising temperature, sore throat and headache.

34

His office was the last on the right. I was suddenly snapped out of my illness-induced, foggy observations by a sharp voice, a voice trying simultaneously to be quiet and forceful. A voice which could only belong to one man. I stopped a few feet before the open door of his office, hoping that his conversation had masked my approach. Curiosity overtook me, and I concentrated on picking out his words. If nothing else, I might have something interesting to tease Joy with later. I tried to stop myself shaking as I leaned against the wall and tuned in.

"You say that, but I'm hearing a lot of words and no action…No! I want results not excuses, goddammit. He's not bloody Houdini. He's Mr. Devlin, you understand? *The* Mr. Devlin…yes I'm fully aware, but you let me know the instant- Yes…yes that's right. I hope so too."

The conversation ended there. More intrigued than ever, I pushed myself off the wall, still all too aware of how weak I was. I made sure to make a bit of noise as I walked the final distance to his office. I didn't want to surprise him, and I didn't want him to think I had actually heard anything. I turned through the doorway, anticipation raising my pulse as I saw the beleaguered Mr. Watts. Though his office was small compared to the meeting rooms on this floor, it was certainly more impressive. What it lacked in size it made up for in lavishness. No wall was without artwork, so outlandishly abstract that it may as well have been a picture of printed money framed in gold. I'd never held much fascination with art like childhood finger-paintings, and knowing they sold for hundreds of thousands made me feel like I missed the joke somewhere. In the far corner stood a grotesque African statue, and even that could not completely take my attention from the state of Mr. Watts.

As if in some sort of dream he stared at absolutely nothing, seated behind his beautiful oak desk in his high back leather chair. He hadn't seemed to register that I was standing in front of him. He looked pale, drawn and disheveled which, while worrisome, instantly made me feel better about myself. With all the confidence of catching someone in an awkward moment, I leaned back and knocked on the already open door. His trance broke in an instant, and he regarded me with the cold revulsion to which I had become so accustomed. Despite his sweating brow, he now sat there every inch the son of Lord Watts.

"Clarissa."

The venom with which he spat my name sent a cold chill down my spine. I suddenly felt like I was under a microscope, forced against a wall with no escape. Mr. Watts used this advantage, rising from the chair and moving around the desk to stand less than a foot away from me. He turned his nose up and looked down on me with disdain, maybe even loathing, in his eyes. His calm and controlled voice was so different from what I'd overheard, and it frightened me.

"What is it that makes you think you can waltz into my office without an appointment? Look at the state of you. If I'd been with a client I would not suffer this embarrassment."

"Mr. Watts, I –"

He held up his hand to cut me off, and took a good few seconds to let his eyes wander all over my haggard appearance. I knew what it felt like to have someone undress my body with their eyes, but this felt like his were tearing down the wall around my mind. The scent of Old Spice now made my head spin.

"I'm not a very hopeful man, Clarissa. I'm a realistic man, but in your case, I'm going to make an exception. I'm going to hope that you took the stairs to get here, and that you are remarkably out of shape. I see no other explanation for your... clammy appearance. Your hair is mildly wet, too. Rest assured I will be making inquiries. If I discover that you are here, sick, infecting my patrons, or that you are abusing the use of my hotel rooms…well. Then it is you who will need to hope."

I silently cursed the fact I hadn't had more time with the hotel hairdryer, but I couldn't think of much else besides what Mr. Watts' had just said. Now I was sick, wet, nervous, *and* terrified.

"Please, Mr. Watts. I…I know I should have called ahead, but I wanted to let you know in person. It's the Devlins. You said to tell you immediately so I raced here and…"

His hands came in a blur and he gripped my shoulders so tightly that I would have screamed had I not been shocked into silence.

"What about them? When did you see them? Are they back in 427?"

His eyes were wide and desperate, and I could not tell if it was fear or something else completely. I tried not to let the pressure on my shoulders freeze me up, but I already felt ready to collapse. Then the words flew out of my mouth with almost unintelligible speed, recounting Mrs. Devlin's entrance, her physical appearance, and her request for the room key. His fingers tightened on me more than I thought possible.

"And you told no one else of this and came straight here? Were either of you seen?"

"N-No. Joy was in the luggage room. I was the only one at the desk, and then I came straight here. Mr. Watts, I was trying to do the right thing."

He looked at his hands as if just noticing where they were, and jerked them back in disgust. "Good…good…" he muttered. His eyes wandered for a moment, gazing right through me like he'd forgotten I was still there. Then those desperate eyes locked onto me, narrowed, and fear stabbed through me like a knife.

His entire character changed, and he whispered to me in a calm and composed voice. "You did do the right thing, Clarissa. It's very important that no one else knows about this. Not Joy, not anyone. You don't speak ever about what you saw, understand? I want you to stay here until I get back. I'm going to deal with this…"

He turned to leave through the door, then stopped as he remembered something and turned back to me. His eyes had narrowed to slits now, the all-too-familiar cold derision back in his voice.

"Don't even think about touching anything. I won't be long."

With that he turned and left. I had been holding my breath again, and it rushed out as his footsteps echoed down the corridor. I thought I might have been holding it since the moment he rose from that chair. Then the shock wore off, and the pain in my head and throat, in my entire body, reminded me forcefully that they weren't going anywhere soon. I made a plan to go to the drug store after work. I couldn't continue on like this. I sagged against the back wall, careful to avoid the paint factory explosion that was the art piece hanging there.

Finally feeling calm again, I thought about just what exactly had happened, and recognized the amazing opportunity staring me in the face. I was in Mr. Watts' office, without Mr. Watts. I wondered if any employee in the history of this hotel had ever been where I was now. And somehow, curiosity overtook my fading fear. It couldn't hurt to look for clues as to just what on earth was going on.

I walked behind the desk and sat in the chair, marveling at both how comfortable the chair was and how good it felt to sit down. I gave a loud sigh and relaxed into what may have been the most comfortable chair ever. And it was a damn office chair.

I knew I didn't have a lot of time, so I glanced over the polished, well-maintained oak desk, void of anything interesting. There was a small paperweight with no paper to hold down, an inactive and currently redundant desk lamp, and a computer screen with mouse and keyboard. I moved the mouse and the screen flickered to life with a box asking for a password. That was a long shot.

Then I saw the two side drawers on the left. I pulled open the top one. Empty. This was ridiculous. No bottle of alcohol, no chocolate, no gun. Just an empty drawer and a severe lack of information. Closing it, I tried to open the second only to find it jammed. No, not jammed. Locked. There was a tiny keyhole on the side. I smiled despite my headache. Nobody locked an empty drawer; there had to be something in there. Then I heard the footsteps.

I leapt out of the chair, shoved it back into position, and thanked God the computer screen had turned off again. The footsteps were heavy and hurried, typical of a man constantly announcing his presence. Typical of Mr. Watts. He burst through the door in a state of greater disarray than when he left, strode to his desk, then turned and looked at me as if he had no idea why I was there. Any color his face might have had was completely gone now, and the sweat had worked its way well into his collar.

His cologne, though never pleasant, was now blended with sweat and maybe perfume, something sickly sweet that almost made me gag. As I watched the sweat running down his face, I noticed that one side of his face was unusually red, and on his neck were what looked like scratches. Three distinct red lines were etched there, and I did my best to hide my surprise.

Clearly the meeting with Mrs. Devlin had not gone as planned. His eyes followed mine and his hand jumped up to cover his neck.

"Clarissa! What in the hell are you still doing here? Go

home, you're done for the day. Go see a doctor or rest or something. I'll see you tomorrow. And your future depends on keeping this meeting to yourself. Are we clear?"

  Unsure if he was talking about my job, my life, or both, I quickly left without another word. My head was spinning from both the literal pressure and the unexpected aggression. I almost ran to the elevator, punching at the call button suddenly understanding why Mrs. Devlin had done the same. When the elevator arrived I stepped in and pressed for the Lobby. I leaned my head against the cool metal wall and tried to catch my breath. I now had the day off, and no idea how I was going to spend it.

CHAPTER 5

I paid no attention to the curious glances from the doorman as I made my way out of the revolving exit, on my way to the station to catch the train back home. It was already made clear to me that I looked a mess, and thanks to Mr. Watts, I could actually head home and give myself some much needed TLC.

Who cares what the staff think! I thought to myself, *Let them wonder why I'm being sent home!* I bet inwardly that they wondered why they didn't get to go home early themselves. I hoped they didn't think it was favoritism, as that would be far from the truth. After today, I felt lucky to just be leaving early, rather than permanently.

I made my pit stop at McDonalds, and couldn't help but think of Jim, and the way he flirted with me this morning. I usually headed straight to the bathroom with my eyes fixed to the floor, but I found myself searching Jim out, to see if he was still working. I couldn't see him, and I didn't dare ask if he were around. I did see the manager, though. He and Jim appeared to have a good relationship from the little I could see, but when he was there, I got a sense that he just tolerated my frequent visits. I wonder if Jim had something to do with that. I was really over the customary cheeseburger purchase, to justify using the facilities. I certainly didn't want that now, I was craving hearty home-cooked food. Times like today, I wished I had a family to go home to.

I didn't have to fight to get a seat on the train; traveling in the early afternoon was so refreshing. I heaved a heavy sigh of relief and closed my eyes, leaning my head back against the seat. I tried to relax but my mind was racing from another crazy morning at work, and the unusual meeting with Mr. Watts.

At each stop, a blast of cold air came through the doors from inside the tunnel, and kept me from getting too comfortable.

"Well, well, look who's here!" The familiar voice rebounded off the train walls and startled me.

Looking up, I saw Jim, standing over me with a broad grin.

"Oh, hi," I smirked "Are you stalking me or something?" I spat the words out in jest before I realized how it sounded. Jim's smile softened slightly.

"Of course not ma'am, I always get this train, so that begs the question, are you stalking me?"

"Maybe," I joked.

Jim sat down in the chair opposite and stretched out his long legs, crossing them at the ankles, clearly very relaxed. "Actually, I don't normally take the train at all. My car broke down yesterday just a block away from my apartment, so I had to brave the subway. I can't believe I bumped into you. How about that! Where do you get off?"

"Oh, erm, I get off at Queensbridge," I mumbled, toying with my scarf trim. I was embarrassed about where I lived. "Anyway, how are you?" I quickly added, hoping to divert the inevitable conversation.

"I'm great, but if you don't mind me saying, you look like hell. Are you all right?" Jim furrowed his brows in concern and leaned forward, stilling my restless fingers with his hand.

I wished I could just rest my aching head on his strong shoulder and tell him all about my day! I would tell him all about the weird actions of Mr. Watts, and speculate with him why Mrs. Devlin came in all disheveled. I would tell him about Mr. Watts' secrecy and about those strange scratches on his neck, and I would ask him what the hell he thought could be in that silver suitcase chained to Mr. Watts' wrist. I was dying to spill my guts to someone! Sensing my restless mind working in par with my fingers, Jim said "It's ok, you don't look that bad, still beautiful."

My eyes met his and I think he saw my best smile to date. He caught me off guard and it felt nice. Knowing I couldn't say anything about work, I gave Jim a half-lie.

"I had a rough day at work, and I'm fighting off a cold, so the boss sent me home early. I think I just need a good sleep and I should be back to my normal self."

Looking even more concerned, Jim sat back in his chair and sighed. I could smell the faint memory of greasy fried food lingering on his work clothes, masked by a sexy masculine scent. He wore a very nice black fall jacket, the kind of jacket that convinced me that Jim didn't live in Queensbridge Houses. Before I knew it, my stop was coming up.

"Soooo," I said a little shyly. "This is my stop."

Jim looked amused, then added, "Mine too."

He caught my surprise that he lived somewhere near me. "Don't tell me you're my neighbour too?"

"Actually I live over on 35th Ave. In Astoria. It's a bit of a walk, but I rarely have to do it. I just hope my car gets fixed today." I was relieved and intrigued. It was nice to know Jim was nearby. He made me feel safe. I could feel those dormant butterflies awakening in my stomach.

As we got off the train, Jim turned to me, and looked deep into my eyes before speaking.

"Are you sure you're alright?" he asked, with genuine concern.

"Yes, I-I think so," I answered shyly, before a bout of coughing cut off my words. Struggling to breathe, let alone speak, Jim whipped a tissue out of his pocket.

He keeps tissues in his pocket? I found myself even more intrigued to know him better. I quickly took the tissue and wiped my nose with it before putting it in a nearby trash can.

Suddenly realizing that Jim was reaching for my hand, and not knowing how else to respond, I let him take my small hand in his slightly larger one.

"Look, Clarissa, I'm not dumb. You look sick, yes.....but even more so, you look like someone who is carrying the weight of the world on your shoulders. You can talk to me you know, but seeing as I'm a gentleman, I'm going to pretend that I'm not bothered by it, and just say that I hope you feel better soon, and please get some rest. And....Oh, before I forget." Jim fished in his pocket again and came up with a little piece of paper. "Here's my number," he handed me the note.

"I meant to give it to you this morning, but you seemed in such a rush that I didn't get the chance."

Stunned, I studied the numbers on the piece of paper, and felt myself blushing an even deeper red than my already cold cheeks were. I looked back up at Jim.

"I was hoping, that…when you feel better of course….we could…." Jim all of a sudden looked away from me, down at the sidewalk, as if asking it for help to form his words.

I recognized that Jim had been trying to ask me out for

44

ages, and I knew I needed to encourage him. "I would love to go on a date with you, Jim," I said, surprising both of us.

Jim looked at me, searching for the truth in my words. Satisfied I was sincere, his smile grew so big it seemed to take over his handsome face.

"You would?" Jim asked, and I couldn't stop a little giggle from escaping my lips as I noticed how boyish he looked in this second.

"Truth is, Jim, I was kind of hoping you would ask me."

"You were?" Jim said. "Oh, Clarissa, if I had known, I would have asked sooner! It's just…I have been turned down before, and I didn't want it to happen that way this time, because I really want to go on a date with you."

"I would like that too, Jim." I hugged my coat a little closer as a chilly breeze suddenly kicked up, reminding me I was still sick and needed to be inside.

"Oh, you're cold," Jim noticed, with a frown. "I better let you get on home, before you get any sicker."

"Yea, I just live over there," I pointed in the direction that I should be headed in, but my feet seemed reluctant to help take me there.

"I live over this way," he said, pointing in the opposite direction.

We both stood looking at each other for a long time, then another bout of coughing spurred Jim to say goodbye to me again, before turning and striding away. I didn't really want him to leave, and it felt like one of those times when someone had to hang up the phone first. I was never very good at that.

I watched him go, and felt a kind of joy bubble up inside me. I certainly hadn't felt this way in a very long time, and I felt all my worry and stress of the day lifting. Mr. Watts' strange behaviour in his office, the Devlins' strange comings and goings,

Mr. Watts' neck scratches, all of that didn't matter right now.

As I headed home, I had a bounce in my step. I passed the basketball hoop and wasn't surprised at all to see the neighbourhood kids that should have been in school, playing a game. The basketball bounced my way, and rather than ignore it like I normally would, I grabbed the ball and tossed it up at the back board, making a perfect 3-point basket. I got roars from the kids, amazed at my ability. But really it wasn't that long ago that I too used to skip school and toss balls around. That was my hoop, and if they looked closely at the rusty old paint-flecked pole, they would see my initials scratched into it.

Finally home, I poured vanilla scented bath gel under the running bathtub water, and watched the delicate inviting bubbles lather up. I sunk down deep into the water and breathed a sigh of relief, as my aching muscles relaxed in unison. Remembering that I forgot to give Jim my number in return, I grabbed my phone from beside the bath and carefully punched out a text. I knew I had to do it now before I lost my nerve, or found a million reasons why I shouldn't date Jim.

I re-wrote that text for about twenty minutes before settling on a worthy message.

"Hi, Jim, it's Clarissa. I'm already feeling a million times better, and I'm looking forward to our date!" I hit send then put the phone on silent and hastily placed it to the side, knowing I would check it every two minutes anyway.

I saw the screen flash from the corner of my eye.

"Eek," I actually squealed out loud.

CHAPTER 6

I unlocked my phone quicker than I thought possible with wet fingers. Excited butterflies bloomed in my stomach when Jim asked about my next night off. After responding in the perfect, not-too-quick, not-too-long fashion, I told him that I was free after four o'clock tomorrow evening. He instantly texted me an address with a smiley face and we agreed to meet up at six.

I spent my time in a relaxing bath that night, thinking that at least one aspect of my life looked hopeful. Once I dried off and dressed for bed, curiosity interrupted my normal nightly routine. What exactly was the address Jim had texted me? I looked it up on my phone and discovered that he'd sent me the address for a theater. The simple sophistication of a night watching the stage sounded only too perfect. It took a while for the giddiness of expectation to die down, but I curled up under my blankets and finally managed a much-needed night of peaceful rest.

A low buzz woke me, and I fumbled around my nightstand in an attempt to find my phone. I had been dreaming of Jim, of walking along the streets with no worry but whether or not to invite him back to my place. I let out a groan as I sat up in bed, rubbing my eyes. The clock said it was almost three-thirty in the morning. I drifted off for a moment, phone in hand, before another vibration shook away my drowsiness.

I muttered to myself, debating whether or not to answer the 'unknown number' scrolling across the screen. I remembered hearing once that nothing good came from late night phone calls, that bad news was the only kind that really couldn't wait. Sighing, I pressed the answer button and mumbled a hello.

"Clarissa? Clarissa is that you? Please tell me it's you!" A trembling voice I did not recognize startled me completely out of my sleep.

"Who is this?"

"It's me, Clarissa. It's your mother." The woman sounded irreparably sad. I feel a flush of annoyance at what must be a practical joke.

"My mother left a long time ago. How did you get my number?" Playing along might have been easier, but accepting the fact that my mother was actually on the phone was an upsetting impossibility.

"Oh, honey, it doesn't matter." I bristled at the familiarity in her words, but the frantic tone of her voice stopped me from hanging up. "Don't trust Watts, whatever you do. You have to quit. You can't stay there!" She rushed her warning while I struggled to find a response.

"What are you talking about? How do you know where I work? Who are you?" The questions tumbled out, and before I could ask any more the same shaky tone interrupted me.

"I can't tell you anything more. You just need to know this. You have to leave that job, Clarissa. Please. Promise me you will!"

It was obvious that the woman was crying now, and then

the sound was cut off by the harsh click of the line disconnecting. I sat there in shock, staring at the words 'call ended' that glowed from the screen. Completely awake and more than slightly unsettled, I wasn't quite sure how to react. The only thing I did know was that the woman had known my name, where I worked. She knew Mr. Watts. As unlikely as her claim had been, a simple nut-job playing a prank wouldn't know these things. Could that really have been my mother? None of it made sense, but everyone else in my life had recently been acting just as crazy. Deafening silence smothered my dark bedroom, and I suddenly noticed how painfully cold my feet were, exposed from under the edge of my sheets.

The bright orange glow of the rising sun made me realize that I never went back to sleep. A penetrating pain in my neck screamed out; I hadn't moved for the last few hours either. I was out of time. The thought of going to work formed a sick knot in my stomach, but staying home was not an option. I couldn't change my life based off of a woman's delirious rambling in the middle of the night, whether or not she was that same woman who abandoned me when I was two. All I could do was try to push the phone call from my mind, and push myself out of bed.

***

"Clarissa!" Mr. Watts barked. "I need to see you in my office as soon as you're finished." The employees and other guests in the lobby swiveled their heads to glance at him. He turned quickly to hustle back into the elevator. Movement resumed around me once the doors closed, but the still air was now stirred with whispered reactions. I glanced at the guests in front of me who were checking in, feeling the hot flush creep up my neck. They too would gossip about this once they left the Concierge desk. I could already feel the closest bellhop's excitement to be the first to spread the news of that outburst, and

49

my unforeseeable punishment. Mr. Watts never abandoned his composure in front of the guests. I knew that by dinnertime tonight, the entire staff would have heard some version of how I was summoned to the manager's office.

I chewed on my lip and nerves bubbled up in my stomach. *Again?* I thought. My nerves couldn't take two visits with Mr. Watts in one week. My water was fixed at home, and I definitely had not used the hotel shower a second time. I wondered if I had made some other terrible mistake, if *this* would be the moment he fired me. I ran through a myriad of possible scenes in his office, distracted again from the family standing before me.

"Excuse me? Are you working?" The woman's children snickered in their Burberry coats at her snooty, upper-class remark. Oddly enough, I feel badly for them through my embarrassment. I could never tolerate that uptight, suffocating lifestyle of appearance-focused perfection, private schools, and outlandish parties. Day after day, I watched a variety of people come in and out of those doors, and I couldn't help but notice that the more privileged one's life was, the less fulfilling it seemed to be.

"Yes, ma'am, I apologize for the wait." I faked a charming smile and finished tagging their bags for room delivery. There was nothing left but to turn timidly toward the elevators and up to Mr. Watts' office.

The second floor was even more daunting the second time around, this time I was greeted by the sounds of keyboard typing. As he came into view around the doorway, I saw he was fixated on the computer screen.

"You wanted to see me?" He jumped at my voice, then fixed me with a sharp glare. My body stiffened. The words of my early-morning phone call flashed rapidly through my mind. *Why had she tried to warn me away from him?*

"Yes, Clarissa." He went back to typing and I waited, confused and anxiously alert. He seemed to remember my presence after a few minutes and sighed heavily when he finally looked up at me. "I need you to work until eight tonight." I blink, and my head tilts in its own disbelief.

"But-"

"No buts. I need you here tonight, and that's final. You went home early yesterday, so I don't think it's an unreasonable request." The warning in his voice hinted that I could easily be dismissed for lack of work ethic, and could just as easily be replaced. A first-date was not a sufficient excuse for leaving work. It would have been useless to remind him that he was the one who sent me home, and I couldn't lose this job. So I hid my annoyance and nodded stiffly. I didn't doubt Mr. Watts' capability to dispose of me as an employee if I disappointed him in any way whatsoever. Still, there was something off here.

"Good. Get back to work." His dismissal left no room for questions.

The hours dragged on, and when it finally came time for my break, I rushed outside to give Jim a call and a heads-up. True to form, he picked up after only one ring.

"Jim? It's Clarissa."

"Hey! What's up?" He sounded cheerful, but I knew the disappointment in my voice was only too clear.

"About our plans tonight...I actually have to work late now..." I hoped that he would also be able to hear my regret, and that I wouldn't have to give more of an explanation.

"Oh. Well, that's okay. Some other time, maybe?" A strange mix of hope and concern poured through the phone. I managed a smile, pleased that he wasn't giving up on me just yet.

"Definitely!" I said, just as Mr. Watts made eye contact

with me through the window and tapped his watch impatiently. He just wouldn't leave me alone! Irritated again, I sighed and returned my attention to the call. "Can I call you later, once I'm off, and we can reschedule?" Even I could hear the subtle desperation in my voice, and I cringed.

"Of course, Clarissa. I'll talk to you soon." The line disconnected, and I felt remarkably the same as I had when the woman calling herself my mother hung up on me that morning. The cold outside pierced my thin uniform and I shivered, once again overcome with a sense of overwhelming vulnerability.

CHAPTER 7

I walked slowly back into the hotel, my legs heavy as stone. My nerves were frayed, and I dreaded the thought of what came next. Once I reached the counter, Mr. Watts cut me off and walked briskly to the fax machine. He narrowed his eyes into slits as I slinked around the desk, then grabbed a pile of papers from the fax machine and flipped rapidly through them. He stopped abruptly as his eyes caught onto something in the stack, and I watched his face change. His eyes grew wide as beads and sweat formed quickly on his forehead. He glanced around nervously, then raced from behind the desk with the heap of papers toward the elevators. I assumed he was heading towards the privacy of his office, but instead he made his way towards the conference room just in sight of the front desk.

I watched him through the glass panel wall as he snatched the conference room phone. The phone on my counter gave a shrill ring and I picked it up before it could ring twice. I already knew he was on the line, but I snapped into auto pilot and gave my usual "Thank you for calling The Regency. How can I help you?". Before I could finish, Mr. Watts interjected. "Clarissa, if anyone asks for me I am off the property, understand? Off the property!"

I jumped in spite of myself and stammered, "Ye-yes, Mr. Watts." He slammed the phone down and walked to the glass door, narrowed his eyes at me again, and closed the blinds. I shivered despite the comfortably warm lobby.

"Wrong number?" Eduardo the bellhop asked as he passed by rolling a luggage cart.

"Huh?" He nodded at the phone suspended by my hand, and only then did I realize it was still there. I dropped the receiver back in the cradle as if it were a hot brick. I had to find a way to distract myself through the rest of the shift.

The best project I could find to keep my mind off of Jim and the mystery woman claiming to be my mother was to delve into the listing of upcoming operas to recommend to the guests. I wondered how it must feel to spend that much money without a second thought just to listen to people sing in a foreign language. I wondered how it must feel not to worry whether or not your most extravagant meal of the month would be peanut butter *with* jelly, or tuna fish.

Lost in thought, I did not realize how quiet it had been until I smelled something that did not belong there. The odor traveled up my nostrils and into my gut, waking waves of nausea. I coughed and gagged, swallowing the sour taste back down, and willed myself not to throw up. The back of my neck prickled and I glanced up. I wondered just how long he had standing there in front of my desk, but a second breath of air confirmed that the stench had arrived with the person.

He was extremely tall, with an angular face above a pale blue suit that made him look rather boxy. His skin was so white it bordered on transparency, and the wispy strands of thin hair on his head were platinum white. He wore sunglasses despite the fact that it was now night, and his thin lips were grey and cracked. The odor of sulfur and wet trash came off him in waves. I wondered if he was homeless or just crazy. Maybe even both. *What was he doing at this hotel?*

The man held something heavy below the counter, his right arm pulling him down making his already run-down appearance even weaker. I assumed it was a suitcase, but seriously doubted that this man had the means to stay in a hotel like this. I was not sure whether to scream or call for security. Unable to form the normal words of greeting, I nervously glanced around the lobby. It was empty, except for myself and this character from a Creep Show comic. I stepped back as he reached down and slowly raised the shiny, metal briefcase that was handcuffed to his right arm. Then he lowered it to the counter with a slam. I tensed, prepared to run for the door, but found that my legs were glued in place. My eyes grew wide as he leaned forward on the counter with both arms bracing him for support.

"Get me Watts," he hissed. The shiny handcuffs clanged against the metal briefcase. It was identical to the one Mr. Devlin had, only the handle and sides of this one were smeared with small streaks of red.

I recoiled and covered my mouth with my hand. I knew security cameras were always focused on the front desk, and I prayed silently that security or Mr. Watts would come to my rescue. There was no one else around. The lounge adjacent to the lobby was usually filled with guests enjoying the late happy hour, but tonight it was uncharacteristically deserted. The bartender Louis had already gone home. I felt something like an anxiety attack creep closer by the minute.

"Get me Watts." the man repeated, his voice even lower.

He grimaced, showing yellow teeth.

"He's not here, Sir," I managed to squeeze out, fighting back the nausea and the panic. I tried to slow my breathing, in an attempt to reduce the inhalation of that disgusting smell. He stared at me, growling low in his throat for what seemed an eternity. Everything felt frozen, and I was thankful for the marble counter top that sat between us. I could not see his eyes behind the sunglasses, but felt the intensity of his glare.

"You tell him I will be back," he snapped, slamming his hands on the counter again. I backed away and felt for the wall behind me.

"Yes, Sir, " I stammered, nodding vigorously. He finally moved away, jerking his wrist back. The briefcase crashed to the ground, pulling him sideways with it. He picked it up in controlled movements, turned, and walked in long strides through the doors. The awful odor lingered for a few more seconds, but then even that was gone. I pushed myself away from the wall and ran to the wastebasket under the computer. There I emptied what little contents there were in my stomach.

Once I regained my composure, I glanced towards the conference room and saw the blinds snap back into place. I wondered how long he had stood behind the safety of the glass, watching me squirm. But Mr. Watts said nothing, and he did not leave the room.

Fortunately, the rest of my extended shift was boring and normal. I had a lot of free time in between the late-night check-ins to think about Jim. *How would he handle it if I told him about all the strange things that had happened in the past couple of days?* I honestly wouldn't have been surprised if the information chased him away.

Mr. Watts never reappeared that night, and before long, it was time for me to leave. I grabbed my jacket and headed out, barely taking two steps out the door when a hand gently touched my arm.

"May I walk you home?" I looked up to see Jim standing at the curb, holding a single yellow rose. I couldn't hold back a smile even if I wanted to.

"Jim! This is a really nice surprise." He was cleaned up and bright-eyed, and had clearly made an effort. I took the rose from him, leaned in, and gave him a tentative kiss on the cheek. He turned his face quickly, as though he knew he needed the momentum, and caught my lips with his. It was another surprise, and I wanted to lose myself in his warmth. But I was very conscious of my surroundings, wary of showing affection right outside of the hotel, of being seen by the wrong person. I grabbed Jim's hand and pulled him away from prying eyes. My normal days had suddenly become so strange that I really didn't want anyone to know about Jim yet. I was afraid of ruining my chances with him, and was suddenly grateful that I hadn't even told Joy any more about him.

"Do you need to change?" he asked.

"I'll just throw my hoodie on over my shirt, and I can switch into my sneakers on the train." His concern for the stresses of my job was heartening.

"Does that mean you don't need to stop by my work to change anymore?" He sounded disappointed.

"Maybe not as often now its getting a bit colder, but we could make up for it outside of work?" I couldn't help but giggle at the suggestion.

Firmly out of sight of the hotel, I relaxed my pace. Jim took the opportunity to gently guide me back against a wall, pinning me between him and the cold concrete. He kissed me again with a delicate passion. I felt everything he had tried to share and every word he had tried to say through that one kiss.

"I'm sorry about our date," I said, looking into his eyes.

"It's okay. We can go to the theater another time. I figured it's not too late to do something though, if you're still up for it."

Spending time with Jim was exactly what I wanted, but what I really needed was to relax and put my feet up.

"I'm not really dressed for going out, but you can come over to my place. Maybe we could watch a movie?"

He grinned, tightening his hold just a little around my waist. "That sounds great. I finally have my car back, so I'll drive. And take-out is on me."

I grinned the whole time, enjoying the change of scenery on the drive home. Jim knew all the shortcuts in my neighborhood and took very little time in getting me home.

Being around him put me completely at ease, filled me with a sense of peace and confidence that I rarely felt. I was embarrassed at first to show him my apartment, but he was so easy-going and positive that all of my hesitation was swept away. He introduced himself to the kitchen and ordered me to relax. We sat on the couch to eat dinner out of plastic take-out boxes, talking so much that we didn't watch a movie at all. We flipped through some music videos for background noise, but all of our attention was focused on each other. He talked easily, listened openly, and never pried too deeply into my personal life. I was grateful for that. Then when our bodies moved closer, the television completely ignored, I discovered that he really was a great kisser.

Midnight came around before either of us realized. I playfully begged him not to leave even as he walked down the corridor to the stairs. I had to remind myself that his shift was earlier than mine the next day, and that sleep was important for both of us. He promised a real date in the next few days, and when I closed the door behind him, I had to keep myself from screaming in excitement.

As wonderful as the night had been, sleep did not come easily. I made full use of my queen size bed, and tossed and turned for what must have been hours, dreaming of my mother's voice and her warning to stay away from the man with the bloodied briefcase. I woke up in a sweat and glanced at the clock. At two in the morning, I'd only been sleeping terribly for an hour.

I recognized the sounds of movement in the living room, and panic rose up in my throat. I reached blindly through the dark into the drawer of my bedside table, groping for the flashlight. I felt the rickety unit wobble, and then the glass sitting there toppled to the floor. The flashlight had become my best friend, a casualty of faulty electricity in this building, and sometimes even my inability to pay the bill. I grabbed it and slowly stepped out of bed and onto the cold, wet carpet. I bit my lip to keep from cursing, and silently wished Jim was there. My eyes adjusted slowly to the dark as my pounding heartbeat echoed in my ears like tribal drums. I dropped to the floor, inched across the carpet, and sat with my back against the wall with my bedroom door within arm's reach. I reached up and turned the knob quietly, holding my breath. There was a feint glow from the living room, and the panic doubled. I knew I had turned off the living room light before going to bed. I opened the door wider and pulled myself up. What I saw there felt like a scene from a movie, with Mrs. Devlin in the lead role.

A strange glow surrounded an image of her, hovering inside my house. She was kneeling down in a wooded area, digging furiously into the ground. Clumps of dirt and grass came out in her clenched fists and were flung over her shoulder. I clamped my hand over my mouth to muffle a cry of horror. There was no way this was real, no way it wasn't an hallucination.

"Where is it?! Oh my Lord, where is it?!" She yelled, completely beyond hysterics. She wore the same jogging pants that I had seen her in last. Her normally flawless makeup ran down her cheeks like ink on blotting paper, hair ratted like a bird's nest above a face moist with dirt and snot. She cried in loud, wailing sobs. I was too stunned to move, shocked by the unwelcome vision of the normally impeccable and stoic Mrs. Devlin, now frenzied and completely out of control. An hallucination it had to be, however realistic.

I watched as she sat back on her knees and gulped in huge lungfuls of air. Once she quietened down, crying silently with her eyes closed, I dropped to my knees. Almost on cue, her eyes snapped up and I froze. She looked in my direction and I was sure she was staring right at me.

"Who's there? Hello?" I watched stupefied as Mrs. Devlin scrambled to her feet and glanced around as if trying to find a place to hide. She stiffened and walked backwards in halting steps. Her left side was turned to me, and the glow remained around her as a shroud of light. Whatever she saw was not part of my vision. She was under the spotlight as I inched up slowly, fear hanging thickly in the air between the world's of my reality and this waking dream.

"Who's there? Oh, God. No. Not you. Please...Not you!" She screamed in terror, face contorted in agony. "Help me, please! Somebody help me!" Her arms were braced behind her, backed into an object that I could not see. I felt a rush of both dread and pity, and I dropped the flashlight, clamoring forward to rush to her aid. Even though the sight of her was only a few steps away, I felt like I was running a mile. The closer I strove to be, the farther away she became. there was a rough shove against my back and I fell into quiet darkness with Mrs. Devlin's shattering screams fading in the distance.

The alarm clock woke me in a panic. I rolled across the bed from the lower corner I had somehow maneuvered myself into, and reached towards the offending sound. I was hyperventilating as the sweat poured down my skin. *Seven o'clock already!* I depressingly slammed the alarm's off button in frustration. I heard the garbage truck in the alley and the yowling of city cats. *Great,* I thought. My head was pounding, and I rubbed aching fingers into my temples.

"Why am I so sore?" I said aloud. "That was a terrible dream." I would have liked to make sense of the nightmare, but trying to recall the details worsened the headache. I moved to get out of bed for a Tylenol, and my hand pressed into something gritty on the mattress. I threw back the covers and turned on the bedside lamp. My heart dropped to my stomach when I saw the dirt and grass under my legs, and the broken flashlight on the ground beside the bed. When I jumped in surprise to the floor, a cold puddle of water squished under my bare feet. My wavering scream broke the silence of the apartment building.

CHAPTER 8

I moved away from the bed in an attempt to separate myself from this madness. I tried to take it all in but I didn't understand what was happening. *Had I done something to Mrs. Devlin? Was it really just a dream?* Before panic could set in, I rationally decided to get the vacuum from the front closet in the living room; not thinking about what hour in the morning it was. As I stepped across my bedroom threshold, I saw a body on the living room floor blanketing a pool of blood and sprinkled dirt. The body was dressed very well, designer everything. I stood still in utter shock, a cool breeze alerted me that my front door had been busted in. *What the hell happened last night?* I reached for the phone, my hand was shaking uncontrollably, making it even harder to focus on the keypad.

I had no idea who to call, I knew it should be the police, but I was afraid. Pacing the kitchen I dragged my spare hand through my tousled hair. I contemplated running to my neighbour but thought better of it. I had no choice but to call the police. There was a dead body on my living room floor!

The 911 operator was my first sense of relief after hearing her voice. She asked for the nature of my emergency, so I erratically described the scene in my living room. I consciously left out the dirt I found in my bed. I didn't want them knowing more than I did.

After dispatching the necessary personnel, she assured me everything would be alright and not to move anything around in the living room. I had two thoughts after we hung up: *Can I clean up the dirt in time?* and *who the hell was that woman?* My curiosity overwhelmed me. It wasn't the first time I had seen a dead body but walking closer to it seemed to go against my usual sane logic. Moving anything around, especially the body, was against the law but I had to know if I knew her.

Carefully, I grabbed the shoulder of the woman just enough to see her face. A slight glimpse of her profile was enough to make me shriek in terror a second time. My shove moved the lifeless person from her stomach to her back. Lying before me was the cold, dead body of Mrs. Devlin. I froze in the living room corner. *Why, of all people, would she be there?* I thought. I could feel my lungs begin to gasp for air as panic began to set in. Rushing toward the closet for the vacuum, I stubbed my toe against something light, hard, and cold. Apparently, my klutz is still in working order even at a time like this. After retrieving the vacuum, I went to see what it was I tripped over. How I didn't see it before, I'll never know. I'm not sure where it was when I first came into the living room, but now it was in the middle of everything. I had stubbed my toe on a metal briefcase. It had been opened but its contents were nowhere to be seen.

Looking around for anything else that might be relevant, I was finally able to take in the fact that my apartment was messier than usual. Someone had gone through my things. I raced back to my bedroom to check there as well, but it seemed completely untouched. I quickly vacuumed my bed, hoping to avoid any suspicion being drawn to me. I kept fighting back the panic that was trying to disarm me. If I didn't know how involved I was, there was no way in hell I would rely on the police to figure it out. Thankfully, the police were taking longer than I was told, so I sat down on my bed, away from the crazy scene sprawled across my living room, and waited. *Why me? Why here? Why her?*

My foot tapped the floor and I stared blindly at the colourful Ikea wallpaper in front of me. Curiosity started rearing its ugly head again and I pondered what Mr. Watts would make of all this. I tried to sit and wait, but the desire to try and understand something, anything, drew me back into the living room. Mrs. Devlin had a small purse with her that held a modest wad of bills and a few credit cards. The cards were in her name, but it appeared that she had no actual form of identification. This woman was just as much a mystery to me now as when she glided through the hotel with all her airs and graces. I wished I knew something about her, and curiously reached to see the gold locket she wore around her neck. I had never noticed it until now. I guess she usually kept it hidden. I was nervous getting that close to the body but I knew this was my only opportunity to learn something about Mrs. Devlin.

Slowly opening the locket, I revealed a picture of a handsome young man who was obviously Mr. Devlin. The other was of a young girl. Concentrating more, I could see her face clearly. It was me! I carefully removed the chain, after battling to unfasten the tiny clasp with uncooperative hands. I quickly headed back to the safety of my bedroom. My bed provided me little comfort as I waited for the police. The heaviness in my chest hurt as much as the lump in my throat. *Could she be the woman on the phone? What was she warning me about? Why didn't I recognize her voice?* I had so many questions that I will never have answered now. One question sharply pierced my conscience: *If Mrs. Devlin was my mother, did that mean that Mr. Devlin was my father?*

My train of thought was halted by the telephone ringing. It startled me despite expecting it to be the police inquiring for more information. Apprehension crept over my shoulders when I heard Mr. Watt's voice on the other end.

"Clarissa?" he asked.

"Yes, sir. It's me."

"Is everything alright?" His voice seemed to care a little more than usual. He winced when he talked. It was as if he was injured; trying to fight back the pain.

"Yes, everything is fine. The police are on their way." *Damn, why did I tell him that?*

"Clarissa, I'm coming over."

Before I could stop him, the line went dead. I began to panic. I felt uneasy around Mr. Watts.

Why on earth did he even call me? It was going on 6:00 am, does he know already?

I prayed that the police would arrive before Watts did, when I heard a knock at the front door.

"Ma'am, this is the police. May we come in?"

I just about torpedoed myself at the door. Although it was busted and slightly cracked, the detective was polite enough to knock. He was an older gentleman, well kept, with a stern look on his face. I walked him through everything that had happened. I told him I was getting ready for work when I came out to find the body.

"Do you know her?" he asked.\I

"Barely. She was a guest at the hotel I work at." *Shut up, idiot!*

Why was I so apprehensive? I did nothing wrong, right?
The detective kept looking around the room while the crime scene unit processed the scene.

"I see cards and cash, so robbery is out." What is that - dirt?"\l
After seeing the cards and cash in the purse, his stare became a little colder and a lot less subtle.

"Ma'am, we'll need to keep this area available for a homicide investigation. Is there somewhere, in town, that you can stay for the time being?"

It seemed like the longest second between when he finished his question and when I started my response.

"Yes, I can go to my boyfriend's place."

Was he my boyfriend now? I didn't even know if he'd be okay with it. I gave them my number and told them I would get back to them with Jim's address.

I went to pack a few things to hold me over for the next few days. I picked up a razor, not wanting to get caught off guard with Jim. Spending more time with him lately had done nothing to dampen the desire I had for him. I couldn't imagine spending even more time with him and not ripping his shirt off. As I fumbled around my room I realized that Mr. Watts hadn't shown up after all. It was now approaching 8:00 am, so I called work to tell them I wouldn't be coming in later. I hurried to McDonald's, searching out Jim. If there was ever a time for a friendly face, it was now, and it was his.

He saw me fly through the doors, and I was welcomed with a slightly puzzled smile. Jim was happy to see me but, of course, didn't understand why I was there so early.

"Clarissa, what an unexpected surprise. What brings you here?"

I forced a smile, "I just couldn't wait to see you again. In fact, I was hoping you could take me out to breakfast somewhere?"

He agreed and said he was due a break anyway. I gave him a summary of the situation.

"My apartment is being fumigated for bugs and I need a place to stay for a few days." *Why was I lying? It was Jim, after all.*

I figured he'd be a little less cautious if I wasn't involved in a murder. He happily agreed and gave me his address. I told him I'd meet him there later. I couldn't believe how effortlessly I lied to Jim. He didn't deserve anything but my honesty, but protecting myself had always been what I had to do to get by, and I wasn't about to let my guard down now.

Jim's apartment was in a better part of town. It wasn't much, but the two bags I did pack sure got heavy after a while. Thankfully, I rode the elevator to his floor. The spare key was taped above the door frame just like Jim said it would be. His couch was ever so comfortable, I could have happily stayed put and tried to ease the tension gripping my forehead but, I knew Jim would be home soon, so I had to make myself ready. Slipping in and out of the shower was hard enough, but I added the chore of shaving. We both knew I'm simply a guest and I wasn't expecting things to progress with Jim, but the thought occurred to me that It could. If Jim and I became more intimate, I would feel so embarrassed if I wasn't perfectly groomed. I got everything done rather quickly with about two and a half hours to spare. Sliding back onto the couch, I rested my head on the arm. It felt so nice to just stop and pretend the day hadn't happened at all.

My mind kept going back and forth about Mrs. Devlin. I didn't know her but seeing her lying there was incredibly sad. I toyed with her locket feeling the cool metal in my hands. I shouldn't have taken it, but it was all I had of her, and there is a real chance she could be my mom. None of it made sense and the endless questions swirled around my head until I fell asleep. I awoke to see Jim in his kitchen preparing something that smelled quite delicious. I sat up to reorient myself of my surroundings. *Had all that really happened? That wasn't just another bad dream?* Jim noticed me getting up,

"Good morning, beautiful. Or is it good evening?"

That's one thing I needed - a smile, and Jim's never disappointed. I went to take a peek at what he was making. The smell was enticing. A little Chicken Alfredo was on tonight's menu. Until then, I hadn't been hungry at all.

"I never really get a chance to show off my cooking skills. I figured this is the next best step to a proper date."

I leaned against his fridge and just smiled at his almost corny charm and sweetness. He slid closer to me to get me within arm's reach. He lightly pulled on my shirt to guide me close to him for a kiss. I can't believe I had already forgotten how good his kisses were.

I set the table, and he served our food with one of the worst French accents ever. I didn't think to remind him we were eating Italian. The food was so tasty, and the company was even better. I joked that perhaps Jim should open his own Italian restaurant.

"I've worked too hard to get to where I am now. Maybe I'll just submit a new menu item," he laughed.

We moved to the sofa to debate which movie we would end the evening with. When we sat, we couldn't take our eyes off each other. The air was heavy with anticipation. We sat calmly looking into each other's eyes when he leaned in for another kiss. As soon as we locked on, we never wanted to pull apart. He reached out to hold my chin, then guided my face to the side so his kisses could move to my neck. God, if only he knew how my neck was my weak spot. My body was ready for him. With each kiss, my arousal level rose. I slid my hand up to Jim's crotch and found that he was very excited as well.

He stayed on my neck for a little longer, lightly biting it every now and then. When he did, it drove me even crazier. He moved his hand down from my face to my chest. His strong hands were very welcome, I felt myself holding my breath with each caress. I wanted to pull him into his bedroom, but I wouldn't move. I wanted to enjoy every minute of this. His hand then moved to between my legs. My heavy breathing and light moaning was evident enough that I could have climaxed there and then, but somehow I held out. His hand found its way under my blouse, then back to my chest. I'm not sure if he was surprised to find that I forgot to put a bra on after my shower.

I reached for his pants zipper when, suddenly, an image of Mrs. Devlin's dead body flashed before my mind. I tried to ignore it and continue with the task at hand. I managed to get the zipper down. I reached in to feel Jim and maybe try to drive him a little crazy like he was me. Another flash of Mrs. Devlin appeared to me. This one was harder to ignore. Suddenly, I was brought back to the dream of Mrs. Devlin screaming at the light. I couldn't escape it. I had to fight back. The light got closer to Mrs. Devlin as if it was about to consume her. I ran towards it screaming, "NNOOOO!" and pushed at it. I snapped out of my vision to find myself standing up from the couch while Jim was still sitting with a bewildered look on his face. I could see he was wondering what he did wrong. I felt so bad.

"Jim, I'm sorry. I just have a lot on my mind. Please forgive me."

"Of course," he said somewhat hesitantly.

He offered me his bed while he slept on the couch. I

wanted to bring him in with me but I sensed a timidity about him after my outburst. He had a very nice queen-sized bed, very luxurious, a bit like the ones they had at the Regency. I slipped into a nice little negligee and laid down. I soon fell asleep trying hard to remind myself I had to work the next day. I woke up around three the next morning. I heard Jim moving about, getting ready for work. He grabbed a few things from his closet and went to the bathroom to take his shower. I thought about getting up and busying myself with a cup of coffee, but the bed was too inviting for me to leave.

After tossing and turning so much I could use a shower myself; *I couldn't just join him, could I?* Out of nowhere, my sex drive revved back up to where it was last night. I was still laying on my side, looking at the bathroom door. I began to imagine Jim in the shower and what I might do if I were in there with him. My hands began to caress my body at the thoughts I was having. *Should I just jump in there with him? It could save water at least, right?* I heard the water turn off. Jim was done, but I wasn't. He turned the door knob and exited in nothing but a towel around his waist. I sprang up to sit on the edge of the bed; my eyes relaxed but focused on him. Fresh out of the shower, and he was all mine.

"Oh sorry, I didn't mean to wake you. I'll be real quick"

Before he could finish his sentence, I got off the bed, and reached for his towel, reeling him in close.

"Please take your time."

Something had come over me, but neither of us was complaining. I ripped the towel off to see Jim in all his glory. I reached my hand down to stroke his erection while I kissed him. I wanted him to know how much I craved him, and to make up for last night. His hands made all the same moves that they did the night before. His bites on my neck were intensified when he moved my head to the side by pulling my hair. It was rough, but I felt completely safe. We moved to the bed. Jim gently shoved me on my back to pin me beneath him. His lips worked mine a little before he slowly moved down to my breasts, and fondled my nipples with his mouth. He was teasing *me* now, and I loved it. His kisses went all the way down my stomach, then he positioned himself between my legs. His mouth hovered right in front of me, pushing my legs apart with his firm grip. His breath rushed out against me, getting me even more exited. We breathed fast, as if we were making love on top of a mountain.

His eyes locked onto mine as his mouth began to work. I couldn't help but moan. I thought for sure I was going to orgasm but I fought it off. My hips began to rock back and forth which slightly threw Jim off. I quickly reached forward to hold his head down and keep him in place. Just as I was about to climax, he stopped; a further show of torturous teasing. For not being the dating type, he knew what he was doing. I grabbed his jaw as firmly as I could to move him back up. My legs wrapped around him like a bear trap. I wanted him inside me now. We both knew how long it had been for me, and Jim didn't seem like the active dater.

He got my hint, and quickly slid inside me. It felt so good. His thrusts started off slow but deep. My nails began to dig into his back. I kept repeating, "Oh god, don't stop. Don't stop. Don't stop." His thrusts became slightly faster and harder. I tried not to scream because of the time of day, but my body decided otherwise. I was close to orgasm and I could sense Jim was too. My hands shot down to the bed and I grabbed the comforter in anticipation. Jim gave a final hard thrust which caused my release.

We had reached orgasm at the same time. I began to pray that this wasn't a dream. Jim plopped down beside me on the bed. Our eyes locked again, offering each other a satisfied smile.

"Well," Jim said. "I guess I need another shower now. Care to join?"

CHAPTER 9.

After this morning's workout, my body was entirely drained, both physically and mentally. I called work again to let them know I had a family emergency and needed a few days off, but Jackie in personnel told me that Mr. Watts had already informed them I would need some time, and due to the circumstances I would still be paid for those few days. I was too elated to think about why Mr. Watts had yet again got involved in my personal life. Nevertheless, I dreaded seeing him. I still wondered why he had telephoned me at such an unsociable hour, and why he had said he was coming over. Too much had happened lately and my mind was in serious danger of becoming a tired old engine. My thoughts were slow, I found it hard to connect the dots, and all I wanted to do was run away.

Staying with Jim was a welcome distraction and we were already becoming a whole lot closer. It was easy to let my guard down with Jim, he was there for me even though he had no idea how complicated my life was. I asked Jim if it would be okay if I spent the day in his apartment while he was at work. I actually told him the truth for once, that I needed more sleep and had decided to take a couple of days off in an attempt to relax.

"That's fine," he said. "But I better get a move on or I shall be late for work - much as I would like to stay here with you for a repeat performance of this morning"

I smiled as I said, "Who knows what delights you might come home to?"

He looked at me with such fondness. No, fondness was the wrong word. Could it be ... dare I say ... love. No, it's too early in the relationship to be thinking like that. On one hand, I was thinking of a dead woman, and on the other, thinking like a giddy schoolgirl with a crush on her teacher. My mind was in such turmoil, like a woman trying to organize a yard sale single handed. Clothes and clutter everywhere, but in no order. Should I keep the glass separate from the china, men's clothes separate from women's and so on. I just could not think straight, but I knew I had to - and quickly. Yes, I was going to use today to sort myself out ready for the inevitable questions from the cops.

I kissed Jim lightly on the lips as he was about to leave for work, but he took a firm hold of me and pressed his lips hard down on mine. Such passion caused my body to betray me by responding far too willingly. Reluctantly I pulled myself away.

"Carry on like that and I won't let you leave. I've been alone for so long I had almost forgotten how good a man can make me feel." A frown creased Jim's handsome face.

"I don't like the thought of you and any other man doing what we did."

"Don't stress yourself, none of them could measure up to you. Besides, by comparison they were amateurs, all amateurs," I grinned.

That seemed to satisfy him, and he went off to work with a smile on his face. I nuzzled back under the warm duvet and drifted off. My rest was arduous. Images of Mrs. Devlin, laid out cold on my living room floor would invade my senses when I least expected it. I was surprised also that the cops hadn't been to see me yet, even though I had given them Jim's address when I made my statement.

I was not functioning well. I needed to come to terms with all that had happened, as it was affecting me to a greater degree than I first realized. Perhaps Mr. Watts knew I wouldn't be strong enough to handle this. I didn't like to be perceived as weak, and the more I thought about it, I felt insulted by Mr. Watts' generous offer to take time off. The man irked me. I had never liked him from the moment we first met, when I came for my interview. I needed a job in that particular hotel because it was the only link with my history. I had done my homework. I quickly figured out that Mr. Watts had an eye for the ladies. I noticed all the female staff were young with film star looks and figures to match. That couldn't be by coincidence.

Before I started working at the Regency, I had made it my business to have tea in the main restaurant at least once a week so that I could see how things were done, and to be ready when the occasion presented itself. I couldn't afford to dine there, but afternoon tea was something I could manage with the little savings I'd amassed. I studied the staff; how they spoke, what clothes they wore and so on. It was pure luck that one day, I was trying out a new tea when I heard Mr. Watts, who was also sitting drinking tea, speaking into his mobile. He was talking to a man named Mr. Devlin, and it appeared that his relationship with this guest went above and beyond normal. At least that's what I thought based on the little knowledge I had of the hotel industry. At the end of the conversation I heard him say,

"Goodbye Mr. Devlin. The Watts Regency Hotel will make sure your suite is prepared for your return, and I personally will supervise moving everyone from that floor so you will not suffer any disruption to your routine. I look forward to welcoming you back on the seventeenth."

I continued to flick through the paper when I noticed an ad for a Concierge position at the Watts Regency. I couldn't pass up the opportunity, so I made sure I was fully prepared and ready to dazzle. And dazzle I did, because Watts was almost drooling as he offered me the position. When we shook hands, he felt clammy and limp wristed. It was like shaking hands with a dead fish. I quickly made for the door because I felt uncomfortable being in the same room as this creature who made my flesh crawl.

Since working there I also learned to hate the way Watts toadied round his 'special' clients. He was so deferential and servile to them, but he treated his staff with the utmost contempt. He never passed up an opportunity to exert his authority; that was how he liked to show who was in control. I had also not found anything that linked me to the hotel, until yesterday, finding Mrs. Devlin sprawled across my floor. Despite how disturbing things were, I could finally be catching up with my past.

Alone in the apartment, I unpacked some more of my stuff and chose some comfortable clothes to wear, which I then laid on the bed before taking a shower. It was as I was drying myself that I heard the front door bell ring. I cast about looking for a robe to put on but whoever was at the front door was impatient. Thinking it must be Jim I went to answer wrapped only in a towel. Imagine my surprise when I opened the door and saw a rather large, expensively dressed, middle-aged woman smiling at me. Her face rapidly changed when she saw it wasn't who she was expecting, because now she was wearing a very frosty look.

"Who are you?" She said, looking as if she was sucking a

lemon.

"I might ask the same of you," I replied matching her frosty glare.

"What are you doing dressed, or, rather, undressed, in my son's apartment?"

"Oh, oh really ..." I stammered. "I'm sorry, I didn't know."

"You don't know, you are in my son's apartment?"

"Of course I know this is Jim's apartment. He's letting me stay for a few days while my apartment is being fumigated."

"What! What sort of hovel do you live in?"

I didn't like her tone, and I would have liked to answer in the same vein but I had to try to recover some ground. If Jim and I were to continue with our relationship, which I now realized was something I wanted very much, I would have to eat humble pie. So, I reluctantly went into operation climb down.

"I'm so sorry I didn't mean to be rude, it was just that I was wrong-footed when I opened the door as I was expecting it to be Jim."

"So I guess he is not home then? Has he been changing his shifts around to accommodate a ... a ... floozie?"

Who's she calling a floozie, I thought. If she carries on like that, there could well be another body lying on the floor before too long. But I made a supreme effort to banish such thoughts from my mind as she barged her way past me.

"Would you like a cup of tea?"

"No, I would not."

"A biscuit?"

"No!"

"Well, if you're sure ..."

"I am here to deliver my son's favourite meal. Chicken soup. For future reference, it's as well for you to know that I take

77

care of all my son's needs."

Not quite all, surely, I thought ... and from what I know of him he doesn't need chicken soup either, as I remembered with amusement his prolonged athleticism this morning.

"I'll put the soup in the refrigerator so he can have it for his supper, but I'm afraid there's only enough for one," she said, rather pointedly.

I looked at the large Tupperware bowl thinking it contained enough soup to feed an army if they weren't greedy.

"That's okay," I said brightly "I'm cooking dinner tonight, but I'll try to use up your soup as a starter or I'll add something to give it some body." Which, I readily admit, in the circumstances, was an unfortunate choice of words, but she wasn't to know that.

"He's very fussy. He only likes his mother's food."

"Oh, well how difficult can it be to make chicken soup?"

"Very difficult if you want to make good chicken soup."

With that, she strode into the kitchen and put the precious soup in the refrigerator. Then she retraced her steps to the front door, but not before running a critical finger over every surface she encountered, tut-tutting as she went.

"Goodbye, lovely to meet you," I said ingenuously. She grunted by way of reply.

Alone once more, I quickly got dressed and decided to go for a walk to clear my head. I don't know how it was I ended up outside Queensbridge Houses. I certainly had no desire to go in. I thought I was just walking about aimlessly. I wanted to find some inner peace, so how I ended up here was quite beyond me. Even though it was deathly cold, I could see Suzanne sitting on an old chair out on the green that surrounded the apartment block. She was pulling on a cigarette, and seemed pretty relaxed considering how cold it had become. At the same time she was watching her son train his dog. Because it was a Mixed Pit Bull Terrier, almost all of the inhabitants except me had complained about it because they were afraid of the beast. I had grown fond of it, as it always greeted me with a friendly tail wag.

Pets weren't normally allowed, but Justin was autistic, and the dog had helped enormously in bringing him out of his introverted world. Because of this, Suzanne had persuaded the manager of the apartments to let him keep the dog. He agreed, but as it was a Pit Bull, and in deference to the other residents, he would only allow it if Justin promised to take the dog to training classes. Suzanne and the boy readily agreed, and true to his word he went religiously every week. In fact, Justin spent some part of every day on the green training Bullseye. He had even recently started to compete at obedience shows and had done a bit of winning too, which was good for a fourteen-year-old lad battling autism.

As I stood unseen from my vantage point, I watched Justin putting the dog through some kind of scent exercise. Justin used a pair of tongs to lay out ten cloths, and then he gave his mother two cloths to put her scent on. Using the tongs again, he took one cloth from his mother and laid that out while the dog was left in the down position behind Suzanne's chair so that he couldn't see where Justin put the cloth. Next he brought the dog round and got him to sit about fifteen paces away from the cloths. Suzanne then gave her son the other cloth which Justin took hold of by two corners and this he placed over the dog's nose. Then I heard him command "Go seek" and the dog quickly found the correct cloth. It was all I could do not to clap, but I knew Justin wouldn't like it. Like myself, most people on this estate wisely kept themselves to themselves.

Justin seemed happy with what he had achieved and released the dog to have a mooch about on his own. The dog was happily running about nose to the ground when he suddenly stopped and started digging furiously, throwing earth in all directions. I guess that is natural behaviour for dogs, but I had never seen Bullseye do it before. Justin was looking surprised too as if he had never seen the dog behave like that either. I was curious to know what had made the dog start now.

I carried on watching until Suzanne got up and called Justin, who then called Bullseye, but the dog carried on digging. That was unusual because normally the dog would come racing back to him. Justin then went and attached the dog's leash, so the dog reluctantly stopped his digging and the three of them went inside.

Now that I had nothing to hold my attention, my mind drifted back to some recent and some not so recent events. Perhaps it was seeing the good relationship between Suzan and her son that triggered me into thinking about my own childhood. It had not been happy. The words of one of the of the therapists I saw as a child came flooding back.

Speaking to one of her colleagues I heard her say "She said it was an accident, but I am not so sure, because it wasn't the first time the girl had upset her. And we both know Clarissa has a low anger threshold, so I think its perfectly possible for her to have orchestrated this so called accident. In any event, as a precaution, we are going to move Clarissa to another home."

Once settled, if I can call it that, in yet another care home, I resolved to find my file. That was the only way I was ever going to find out why my parents had abandoned me and with luck I might also find out their names. I knew the file was kept in the manager's office, so one night I broke in and very quickly found it. However, I didn't get time to study it in great detail before being discovered but I saw enough to interest me. On opening the file, the first thing I saw was the name; Watts Regency Hotel. That is why it was imperative for me to get a job there one day, in the hope of finding some clue as to why my mother abandoned me.

Over the years, I had made up all sorts of stories in my head. One was that my mother was a princess forced to marry a prince from some far away country. Another was that aliens had abducted her, but when it came down to it, the plain, unpalatable truth was that she just didn't want me. I started to feel the old anger rising, so I turned my attention towards my father. He was a big shot in the city; a millionaire, sometimes a billionaire, depending on how I felt about him at the time. He didn't know I existed as my wicked mother had kept it from him. Then, he did know but like my mother he didn't want me either. I felt myself flush hot with anger at this double betrayal, but I tried to calm myself before making my way home. What am I saying? It's Jim's home not mine. I was starting to feel like it was my home too, and that was dangerous because whenever I felt like that something happened, and I got moved on. I don't know how I would cope if that happened this time.

When I eventually got back Jim was already there with two other men. One of them came towards me and said, "Clarissa Clements."

"We want to have a chat with you down at the precinct. There are a few questions we would like to ask as there are some inconsistencies in your statement."

"Will you please tell me what this is all about and why it's necessary to take her to the Precinct? Can't you question her here?" said Jim, looking anxiously into my eyes.

"Yes, I'm afraid it is necessary," said the other man. "But don't worry she's not being booked ... not yet at any rate," he added rather ominously.

Then I was led away but I turned back expecting to see Jim's anxious face, but what I saw was a look that took me

81

completely by surprise. Was it ... was it ... could it be ... relief?

The police didn't keep me long, they went over and over my statement. They seemed frustrated that I knew so little about what had happened.

"You slept through it all," the good cop considered that this could be true with utter disbelief. I thought about this over and over during the ride back to Jim's. *How did I sleep through it all?* The only good thing to come from my encounter with the police was that I was informed I could return to my flat in two more days. I didn't know how I felt about that.

"Clarissa, you're back. I was worried about you."

I searched Jim's face looking for sincerity in his words. It was there, but I had a reservation that there was something he wasn't telling me. The irony in that was ridiculous - here I was about to lie to the man I was falling in love with.

"I'm sorry Jim, I should have told you earlier about what really happened. I didn't have fumigators in my apartment. I was broken into. My place was turned over pretty good, and the police wanted to do a full investigation before I returned. I know I should have told you, I just didn't want you to worry unnecessarily."

"You should have told me Clarissa, now I know why you've been so jumpy. Come here ..."

Jim embraced me with the tightest bear hug I could handle. In truth, he could never squeeze too hard. My life had lacked a hell of a lot of hugs, and I was due my share. I thought about the relief I saw on Jim's face earlier, and considered that maybe his mother had called him, casting a spell of doubt about me - the floozie. I knew we would have to talk about his mum at some point, but for now, I was going to enjoy my time off at Jim's place.

CHAPTER 10.

The days passed much more quickly than I would have liked, landing me back in my apartment. It was a strange, cold feeling, returning 'home'. All of the security and warmth that Jim's place had was absent here—here, where I grew up. But what did I expect? Mrs. Devlin's dead body was found here. It will never be possible to walk through the rooms without remembering her lying there, without remembering the dirt in my bed, without remembering the fear in her voice.

"NO! NOT YOU!"

There was no way that was only a dream. I woke up with dirt in my bed, for Heaven's sake. I didn't have a history of sleep walking. The only way I could have got dirt on myself is if I was actually there, wherever there was ... *but how did I get back into bed? And to whom was she screaming at— who else was there?*

The police had finished their investigation with nothing turning up, but yet I was on edge. It felt as though at any moment they would burst through my door and cuff me, even though I didn't do anything wrong. Being here was causing anxiety to grip my heart.

When I got the call informing me that I could return, I considered asking Jim if he wanted to stay at my place for a while. I couldn't keep staying with him, even though I'm sure he would have been more than fine with it—but I didn't want to be home alone, either. I could almost laugh at the memory of my childhood therapists praising my resolve through some horrendous times. If only they could hear my thoughts now.

Fiddling with the locket, I lay down on my bed and stared at the ceiling. Mr. Watts had called me on the second night of my stay at Jim's, telling me in his most professional voice that I would not return to the hotel until Thursday. He gave no further explanation and hung up. The message left me confused. I already knew this, and I'm pretty sure he was aware of that. It was like he wanted to say something, but couldn't. His voice gave nothing away and now back in my apartment, it just fueled my anxiety further, lacing my erratic thoughts with suspicion.

I wanted to ask why I was still being paid, but that simple question would lead to a hundred more. If I dared to approach any topic with Mr. Watts, I was afraid that stepping over our cordial boundary would leave an invisible line wide open. I couldn't push too hard just yet, not now that I was so close to finding out something about my past.

My mind drifted back to the incident. *How many people knew of Mrs. Devlin's death? Did they know where she was found?* Even though she had no formal identification, the number of credit cards with her name on them said enough. *What about Mr. Devlin? How could I even face him?* My hands suddenly felt very clammy, as though they were caked in dirt. Quickly sitting up, I rushed to the bathroom and washed my hands. I needed to do something to get this whole situation out of my mind, but I couldn't go back to a therapist.

CWC – The Concierge

What would I even say? *"A dead body was found in my apartment the other day. My boss knows something—what, I am not sure—but it might be related to the creepy guy who came into the hotel. Oh, and that dead body might be my mother."*

Splashing some cold water on my face, I stared at my reflection in the mirror. My ash-brown hair looked positively limp, my brown eyes horribly dull, and my skin ghostly pale. I didn't look like this at Jim's. Moving out of the bathroom, I threw myself back onto my bed, ignoring the springs' cries as my weight crashed down on them. The glowing-red numbers of my clock read seven in the evening. Tomorrow was coming too quickly. Tomorrow I would return to the hotel and greet guests with a smile. Tomorrow I would work efficiently as if nothing had ever happened. Tomorrow I would be back where everything began.

***

My cheeks ached as I smiled goodbye to a young couple, nodding a "you're welcome" as they followed my directions to a local restaurant. Nothing was different. Everyone acted exactly the same. The lavishly rich folk came and went, ignoring me unless they needed something - as usual. Mr. Watts was nowhere to be seen, but no one else gave that a second thought. Unless the Devlins were arriving, he really had no other reason to be out on the floor. I, on the other hand, had my eyes peeled for him. I had no clue what I would say to him, but I needed something to soothe my mind, and for some reason, I thought that just seeing his face would give me some answers.

Mrs. Devlin's locket rested heavily around my neck. I didn't want to wear it, but for some reason, I didn't feel comfortable leaving it at home. In fact, I didn't feel comfortable leaving anything in that apartment. Mrs. Devlin was yelling at someone in my dream, which meant someone else was in my apartment. I considered leaving it in my bag, but I did not trust the other employees enough. If they knew that Mrs. Devlin was found dead in my apartment, they would do anything for tidbits of information, including taking a quick look through my stuff.

I buttoned up my shirt all the way and tucked it inside. No one could see it. Even so, it was a heavy burden that consumed my mind, but my train of thought was broken when two hands rested on my shoulders from behind, making me jump. They slowly relaxed when I realized someone was giving me a massage.

"What's with you, Clarissa? You seem out of it." Joy inquired.

Releasing the map I still held tightly, I placed it back in the drawer and turned to face her. Worry consumed her eyes, but the small bit of curiosity that danced in the background was not missed.

So goes the life of a hotel employee, always wanting to know what's happening with everyone. I wanted to throw the question back at her—*where had she been lately?* My mind was on overdrive, singing in a tantalizing voice that it was all too much to be coincidental that she would return when I did, but I forced those thoughts out of my head. Everyone was under scrutiny now, not by choice, I just lacked any ability to trust. This had become evident to me more than ever after lying to Jim so many times.

"Do I?" I asked back, trying to seem as nonchalant as possible.

Humming a "yes," her eyes briefly scanned the area before landing back onto me.

"Well, I'm glad that you're feeling okay, I know that losing a family member can be tough. I felt bad, actually. I asked Mr. Watts where you were one day because the fill-in was helpless, but he didn't want to tell me. After a bit of persuading, he finally relented and told me your aunt had died. I haven't seen him around much since though," She quickly added.

"Oh."

"But do you want to know something strange?" she suddenly whispered. She crouched down so that we were eye level with each other. Excitement sparked in her - she belonged in this industry without any doubt.

"When Mr. Devlin checked in on Monday, Mrs. Devlin wasn't with him. He seemed really haggard. Well, not too much, but you could see it in his eyes."

"Strange." I commented as nonchalantly as possible. "By the way, what have you been up to? Are you okay? You were absent for a while yourself."

The cunning look in her eyes was replaced by one of sadness. "I'm fine, just some family stuff going on. I don't want to add my issues on top of yours ... just know that I understand what you're going through."

I instantly felt guilty for quizzing her. Maybe she really did have family problems. I mean, didn't everyone? Looking around again, she straightened up. Sadness erased off of her face, she sent a wink my way and walked into the stockroom. I turned my attention to the miscellaneous papers in front of me. I was riddled with remorse thanks to Mr. Watts' lie. No one had actually died in my family. Well, maybe my mother, but that was still unclear, and Joy seemed to be going through some real problems.

The elevator dinged, bringing me out of my thoughts. My attention turned to the doors and I watched as Mr. Watts walked out. He was put together from head to toe; I couldn't imagine that this was the man who called me that night. The devil on my shoulder slyly asked what floor he was coming from—*perhaps the fourth?* The memory of his and Mrs. Devlin's argument came to mind, but when his eyes met mine I pushed it away. Subtly changing his path from his office to my desk, he stopped and raised an eyebrow.

"How are you feeling?"

I wanted to laugh. Concern (real or not) sounded so strange coming from him, and what was that question even referring to—'my aunt dying', or finding a dead body at five in the morning? I gave a typical "I'm fine" response and observed as he nodded and turned towards his office. My eyes caught a glimpse of some metal hanging from the inside pocket of his coat and my mind immediately supplied an image of handcuffs. How easy it was for him to lie about a death in my family made me sick. He was involved, there was no question about that anymore, but how involved was he?

"Don't trust him." The woman on the phone had warned me, and now my subconscious was doing the same.

After completing mundane task after task, the day was almost over. Mr. Watts never returned from his office and I didn't have any desire to confront him, yet. *Why were there handcuffs - if they were even handcuffs, in his pocket? Were they the same ones that were on Mr. Devlin and that creepy man's wrist?* This hotel housed some really strange activities, and I was ready to leave for the day. I texted Jim during my break, and we made plans for dinner at his place. I also had a change of clothes in my bag, just in case. I wanted to bitterly laugh at how I was acting. Why couldn't I just bring myself to ask him if I could stay the night again instead of planning on sleeping with him to stay?

Every hour that passed, all I could do was think about how much I wanted to forget everything that happened. As someone who worked at a hotel, I had a natural interest in the latest gossip, especially when it revolved around the wealthy and well-to-do ... but this was too much. I wanted to know about it, not be in the middle of it. And depressingly, I was finding out more about everyone else instead of what I really wanted to know about.. me! Sighing, I unbuttoned the top button of my shirt, feeling immediate relief as the fabric pulled away from my skin. It wasn't the most professional thing to do, but as far as everyone else knew, my aunt had died—I was allowed to act a little strange.

Organizing the paperwork at my station once more for good measure, I was about to grab my bag when someone stood at the desk in front of me. Looking up with a smile, I was surprised to see Mr. Devlin standing there. The surprise was short-lived as my heart quickly picked up in fear. It was Thursday. He should not be leaving until tomorrow, yet here he was holding his key out to me. Joy was correct, he did seem tired. Designer labels could not hide the dark circles under his eyes. Taking the key from him, I smiled, bid him a goodnight, and turned around to hang the key up. However, when I turned back, he was still there. His eyes did not look through or past me like they normally would, instead they stared right into mine.

"Is there anything else I can help you with, Mr. Devlin?" I uncomfortably asked with a smile. His expression slowly shifted from one of harsh examination to one of exhaustion, as if he didn't realize he had been staring.

"No." He shortly replied.

Giving me a nod, he took a few steps towards the exit, my eyes quickly scanned the room to assure myself that no one had watched our exchange just now. The Devlins didn't make conversation with just anyone, and even that two-line interaction was out of the ordinary. I was already on my toes at work because of the call from Mr. Watts, I didn't need any other employees spreading rumors or gossiping about me. My heart stopped as he turned around once more and looked at me.

"The chain is twisted," he stated, then continued on his way.

The doorman opened the heavy oak doors for him and he walked out in a stately manner, as though nothing was wrong. Rich people always had to keep up their appearances. I watched the doorman nod his head in respect as Mr. Devlin passed. His chauffeur opened the door to his shiny black car; what kind it was, I had no clue, and they quickly made their departure.

Reeling back to his leaving comment, I could only wonder what it meant. The world seemed to enjoy speaking in riddles and I was done trying to decipher them for the day. The thought of my dinner with Jim in an hour soothed my mind. Rubbing the back of my neck with my hand hoping to relieve some of the sudden strain, my fingers grazed upon the clasp of the locket. Gripping it between my thumb and pointer finger, I fiddled with it nervously. Sliding my fingers back and forth, I moved down towards the frame, only to realize that the chain started twisting inwards.

'The chain is twisted.' Grabbing my bag and checking out for the day, I practically ran towards the subway station. Mr. Devlin saw the locket.

MRS. ROSEMARY DEVLIN

Checking in at The Regency had become an ordeal for Rosemary Devlin over the past few weeks. Each time she walked through the doors to the plush foyer and headed for the concierge's desk, she knew there was a chance she'd come face to face with Clarissa.

She had known the minute she saw the pretty new concierge for the first time. One flash of those troubled brown eyes confirmed it. The same gaze she'd wanted to see for so many years in her own daughter's face. The first time, she was shaken by the almost overwhelming desire to grab the girl, hold her tight, and tell her everything would be all right. But more than forty years of strict social etiquette had quickly brought down those emotional shutters. She quickly trained herself to ignore those urges, and now she looked straight through the girl like she was any other anonymous hotel employee. Rosemary knew it was the closest they would ever get.

She hadn't always been this way. Once, a lifetime ago, she and Patrick had been so carefree, rebellious, ready to take on the world in spite of the things expected of them. He was the bored, pampered adopted son of a family whose wealth had been illegally earned, smuggling alcohol during Prohibition. At that time, they would have been looked down upon, but the family's respectability had grown as quickly as his grandfather's bank account. Patrick himself got his thrills from driving the cherry Eldorado too fast up the New England coast, frequenting the sort of places that his neighbours in Park Avenue never knew existed. He gained more life skills from his family than he realized, and when he found himself standing on his own two feet, his ingenuity stepped in.

Rosemary had rebelled against her boring and comfortable existence. Daddy's plan for her had involved walking down the aisle of a high-ceilinged Presbyterian church, with a rising young merchant or investment banker waiting for her at the altar. She had kicked ferociously at that layout, and spent her days instead at art school, her nights in Greenwich Village's questionable jazz clubs.

Black Capri pants and turtleneck had set off her caramel blond ponytail and kitten-flick eyeliner the night they met, drawing admiring glances from many of the would-be beatniks who populated those clubs. Not least among them was Patrick. Knowing this type of guy was forbidden fruit made the attraction all the more powerful as she climbed onto the low stage to recite her poems, staring at him unflinchingly. Ignoring all the others, she had left with him that night, and that had been it.

Soon they were spending every spare moment together. They were inseparable, sharing everything, convinced that no one else in the world could understand each other as they did. Secret looks betrayed their palpable connection, whether they enjoyed the grit and glamour of the city, the casual luxury of the Hamptons, politely dominating in mixed doubles tennis games, or sipping the specialty, and potent, Long Island Iced Teas on the terrace.

They soon learned they could never be together as an ordinary couple. And the socialites of their world could never know about them. No one would understand. They tried to dampen their passions, but the bond was too strong. Once they had crossed that invisible yet electric line into the forbidden, nothing was ever the same.

Needless to say, Rosemary never revealed the name of her child's father, and the pregnancy had been hushed under the threat of scandal. Her mother, in an incredible attempt to protect her, padded out her waistline and confided to her Bridge group the shock of being pregnant once more herself after turning forty. Rosemary had then been whisked away to a finishing school in Europe, far away from wagging tongues and prying eyes.

Once Violet was born, Rosemary had thought her life was complete. Family friends were delighted by the young woman's devotion to her unexpected baby sister, none of them aware that the love and trust in the child's brown eyes were directed at mother, not sibling. Rosemary would meet Patrick, with Violet in tow, and they doted on their perfect daughter, wishing they could be a family together.

As the girl grew, she embodied more and more of her mother's rebelliousness. By the time she was nineteen, Violet declared that she would not attend the Ladies' College that had been the chosen path for her. Instead, she wished to get a job and make her own way in the world. Thinking she'd gained her independence, Violet was unaware that the secretarial position with some high society doyen, the position that made her so happy, was only the product of so many pulled strings. The only thing that mattered was that the family was happy, assured by their success in deliberately keeping Violet away from the riffraff. Everything seemed to be going well, the pretty bow around an ugly accident.

Until that night. The night that Violet had come home tear-streaked and hysterical, pregnant with a bastard child.

Rosemary had begged her to go to a home for expectant mothers in New Hampshire, where she could spend her confinement in peace, free of society scandal and cruel accusatory fingers. Then she could hand over the inconvenient fruit of her indiscretion when it was born. Rosemary had honestly thought she was saving her daughter, protecting her from a ruined future. Little did she know it was the last time they would ever speak.

Violet's answer had been stunned silence, and a glare thick with disgust. She had stormed outside and into the back seat of a battered black Ford, a thin and pale man waiting quietly behind the wheel on the gravel drive.

Rosemary had never expected to see her daughter again, had been even more unsettled the day she recognized those same eyes of The Regency's new concierge.

CHAPTER 11

I stopped two blocks from Penn Station and leaned against a flier plastered lamppost. I was sick of all these riddles. Everyone else seemed to know more than I did.

The woman who claimed to be my mother knew that Mr. Watts was not to be trusted. Mr. Watts clearly knew something about how the body of poor Mrs. Devlin had ended up in my apartment. And now Mr. Devlin knew that I have Mrs. Devlin's locket.

The wind picked up, pulling at my jacket collar and my over-night bag. One by one, clues popped into my head. The strange faxes for Mr. Watts. The strange visitors for Mr. Watts. The locked drawer in Mr. Watts' office. Not to mention the Watts Regency Hotel being listed in my adoption file.

It was time to bust open some riddles, and there was only one place to start looking.

Cinching my collar closed, I turned back towards the Watts Regency Hotel and marched into the wind. Jim would have to wait. He'd understand – or would he? This wasn't the first time

I'd have bailed on him. I paused, passersby bustling on past me. My resolve was torn between finding answers and Jim. The initial excitement of the idea of breaking into Mr. Watts' office dwindled. The warmth and certainty of Jim's house made an alluring case.

If I hurried, maybe I could have both. Besides, I'd already missed my train. The wind nipped at my exposed cheeks and nose the rest of the way there. Tomorrow I'd wear a scarf.

I lingered outside the Watts Regency Hotel. I hadn't come up with a reason for returning to the Regency yet. I could see inside that Joy is at the concierge desk helping a man in a pale blue suit.

Plan-less, I gave the doorman a shrug and a smile. A familiar and sickening feeling overcame me. It was that creepy guy again. Granted I couldn't smell him this time, but his presence made me anxious. I'm glad it was Joy who had to deal with him this time.

"Mr. Watts is in the conference room," said Joy, pointing to a room with closed blinds kitty-corner to the concierge desk.

Mr. Watts must not have told Joy he was out, and I anticipated that he would not be happy.

The creepy man, oddly still in his same light blue suit, that now looked pressed and sharp, entered the conference room. The lobby tensed for a few quiet moments until the yelling began.

Each hotel employee's attention was fixed on the conference room door, except for mine. I walked, as casually as I could given the circumstances, toward the north stairwell. It was a quick hike up to the second floor even with my over-night bag over my shoulder.

The walk along the vacant floor toward Mr. Watts' office was eerier than usual. I kept expecting all sorts of unusual characters to pop out: Mr. and Mrs. Devlin, the creepy man, even

Jim's mom. Who knew – she could be part of this too. Logic told me it probably wasn't so, but she hadn't been nice and I liked to think of her being mixed up in all of this, so I could further justify my instant dislike of her.

At the end of the hall, the door to Mr. Watts' office sat ajar. I listened for a moment and heard nothing but the heater. I gently pushed open the office door, ready to bolt at the first sign of danger. The door swung open. There was no danger. Only the usual furniture, though Mr. Watts chair seemed to have been pushed much farther back from his desk than needed.

I put the door back in its slightly ajar position, tossed my over-night bag in the corner, and made my way to the other side of Mr. Watts desk. My heart was doing cannonballs. A persuasive thought leaped into my head. *I didn't have to try to open the drawer, It might not open. There might be only boring files in there. I could leave now and not even be late for dinner with Jim?*

I looked down. The drawer in question was open, … and empty. My heart fell. This ridiculous bit of espionage had been pointless. I shouldn't have bothered.

"At the end of the hall," said Mr. Watts.

I froze. He must have been in the hallway, and with someone too, probably that creepy man. I spun around, hoping to see a way out. No windows, no other doors, no secret passage ways. I had one very childish idea, and with no other offers, I got on my knees and crawled under Mr. Watts' desk.

"Mr. Creed, I assure you there's no funny business, as I agreed with Violet, the papers are being prepared" said Mr. Watts, his voice rich with the false sincerity she often heard him put on for hotel guests. I can hear their footsteps enter the office.

"Hmph," came from the smelly man with light blue pant cuffs, Mr. Creed.

"There have been a few hiccups yes, but the documents will be in your hands momentarily," continued Mr. Watts. I can see his polished shoes coming around the corner of the desk.

"Good heavens," squeaked Mr. Watts. In my inconspicuously curled up position, I dare not lift my head. I do not know if he is shocked because the drawer is empty or because I am under his desk, or both.

"What 'hiccup' is there this time?" asked Mr. Creed. The disdain dripping from his voice was nearly as toxic as his stench. This would be a bad time to throw up.

"It seems I've had a bit of a miscommunication with our Mr. Devlin, I need to speak with him first" said Mr. Watts. He pushed his chair back into its proper place, sealing me from sight.

"I s'pose you'll be wanting me to give you 'a little more time', again," said Mr. Creed, stepping closer to my hiding space.

"I've acquired, inquired, and bent over backwards on behalf of Violet, I think you know how much I care for her, even if she doesn't exactly realize at times. I should be afforded some leniency and patience here and there." Mr. Watts sounded demanding, but I could see his ankles trembling. Perhaps Creed didn't know it, but it certainly looks like he was hiding something.

"We'll just have to see what she says about that," said Mr. Creed. I could see his shoes turn to face the door. "Don't leave town."

Mr. Creed left the office and I wondered how long I'd have to wait for Mr. Watts to leave before I could get away home free.

"I had hoped to keep you out of this my dear," said Mr. Watts. He couldn't be talking about me. He must be talking over the phone or – my over-night bag plopped onto his chair next to my head. My face burned with humiliation and fear.

"Don't come to work tomorrow," he said and walked

98

toward the door.

"Am I fired?" I asked, still cowering beneath his desk.

Mr. Watts' shoes stopped. "It was irresponsible of me to have hired you in the first place," he said. "But no, you aren't fired."

I popped out from behind his desk. "What does this hotel have to do with my adoption?" I blurted out.

Mr. Watts didn't turn around. "Wait at least half an hour before you leave," said Mr. Watts as he walked out the door.

I slumped into his desk chair in relief and disappointment.

"You're not important, Clarissa," Mr. Watts called back to me. "Don't start acting like it."

I pushed down his all too accurate words, and decided to be grateful instead. I had the opportunity to wait here for half an hour and then walk away like I didn't know anything. And really, I still didn't know anything.

Waiting was boring. I riffled through some files, but found nothing of interest. I traced the dents in the busted open drawer. I texted Jim to let him know I'd been held up at work, but that I was coming. Answer-less and Jim-less, I couldn't bear to wait any longer. It had only been ten minutes, but I wasn't one to stay in an unsupervised time-out.

I grabbed my over-night bag, crossed the eerie hallway, and flew down the steps and out into the lobby.

Mr. Creed was there talking to Joy. They both turned to look at me. Joy gave me a small smile, though her brow showed her confusion. Mr. Creed had his usual sour expression, though his venomous eyes locked on to me.

I ducked my head and walked straight out the main door. I should have trusted Mr. Watts and waited. A block later I checked behind me. I didn't see Mr. Creed, and once inside Penn Station I relaxed more. I texted Jim that I was on my way and resolved to leave the whole matter behind me.

CHAPTER 12

I paused at Jim's door. Breathe in… breathe out. *You need to let this go,* I told myself. *Don't let what just happened ruin your time here now.*

Before I had the chance to knock, the door swung open and there stood Jim wearing an 'I love New York' apron, grinning like an affectionate puppy dog. I couldn't help but smile. This effect he had on me was what I loved the most about him. As he ushered me through the door, I caught the most delicious scent wafting from the kitchen.

"Right," said Jim. "Coat, gloves, hat and bag please. Pass them to me. Tonight, I'm here to wine and dine you."

I laughed - something I had not done all day.

Dinner tasted as good as it smelt. Jim had prepared simple comfort food: fried chicken, mashed potato and beans, and as I ate I had a sudden memory of eating this exact meal with one of my foster families. It was a strong, vivid flashback, *but which family?* I had blocked them all from my memory for so long.

I must have been staring into space for quite some time,

mouth half full, when Jim brought me back to reality.

"Is the food OK? I swear I didn't put rat poison in it," he joked.

I feigned an enthusiastic smile. "It's delicious!"

As we dined, Jim gave me a chatty narrative of his day, with all its ups and downs. I did my very best to show interest, nodding and smiling at the right places, offering feedback when it felt appropriate, but I couldn't quite focus and give this lovely man my full attention.

"Jim!" I suddenly found myself blurting out. "Let's go away for a few days. I have been given some time off from the hotel. Mr. Watts has decided to do a deep clean of the hallway carpets and while it takes a whole day for one floor to dry they have decided to do three floors at once, so occupancy will be low and they'll only need a skeleton staff. Joy really needs the money with Christmas coming up, so she'll be on duty."

Wow, I even surprised myself with that story. I was getting pretty good at this lying game. I hated deceiving Jim, but there was no way I was going to tell him what had really happened today.

He looked at me, tilting his head to one side like a child trying to get the measure of a new visitor. I couldn't be sure, but I felt like he saw right through my lie. Regardless I continued to state my case.

"We could drive down to Montauk, It's off-season now, so it won't be expensive or booked up. We could find a small hotel - nothing fancy - and just relax, take in some sea air, leave behind everything that has been going on."

Jim regarded me with mock severity: "Well, I don't know," he said. "Being head honcho at the local McDonalds is an important job, you know."

A broad grin broke his serious expression as he

continued: "I'm sure I can adjust the roster. After all, I haven't taken any leave all year. Yeah, let's do it, baby!"

I felt my body loosen with relief. *Thank god!*

"I just need to pick up a few things from my apartment in the morning, if that's OK," I said.

"Of course it is," replied Jim. "You know, I think a get-away will do us both the world of good. Let's drink to that. Cheers!" We laughed as our glasses clinked.

The sky was a harsh brilliant blue as we set off early the next day. Winter was definitely on its way and even though the air was crisp and frost covered the grass, there was not a cloud on the horizon. I had butterflies in my stomach - I was so excited to leave the city behind.

We left the lift and climbed the stairs to my apartment, when a sudden rumble and clattering of claws on cold tiles made my heart skip a beat and my eyes snap open in momentary panic. Bullseye came hurtling around the corner. I froze. Jim took three steps back, not quite sure how to react. The dog ran straight towards me, stopped abruptly, and sat at my ankles sniffing my feet. I could feel the heat from his body and thumping heart against my calf as Justin emerged from his apartment, collar and lead in his hand.

"Wow, he really likes you," he said. "I've never seen him do with anyone before!"

Bullseye stayed right where he was, looking up at me, panting. He only moved when Justin shook the lead in his hand and called him for his walk.

Jim peeled himself off the wall as they bounded down the stairs.

"Well, that was interesting." I nodded.

"Just wait here," I told him as I turned the key in the lock. "I'll only be a minute."

Closing the door behind me, I let out a breath and wondered... *did Bullseye sense something I didn't?* "Don't be silly," I scolded myself. "He's just a dog." I gathered my things, locked up and headed out for our first trip together.

Montauk is a three-hour drive from New York located at the southern tip of the fork of the Long Island Peninsula. Some consider it the scruffy younger brother to the glitzy, glamorous Hamptons, but it's fast gaining popularity with the young and hip. Another plus is that once the summer crowds clear out, you pretty much have the place to yourself.

I thought briefly of Mr. & Mrs. Devlin as we drove along the Old Montauk Highway, looking for a cheap and cozy hotel that ticked all our boxes. Would the Devlins' have ever ventured past the Hamptons - I was sure they had a palatial summer house there where she played tennis, and sipped afternoon G&Ts with friends. *Probably not.* Holding the locket, caressing it absently, I mused that even after all the recent events, I was still no closer to knowing much more about this woman.

With a jolt, I felt the car pull up outside the Royal Hotel, a three story Bed & Breakfast sandwiched between two modern designer hotels. It's cladding was grey and weather beaten, with paint peeling from the window sills. It looked like the hotels either side were sucking the life from it, but the lights were on inside giving it a welcoming glow and the Vacancy sign swung gently in the breeze. Jim ran in to see if there were any double rooms and promptly returned, declaring "There is room for us at the inn" with a smile.

I grabbed my overnight bag from the back seat and opened the door. The brisk sea air hit my tired face. I took in a deep breath as we made our way inside to Reception. Whilst Jim organized the room with the front desk, I took a look around the foyer: dark brown oak paneled walls made the space seem like it belonged on a tall ship; pictures of Montauk's historic fishing industry - men with weathered faces and toothy grins. It was so far removed from the foyer of 'my' hotel, but more homely and welcoming than Mr. Watts' establishment could ever be.

"Just follow me," I heard the Receptionist say. We made our way up the first flight of stairs through a set of double doors, up a second flight, a sharp turn to the left, one more set and we were there. Room 21.

Our room had a comfortable double bed, a dresser, TV, small table and two chairs. Nothing fancy - just simple clean lines. The décor did not matter to me anyway, I was immediately drawn to the bay window and the view. I couldn't remember the last time I had been to the beach. Probably one of my foster families had taken me as a child. I pinched myself at another long-buried memory that had come inexplicably to the surface after so long.

Waves rolled in, one after the other, crashing onto the beach. Just a few brave souls were walking along the seafront - dog walkers and locals making the most of the late afternoon sun before night fell. If I craned my neck and looked to the very left side of the window I could just make out the lighthouse. Jim followed my gaze.

"The Receptionist said we should take a walk up tomorrow morning," he said. "They can make a breakfast picnic basket for us."

It sounded great, I loved how Jim was always so thoughtful. I flopped down on the bed like a rag-doll. The past few weeks, even years, finally seemed to be taking their toll. I was exhausted. Jim lay down beside me and I put my head on his chest. Before I knew it, I was fast asleep.

The morning light woke me as it peeked through the pale green curtains. Jim was still dozing. Looking over at him, I felt a pang of guilt - we had driven all this way only for me to fall asleep as soon as we arrived. I would get this picnic basket organized and make it up to him today.

By the time I returned to the room, Jim was up and was putting on his shoes. "I have everything arranged for our adventure to the lighthouse," I told him.

"Great!" he replied. "Ready when you are!"

We headed up the beach embracing the last of the autumn sun, enjoying it's warmth on our faces. We strolled hand in hand listening to the seagulls soaring above. No need for conversation. I liked that there were no awkward silences between us - he understood my need for quite time.

As the lighthouse dawned on us, we found a grassy knoll where I spread out the blanket and laid out the coffee, croissants and fresh fruit from the basket. Sipping my coffee, I felt Jim's gaze lingering on me.

"What?" I said, thinking I had food on my face.

"Nothing – it's just…"

"Just what, Jim?"

He took a deep breath before saying: "Last night, when you were sleeping, you were screaming. I tried to wake you but couldn't. You kept repeating 'Don't let them take me Mummy, please' over and over. It was the first time Jim had ever mentioned anything like this happening as I slept, so I had no reason not to believe him.

I took a sip of my coffee before saying: "Jim, I'm going to tell you all I know. I don't remember my mother or father. I barely remember the foster homes - I know there were a few - and every time a family sent me back I was marched off to another therapist to try and 'fix' my problems. It wasn't until I was eight that I was sent to Queens Bridge houses, adopted by a lovely couple unable to have their own children. They both died suddenly in a car accident a few years ago and that's when I found my adoption file with…."

My voice trailed off. Even though I felt this connection with Jim, something was telling me not to reveal all to him. A voice in my head reminded me that I still had no proof of why Watts Regency was listed in the file - and until I knew for sure I was not going to share it with him, or anyone else.

"I'm sorry if I scared you, Jim." I continued. "I really can't explain why I would have been saying those things. It may just be memories coming back through my dreams. Maybe when we get back to the city I should start seeing a counselor again, it may just help unlock some of these doors in my mind. Maybe the last one I had - she really helped me adjust to life with my adoptive parents. I saw her until the age of 12, and she showed me that your past can never define your present.

Jim seemed satisfied with my answer and we settled back to lie in the sun for a while before walking around the lighthouse and then back to the hotel. We explored Montauk Harbor with its fishing trawlers bobbing up and down before they were prepared to head out for their nightly catch, then stopped at a lovely port-side seafood restaurant for lunch.

I loved it here. The thought of leaving tomorrow terrified me already. *What was waiting for me at work? Or at home, for that matter?* I pushed those thoughts of dread aside as I snuggled into Jim. For now, this felt right and tomorrow was a new day.

***

"Damn" Jim suddenly said.

"What's wrong?"

"Oh I just remembered I left my charger up in the room," he replied. "I'll just run up and grab it."

"Fine," I said, kissing him gently on the lips, "I'll wait here."

I scanned the brochures on the cheap plastic stand: whale watching, shark diving, *Oh my!* Fishing tours… Then I sensed someone watching me intently.

I whipped around, pressing my back defensively against the stand. He was so close, I darted my eyes around him, looking for Jim, someone… anyone. But it was just me and Mr. Creed.

A thin boney finger reached towards me and traced the shoulder strap of my overnight bag. The corner of his thin lips twisted upwards into a slight sneer as if he had seen it before. His skeleton-like finger then moved along my collarbone before lightly brushing aside a strand of my hair to reveal the necklace. He stared at it, then rolled it between his fingers before raising his gaze up to meet mine.

"You have the same eyes as someone I know, but have not seen for a very long time," he rasped. "Remember Clarissa, when you dig up the past, all you get is dirty."

And with that he turned on his heels and walked out the door.

CHAPTER 13

"Is everything ok Miss Banks" the sweet hotel owner asked. She had clearly witnessed my exchange with Mr. Creed. I guess all hotels thrived off gossip, not just the Regency.

I stammered and struggled to formulate a formidable reply.

"Erm, uh-huh, ah, er, yes, yes I am. Actually, would it be ok if we stayed a couple of extra nights?"

Jim approached me just as I was handed back the room key. He smiled when I dangled the keys between my fingers.

"Are we staying in Montauk for another night then?" I smiled and nodded. I was feeling good in that moment, Jim's presence made me happy and I kissed him to show him how I felt.

"Aren't you worried about being fired?" He asked.

"Terrified. But, I don't know, we'll see what happens, if I get fired maybe it's all for the best."

***

The nightmares were back.

I turned on the shower as warm as I could handle it and locked the bathroom door behind me. I had lied so much to Jim but the hardest lie was telling him I was okay when I felt like I was breaking inside.

I had thought I was safe in that moment of courage, I had thought by staying away from home I had banished the nightmares, but I was wrong. When I awoke from the last nightmare, I felt like I had woken up, maybe for the first time in my life. My face was stained with dream tears. I dropped my nightgown on the cold tiled floor and immersed myself in the heat of the shower and for the first time since I was small I let myself cry the tears that I held in every day. They were the tears I felt for being abandoned, they were the tears caught in the memory of my dream, they were the tears because I felt like I was a stranger in the world, homeless and clan-less and I had felt that way my entire life. They were the tears for faded dreams of memories of happiness and yelling and fights that only my two year old self was a witness to.

The dream I had awoken from... it wasn't just a dream, it was a memory. I had been eight, I remembered because 'she' came to see me, even though I was with the nice people, the couple who had adopted me.

My Mother visited when was eight and I knew that I wasn't supposed to talk to strangers, but when the beautiful woman with the sunshine yellow sundress and the sunlight in her hair had gotten out of an expensive car, I had known her on sight. There had been only one moment, one brief pause when both of us wondered if the other would realize, then I had dropped my bag and ran to her.

She had picked me up and hugged and hugged me and we were both crying, me the same tears I cried right now, the tears of thinking I was alone and then realizing that there was somewhere in the world where I belonged after all. She was impossibly beautiful and impossibly young. She pulled me into the car where she had been sitting in the back on the passengers side and she held me as she wept. I knew in the small, still way that children sometimes know, that her pain had been greater than mine and I melded to her while she clutched me to her chest.

A man was in the front seat. I wondered if he was my Dad, but I realized from the way my mother treated him that he wasn't, he was an employee of some sort. She called him her driver and told me that he was safe, he was someone she trusted. She said, "If you ever need help and you can't find me, you ask for Mr. Reed. He'll always know where I am."

She hugged me fiercely after that and I noted that Mr. Reed was watching us in the rear view mirror. I wondered, even then if she was right to trust him. His eyes were strange and I thought that he looked like an evil magician. He was a villain, not a hero. All thoughts about villains faded in the light that my mother seemed to shed all around her. I didn't want to tell her that someone had adopted me, I didn't want her to know that I had given myself to anyone but her.

We had two more encounters after that. One time a year later on my ninth birthday she had phoned me and she had told me with tears that she was doing everything she could so that it could be safe for me to come home with her. The next time I had seen her it was another year later just a few weeks after my tenth birthday. There was no phone call for my birthday that ycar cvcn though I insisted on staying home for the entire day. My 'parents' exchanged worried looks all day on my birthday, they had discerned the source of my birthday phone calls that left me on an emotional roller coaster of tears and joy. I saw her two and a half weeks later but it was the saddest encounter so far and it had only been a glimpse of my real mother at my adopted grandfathers funeral. She had disappeared before I could get to her through the throng of relatives who looked at me with dead eyes that had never truly accepted me. They had told Rita and Jonathan, who I had awkwardly called 'mom' and 'dad' for the past two years, that they were foolish for taking in an orphan, that it was sure to lead to heartbreak.

At only ten, it seemed like I had lived several lives already and now the me that had lived for two whole years with my adopted parents seemed to be less settled than everyone had hoped. I really believed my mother would come for me, I thought she would save me from the next foster home and then I thought she would save me from the one after that, but she never came, and somehow I managed to make this couple my family, until they too were cruelly taken from me, by one careless driver.

Over ten years passed before I heard her voice again... My memory had faded and sabotaged my ability to recognize her, but I think I had known deep down, that it was really 'her' on the phone. Her voice, frightened, more frightened than it had been when I was eight, when she had tearfully told me over the phone that she was trying to make it safe for me. This time she had been frantic and tearful as well and had told me not to trust Mr. Watts, and warned me away from the hotel.

I turned off the shower and dried myself off as quickly as I could. "Mr. Creed..." I suddenly realized what my mother had told me. I never considered I was mistaken, but saying it out loud made me sure. It was never Mr. Reed, how could I have forgotten his villainous face, but now I knew, I had to go find Mr. Creed right now. She had made a promise to me that he would always know where I was and whether I was right or wrong to trust him, I was awake now and I needed to know the truth.

I was barely dry but I jammed my jeans onto my legs anyway. Jim sat up and rubbed at his hair that had become unruly, "Where are you going...again? Are you alright?"

"I've got to find Mr. Creed, I think he knew my mother."

"You said that already, he said that your eyes were like someone's he knows and you said that you were sure he meant your mother. You didn't seem to know why you were so sure he meant your mother..."

I stopped my frantic search for my shoes and looked at Jim. He had been so kind to me, so understanding, and I... I had been so unreasonable and so, well, the kindest word for my behavior that I could think of was, 'mysterious' but I knew that words like 'spazzy' and 'untruthful' were a lot closer to home. I realized that I owed him. I owed him for taking me to Montauk, I owed him for being kind to me and I owed him most of all for believing in me, even when I fibbed about the carpets being cleaned.

I sat down on the bed next to him. I wanted to lie down on the bed and put my head on his lap, or curl up on his chest. I didn't feel like I could, I felt like the scaffolding I had erected from the time I was a child to keep me safe from the world would collapse if I did and I didn't know Jim well enough to trust him to hold me up if that happened. I knew myself well enough to know that I couldn't hold myself up and if he let me fall... I didn't think I would ever get up again.

So, I didn't curl up with him, but I sat next to him and I put a hesitant hand out to him and then pulled it back again. It fluttered in the air between us uncertainly, he sat up and took it in his own hands. I thought that he was strong, I knew that he was just a manager at a fast food joint, but then, maybe that was the perfect prince for a concierge.

"I remembered Mr. Creed, I remembered him the way he remembered my eyes," my voice was full of crumbles and cracks. I cleared my throat and managed to go on, "I remembered

113

seeing my mother, I saw her once, when I was eight. She told me that I could trust Mr. Creed and that he would always know where she was. I was in such awe that day, I didn't pay attention, I thought she said Mr. Reed, but the name Creed is just too similar. All this time the name 'Reed' kept playing over and over again in my head, when the person I was looking for had already found me."

I knew as the words sat between us that I had taken the first step in trusting him. Nothing else had been trust, not sharing a hotel room, not having a nightmare in front of him, only this, the truth. I held my breath waiting to see if he would think I was silly, or just plain wrong. I held my breath and waited to see if he would break my heart.

He gazed at our hands. Two of his held one of mine and my other hand picked at invisible lint on the hotel comforter. "I understand."

That was all he said and I could breathe again. We searched the hotel from top to bottom and asked at the front desk for Mr. Creed but everything led to blank looks and dead ends. We retreated to our room again and I paced and then sat and then paced again. I felt like a feral animal and Jim's silence made me feel terrible. Did he think I was making it up after all?

Finally, in desperation I asked him.

"Making it up? Oh, I don't think you're making anything up, Clarissa."

"Then why are you just sitting there."

"Because I don't know how to fix it. Don't you see, Clarissa, don't you understand that I lo..."

He bit off the word 'love' at the last second. I stopped pacing and we stared at each other from across the room. I was paralyzed with the force of the unsaid word between us, wanting and not wanting. Dreading the utterance and hating him for stopping the word.

He looked at me in the eyes, his voice was quiet and raw with his feelings. "Don't you understand that I love you, Clarissa?"

"You can't." My automatic refusal of love, always, to everyone. I loved him too, I wanted to. It was too soon. I would die without him. I felt all these ways and numb at the same time. Too many feelings had been pushed through me in too short of a time. I was a sleepwalker once more.

"I can. I do. I'm not a prize and I don't have a lot, but what I do have is yours. I've been yours since I first laid eyes on you from across the counter. Why else would I drop everything to bring you here? Why else are you here, Clarissa? You're a beauty and a prize even though you don't seem to know it. Why did you come here with me of all people unless you loved me, even a little bit, in return?"

His impassioned plea seemed to drain all my restlessness into the floor, I sat down on a chair, closer to him than I had been, but still aloof, still alone, "I can't say I love you back, Jim. Can't you see how wounded I am? Can't you see how much it would hurt me to say those words to you?"

"I don't need you to say the words back to me, Clarissa, I just need you to not run away or refuse them when I say it, when I say, I love you, Clarissa Banks."

I didn't run away and I didn't refuse his words. I crept over to the bed where he sat on the edge of it. His long fingers were steepled under his chin and when I walked to him, he didn't move. He was luring a deer in a clearing closer to him and he was afraid to move, he loved me and he didn't want to hurt me. I sat beside him and put my head on his shoulder. I was awkward about it and he unsteepled his fingers and put an arm around me.

"I don't know how to be loved," I said the words and they

dropped into the room like pebbles in a pond. Each one a simple truth.

He kissed my head and held me tight, "I'll show you."

I gasped at the power his words held and lifted my head to meet his gaze. He smiled and kissed me and I let him. After a moment, I kissed him back, and without a flinch I let him tug on the strap of my top, pulling it slowly over my exposed shoulder. He looked into my eyes, seeking approval and with nothing more than an agreeable glint in my eye he spun me around, onto the bed and channeled his love into me with every exasperated touch. Jim owned my body, and my heart. If only I could tell him.

***

Unaware of how much time had passed, we reluctantly peeled ourselves off of the sweat ridden sheets and prepared to head out for some much need fresh air. I told Jim I would meet him downstairs, but never even made it to the lobby door before I saw a derelict shadow on the wall and as soon as I saw that the shadow was carrying a briefcase, I knew that Mr. Creed had found me.

I whirled around and grinned at him. "Mr. Creed! I was looking for you."

His old white eyebrows climbed the many creases on his forehead. "You were looking for me?"

"Do you know where my mother is? I remember you. She said you would know."

It was only a fleeting darkness but a shadow fluttered across his eyes before he cast it aside and nodded. I was too excited to remind myself that I had known since I was eight that this man was a villain and I couldn't think of him as the one who my mother, with the sunshine hair, had told me that I could always trust.

"I know where your mother is."

"Was Mrs. Devlin my mother" I spoke with gravity, picturing her tomb stone. I asked with expectation and sadness "Where is she?"

He scowled. "Mrs. Devlin was your grandmother. You're asking too many questions. I have some papers for you in here, that's why I came back to find you."

"Why didn't you give them to me at the Regency?"

"Are you daft? It's not safe there! You can't go back there."

"Why not? I don't understand!"

"You don't understand? You don't understand?! Lionel is your father!"

"Lionel?"

"Lionel Watts, you call him 'Mr. Watts' and he signs your paychecks, but who knows how long you'll be safe once he figures out that you know the truth."

I fell back into a chair in the lobby where Mr. Creed had found me. I looked at him, his spindly old body was bent nearly doubled and the briefcase he carried weighted him down much the way Jacob Marley had been weighted down by the chains of his crimes.

"But that can't be, Mr. Watts doesn't have any children."

"That's exactly it, that's the only reason you're still alive, he still has time to start a family, but if he doesn't succeed in having children then you will be a danger to *them* and to the family fortune."

"The family fortune..." I repeated his words back dumbly. He smiled at me for the first time and in his smile was such a kind gentleness that I could see why my mother had told me to trust him. He sat down across from me and rested the heavy case that was manacled to him on the floor.

"Yes, the family fortune. You're a heiress, my dear, the

only question now is whether or not you will live to ever realize your inheritance. The Watts are not above murder, as you well know in your twenty one years of life."

"Murder! Mrs. Devlin, did Mr. Watts..?"

"If you mean with his own two hands? Then no, I would say the chances of him getting his hands dirty are slim to none. If you are asking whether or not he was responsible, I would tell you that as a betting man, I would wager what I have that he, or his parents are guilty as hell of murdering your grandmother."

Mr. Creed looked at me with concern. I felt sick and confused. My entire concept of myself, the hotel, the Devlins', my mother and Mr. Watts had been sent into turmoil. I wanted Jim, the only sure thing in my world, he would hold me, he would tell me that I would be all right and I would believe him when he told me that I was.

"I really don't feel well," I managed to say whilst fighting back waves of dizziness. "Is that a new suitcase?" I suddenly felt inclined to ask.

"Your observant, and yes, they come in quite handy, unless they go missing that is. Look Clarissa, I imagine this is a lot for you to take in. It's good though, it's good that you remembered me and it's good that you finally know the truth."

I stood up and swayed on unsteady legs. Mr. Creed watched me with concern but made no effort to help steady me. "Oh, the papers I have for you, I promised Mr. Devlin that I would see to it that you got your copy, Mr. Watts already has his."

"Papers?"

"Yes, the papers. Your dear mother has been on the run for her life ever since the Lord Watts had your adoptive parents killed. He suspected that your mother had been in contact with them and were worried about how much they knew. They couldn't risk anyone finding out about you, they didn't want a bastard on their bankroll who could take everything from under them. Your mother always knew how dangerous the Watts are, but now the stakes are higher."

He saw the shattered expression on my face and apologized, "I am sorry, it's only how people like the Watts think, you see. You weren't expected and Lionel and Violet were playing out of bounds when they made you... Your mother loved you so much she couldn't bear to just leave you alone, she wanted you back, and I'm afraid her desire to have you back has caused her and you and many others besides a great deal of pain... I'm even more afraid that it's about to cause a lot more."

I felt like I should apologize for being such a bother as a baby. The words, 'they didn't want a bastard on their bankroll' had been a punch in the gut, I couldn't apologize as I couldn't find the air to speak. Mr. Creed looked uncomfortable about my inability to talk. He cleared his throat and looked around awkwardly, guests were starting to come down for dinner and he lowered his voice a little to speak his next words.

"I'll meet you up in your room and give you the papers, as I was saying, you're mother has decided to put an end to it. She's hoping that by declaring you their legal heir will put a stop to this once and for all. Frankly, I'm terribly worried she hasn't thought this through and this time her actions will get both you and her as dead as her own mother."

"But what about Mr. Devlin" I asked? I was confused, but got nothing but a tired look in response. I realized there was more to this than I already understood.

He stood abruptly and walked away. I made my way up to the hotel room hoping against hope that there wouldn't be any more surprises.

MR. CREED

Mr. Creed left Clarissa to gather her thoughts, and made his way out of the hotel into the gentle glow of the afternoon sun. As he walked briskly along the promenade to his car he stopped, inhaled a deep breath of sea air, and banked left down the stairs to the beach.

A few steps towards the sea, he slumped down into the sand, taking the weight of the world with him. Removing his shoes and socks one by one, he let his pale and spidery feet rest on the cold sand. It had been a long, long time since he had been to the beach; so long ago he struggled to remember.

He dropped his heavy head into his hands, closing his eyes and listening to the waves crashing onto the beach, one after another after another. *Why am I still helping her?* he thought. *Twenty long years of friendship and she still has me running around like her personal dog.* Loyalty, maybe? It had been unwavering loyalty until the day he saw Clarissa in the hotel foyer.

She was now a fully grown woman, and had it not been

for those eyes he would not have given her a second glance. How had she become involved? What was Watts thinking when he hired her? Perhaps he was unaware of the consequences when Lady Watts found out.

Creed tried to forget his thoughts of Mrs. Devlin's death. It wasn't part of the plan, but if Violet had just told him that Clarissa was working there, maybe he wouldn't have looked for other opportunities.

It was fate only that he had overheard the conversation between the other concierge Joy and one of her colleagues. They were talking about Clarissa, and how Mr. Watts had a soft spot for her, giving her extra time off. At the time, he hadn't known they were talking about Violet's Clarissa. As far as he was concerned, there was no way she could be so close by. But something had changed after that nasty car accident. It left Clarissa alone, and if she inherited any of her mother's suspicious tendencies, it would only be a matter of time before she showed up to stake her claim. Or so he had thought.

He lifted his face slightly towards the sun. He had worked so hard to keep the girl away from this poisonous situation. He'd found that wonderful couple to look after her, appalled by how many failed foster families she'd been through. And he'd risked his own life to bring her mother to visit her that day.

He let out a long sigh. "Violet" he whispered. Her face appeared before him like a mirage, the most beautiful women he had known. "Beautifully messed up."

Originally, he had been hired as Lord Watts' driver. His pale skin, off-putting appearance, and serious lack of qualifications had made it hard for him to find work. Then a friend of his, who worked as a gardener for the aristocracy, mentioned the Watts were looking for a driver. Creed's only skills in trade were as a car mechanic, but fortunately Lord Watts had been impressed with his knowledge and love of motor vehicles. He was hired on the spot, on the condition he tidied himself up. The job itself was mundane, ferrying His Lordship and his son to and from the hotel. He lived in a room above the garage, above Lord Watts' prized collection of cars, overlooking the sweeping driveway and Porte Cochere for the perfect view of the comings and goings of the Watts household.

It had been through that very window that he had first seen Violet, walking Lord Watts' two terriers down the driveway. She stopped every few meters to throw a ball for them to fetch, her laughter infectious even from where he stood. He watched her stop and pick a bunch of daisies from the edge of the drive, twirling one in her fingers. She placed it behind her ear, like some kind of magical fairy, then spun about with the dogs before collapsing onto the lawn and surrendering to their enthusiastic games. She had laughed as they licked her face.

He'd known, then and there, that she could never fall for someone like him. He was pale, scrawny, socially awkward, a nobody. But he didn't care. In his heart he knew that his real job was to protect her, to keep her safe at all costs.

Violet had been hired as Lady Watts' personal assistant (*Ha!* thought the man on the beach, and he snorted. *More like a personal slave!*) a few years before Creed had joined the household. He knew that Lord Watts never approved of Violet, especially when he discovered her affair with his only son who also had full control of their hotel empire.

Lord Watts' wife had been even more ruthless than her husband could ever have dreamt of being. She was like a poisonous arrow that could strike at any time without warning. She had a plan for her son and the family fortune, and Lord have mercy on your soul if you got in her way. They both tolerated their son's affair with the pretty staff member, yet made it crystal clear that it must never be anything more than a fling. One that they could stop at any time they wished.

And that's just what they did. He'd heard the commotion one stormy evening, shouts and screams cutting through the thunder and rain that cloaked the house. He ran to the window to see what was it was. Through the rain-streaked glass, he could just make out a car parked under the Porte Cocher. There was Violet, unconscious or possibly drugged, being carried out and laid in the back of the car by two men. He had grabbed his uniform and yanked it on it on as he ran down the back stairs. Reaching the car just in time, and told the drivers he would take over. They didn't think twice, perhaps grateful for the chance not to get involved, and left.

Creed had driven that car as far away as he could bear before checking on Violet. She had seemed okay, but it was now up to him to look after her.

He could only imagine the venomous words Lady Watts would have dished out to the other staff once she realized what he had done. That poisonous spider of a woman, and she alone, knew it was him who intervened and put an end to her despicable plan. There and then, he'd known that nothing else was important. All he cared about was Violet.

He had pulled over and stepped out of the car and into the pouring rain. Violet still rested in the back seat. The thought of Lady Watts had made him shudder, but he knew that he had finally broken free of her web. He just hadn't known the price he would have to pay for getting involved in this huge mess, or how far he would be willing to go to finally break free from them all.

CHAPTER 14

Dazed, I walked back into our room and Jim looked up from tying his last shoelace. He smiled sweetly. "I know, I've been ages, but I'm ready now - lets go."

"Actually Jim, I just felt a little queasy, and decided to come back and rest for a moment. You must have worn me out last night" I added for good measure. Jim was always very easy, and grabbed the paper to read whilst I rested. After half an hour had passed, I wondered if Creed was coming back with these so called papers after all. I figured there was no point mentioning it to Jim until he actually knocked on the door. Deciding that wasn't going to happen after all, I was ready to take our overdue walk along the beach. I hoped to blow away all the cobwebs and give Room Service the chance to change the sheets we had so thoroughly rumpled with our love-making.

This time, I told Jim I would meet him downstairs, whilst I freshened up quickly. In the bathroom, I splashed cold water on my face – three, four, five times – then looked up at the restroom mirror. Red spots blazed on my cheeks, strands of wet hair stuck to my forehead and little drops of water merged with my tears as they traveled down and dripped off my chin.

My head was spinning. After so many years of searching and wondering who I was, I now knew – and it was just too much information for me to process.

In just a couple of weeks, I had gone from feeling totally alone in the world to learning who my parents were and finding out I could be the sole heir to The Regency and the vast fortune behind it. I also found myself in the midst of a sinister web of lies and greed that had probably cost my grandmother and my beloved adoptive parents their lives.

This wasn't the fairy tale ending I'd dreamed of when I was a little girl. It was a nightmare. Whoever said 'Ignorance is bliss' knew what they were talking about. I allowed myself a bitter little chuckle at the irony of that last thought, then shook my head to see if all the pieces of the puzzle might re-settle into some kind of pattern that made sense. They didn't. They just jumbled up again, with lines connecting them like a drunken spider's web.

I reached for the towel, dried off, combed my hair into submission and touched up my blotchy face with a little powder and paint. The person who was present in my life was downstairs waiting for me, and that was something I could fix.

Coming down the stairs, I paused behind one of the columns, watching him from afar, drinking in his strong, reassuring presence. I closed my eyes and let out a deep grateful breath. Amid all this mayhem and uncertainty, I couldn't believe that I had found such a great guy.

Jim was Jim. Solid, reliable, caring, with a gentle humour and no nasty surprises. Who'd have thought all that could come wrapped up in a McDonald's shirt and name tag – my very own Happy Meal. Instinctively, he seemed to know when I needed my space, and he knew when I needed to be touched. And he knew exactly how to touch me.

I saw him jump as his phone rang, and smiled at his cheesy loyalty when I recognized the "I'm Lovin' It" ring tone. No wonder he'd won 'Employee of the Month' so many times. But my smile froze as I heard him utter a panicked "What?" His face clouded and his shoulders slumped. Something was very wrong.

"When?" he asked urgently. "Where is he now? Can we see him?"

He grabbed a pen from his pocket and scribbled something hurriedly on the Shark Diving brochure in front of him. "I'm out of town, but I'll be there as soon as I can."

Obviously, there was not going to be any romantic stroll down the beach for us, after all.

Jim was shaking visibly when I got to him. Despite his kind, tired eyes and salt and pepper stubble, he looked like a lost little boy when he looked up at me.

"Oh babe, I'm so sorry. We have to leave," he struggled to get the words out. "It's my Dad… he's in hospital. He never gets sick, always the strong one, and now…" A hiccup of fear and suppressed panic swallowed the rest of his sentence, and he doubled over, almost touching his knees with his nose.

I put a comforting hand on his back and said, as gently as I could: "Of course you must go. But you're in no fit state to drive now. Let's get some sweet tea inside you and take a little time before we hit the road." Inwardly, I cursed my New Yorker mentality that had never pushed me to get a driver's license.

Over tea in the hotel's cozy coffee shop, all chintz curtains and potted herbs, Jim sipped his overly sweet tea, and moved an almond Danish around his plate, talking absently about his father.

"You'd never even know we were related. You met my Mom, so you'll know that I'm just like her - but without the permanent wave and sensible heels," he tried to grin through the tears that threatened to break the surface of his composure.

"But that's just on the outside. Mom's all drive and doing the right thing – I think I'm a bit of a disappointment to her, to be honest. But Dad, he's all heart." He let out a bitter laugh. "Pretty ironic really, considering it's his ticker that's put him in hospital."

He fumbled in his back pocket and pulled out a battered leather wallet.

"He gave me this for my 18th birthday," he sniffed. "Best wallet in the world."

Shuffling through the credit cards, receipts and dollar bills, he pulled out a creased, slightly faded photograph and handed it over. It showed a happy family group, hair mussed by the brisk East Coast breeze, grinning at the camera from a plaid picnic blanket on the beach. Though Jim couldn't have been more than 12 years old in the picture, he and his Mom were instantly recognizable – the same sturdy build and steady gaze. With them was a younger boy, maybe 8 or 9, his dark hair flying in the wind.

A jolt of recognition hit me like a thunderbolt as I looked at the fourth person in the snap. A middle-aged man with thinning hair and the beginnings of a holiday beard was buried up to his neck in the sand, laughing at the absurdity of his situation. His dancing eyes bored into me from faded print from the past.

"That's your father?" I asked, praying Jim didn't notice the tremor in my voice.

"Yeah, look at him. The old goofball. I could never get a proper picture of him, so this is all I've got."

A seagull screamed outside the window, and I sank back

into a misty, half-buried memory. Running down a beach, salt water and grains of sand clogging my hair, screaming as the first waves slapped me, but refusing to be the scaredy-cat who'd turn back at their first wet embrace. Determined to make a good impression on the two boys and kind-eyed man, and perhaps even the stern matron who seemed to be in charge of everything, I'd thrown myself in and paddled madly out into the deeper water. The rest was hazy. Brief flashes of cheese bagels, Hershey bars and lukewarm Pepsi on the beach, a long lazy drive back to the city, and the sound of harsh words drifting up from the garden late that night. Then a screaming nightmare - one of the countless ones that haunted my childhood - followed by terse whispered phone conversations the next morning. I was back with the Child Welfare Department before I knew it, and in the child psychiatrist's office by the end of the week. I didn't know what I'd done – but once again, I knew I'd failed to be good enough for yet another foster family.

"Jim, did your parents ever take in children without families?" I asked tentatively.

"Yeah, that was my old man. He'd had a tough childhood, and said he owed it to the world to give other kids a chance. Didn't last long. After the first four or five, Mom put a stop to it – said it wasn't the sort of thing 'people like us' did."

He rambled on, calming himself with happy memories, when the penny finally dropped. He turned slowly to me, mouth agape.

"That was you! You're Clara. That's why I felt I'd known you all my life since that first day I saw you sneaking into the restroom!"

We sat, staring at each other in disbelief, not saying a word. A million jumbled thoughts tumbled through my mind – including the nagging doubt that Jim might somehow be mixed up in everything. But one look at his dumbstruck expression and the pain and incomprehension swimming deep in his eyes told me he knew nothing.

The spell was broken as the waitress appeared by my side and asked it everything was alright and if we needed anything else. "No, thanks," said Jim, shaking himself and putting on his 'strictly business' demeanor. "It was great, but something's come up, so we have to go and check out. Can you ask the lady at reception to add the tea to our bill, and we'll settle up when we check-out in about ten minutes."

"No problem," smiled the girl, with a New England twang, and cleared away our cups and plates.

It didn't take long to gather up our belongings. After all, it has just taken me a few minutes to grab what I'd needed from my apartment when we made out spur-of-the-moment decision to get away. Toothbrush, make-up bag, change of underwear, spare jeans, sweater and hairbrush – no nightdress (no need for one). On the other side of the now perfectly made bed, Jim was zipping up his overnight bag and looking around to check if he'd left anything behind. His phone bleeped and his face clouded with worry as he read the new text message that had come in.

"No time to waste, babe. They're taking dad in for surgery, and I want to be there at his side when he wakes up."

I nodded mutely, then ventured "Do you want me to come to the hospital with you?"

His eyes melted, and he sighed with gratitude. "Oh god, yes. Thank you."

The drive back passed mostly in companionable, if anxious, silence. I occasionally commented on the gorgeous autumn colours of the trees we passed, but mostly left him to his own thoughts, wanting to give him the same space he needed, that he'd always given me. As we approached the city, he started mumbling to himself, mentally steeling himself for whatever would be waiting for him at the hospital. He seemed more and more tense as we drew closer.

"I should warn you, my mom will be there," he said. "I know you didn't get off to the greatest of starts with her, so if you want to change your mind, that's OK."

I assured him that I was more than capable of standing up to whatever his mother could throw at me in order to be there by his side. "And, anyhow, I reckon she'll have other things on her mind than her disapproval of her eldest son's latest girlfriend." I almost laughed at the word, it was the first time I'd called myself Jim's girlfriend out loud.

"I don't know why she was so hard on you the other day," Jim went on. "Sure, she's much tougher and more judgmental than Dad, but she's got a good heart way deep down. She usually only lets her inner bitch out when she feels threatened by something."

I pursed my lips. *Could Jim's mom actually feel threatened by me?* I was beginning to think that while Jim wasn't mixed up in my crazy, complex story, anyone else could be. His mom was part of my past. So far my past has caused me nothing but pain. I willed Jim to be that one good thing. He had to be! I was pretty sure his mom hadn't recognized me anyway.

We drew up into a vacant space near the hospital entrance, parked and walked briskly through the automatic doors. Jim strode to the desk and asked for directions for the Cardiac Emergency Care Unit. He looked back at me, and beckoned for me to follow him.

As we followed the green line on the floor showing the way to the Unit, I felt Jim's body stiffen next to me and his breath quicken as he prepared himself. Pushing through double swing doors, I saw Jim's mother talking to a slim man with his back to us wearing an expensive overcoat and a trilby. Caution told me to let go of Jim's arm. His mother looked up and her lips started to form a tense, relieved smile at the sight of her son, but it stopped as she spotted who was at his side. She muttered something I couldn't make out, and the man she was talking to darted sideways into one of the corridors that formed the endless warren of the hospital.

"Hi Mom," Jim said. "Sorry it took me so long – I got here as fast as I could."

She hugged him tight, gave him a perfunctory kiss on the cheek, then shot me a cold look over his shoulder and cut me dead.

"He's going to be OK, my darling," she said. "But you're going to have to step up as the head of the family until he's back on his feet."

Shooting me another filthy look, but still refusing to recognize my existence, she added with meaning: "You have to be strong for him. You need do the right thing."

I slumped down on a moulded plastic seat bolted to the wall, and watched the two of them as they walked down the hall. Two almost identical backs, the same height, the same sturdy build, the same way of walking – just one was in casual weekend chinos and a Yankees sweatshirt, and the other was in a twin set and pearls.

Once again, I felt alone. I didn't belong here, that much was clear from the icy glares I had received, but I wasn't going anywhere. Jim needed me, and I was going to stay by his side until he turned me away... like so many foster families had when I was a kid.

The hushed swish of a door opening and the click of expensive shoes against the floor tiles brought me out of my thoughts. I looked up to see the man that Jim's mom had been talking to emerge from a room down the hall and head towards the exit. He didn't look my way, but I saw enough of his profile to see who it was.

Mr. Watts. My boss. My father. I shook my head in disbelief at the thought. His left hand had a tight grip on a paper wallet loaded with documents.

Without saying anything to Jim, I stood up and left the hospital. Not quietly or with purpose, I just walked away feeling cold. I angered myself by feeling relieved that Jim would be kept busy for a while with his dad. I just knew I needed to get out of there.

CHAPTER 15

When I reached my apartment, I pulled out a sachet of soup and put the kettle on the stove. I thought I had no more tears to cry until I was suddenly drowning in my misery. I sobbed deep air gasping sobs. After what was meant to be a romantic break, I now felt more alone than ever.

The next day I phoned in sick, told them I'd come down with a serious case of mood poisoning. Of course, I meant food and my little joke was lost in the wind. For the next couple of days, I stayed in my dressing gown and moped around my apartment as though I really was ill. There was this pain in my chest whenever I thought of Jim and it crippled me with guilt at how I'd been. When I had first started at the Regency, I told myself I would never have a single day sick, that I would not risk losing a job that I'd never thought I could land. But now I wondered if Watts had been behind everything, pulling strings so he could keep me close.

Keep your enemies closer…

Was I really his enemy? No, but he was quickly making

one of me. The man who had something to do with the death of my grandmother, and who made my mom fear for her life. A powerful man, Watts thought he was untouchable. As I sat in my chair, eating right out of a tub of ice cream and being terribly clichéd about things in my sulk, I thought about how money made you powerful. Who was I to go against a man of Watts standing, the owner of a hotel? *Oh, but I am someone he fears,* I thought. Keep me close, watch me but never make a move. Maybe there was a glimmer of parental love in the man. I doubted it. Anyone who could kill surely had no warmth.

I physically ached for Jim. I hadn't seen him or heard his voice since I walked out of the hospital. Just a few hurried texts to tell me he was spending every waking moment by his father's bedside. The last text said his dad was doing well and could be coming home any day now - but I guess I wasn't high enough on Jim's list of priorities to warrant a phone call.

On my fifth day of pretend illness, the phone actually rang and I picked it up with a moment of hesitation. What if it was Jim calling to tell me he wanted to end things. Just be friends, maybe. He'd kept his distance over the days, probably busy with his Mom and Dad, and probably getting used to me not being around. When I heard his voice on the phone, my heart sank.

"Clarissa, I've been thinking about this whole situation," Jim said.

Here it comes. Say the words: end the relationship.

I pressed the phone close to my ear. "What?" Hang up, I told myself. If I didn't hear it, then it can't be true.

"Well first of all, I'm so sorry I didn't call you," Jim gushed, sounding like a naughty puppy begging for forgiveness. "Mom was watching me like a hawk, and the last thing I wanted was a scene with us screaming about my right to choose who I love over my dad's sickbed. Please forgive me."

I almost cracked my sullen face as a trace of a smile begun to creep across my cheeks.

"I've managed to book into room 426 of the Regency hotel. How do you fancy spending the night there?"

Sitting upright, I couldn't help but cover my mouth with my hand, stifling my gasp. "You're not serious, are you?" My heart hammered as excitement grew. *Room 426? Right next to the room the Devlin's stayed.*

"Uh-huh. So you fancy going undercover for a little snooping?"

It was dangerous, yet strangely erotic. My skin tingled at the thought. Creed had told me to stay away, and every bit of sense I had screamed at me to turn the offer down. "Yes." The word was out and I held my breath for a moment before letting it out with a delighted sigh. "Have you booked us in under false names, too?"

"Yes, Mrs. Smith. You'll have to wear a disguise, of course."

"Of course," I echoed. Nerves did a funny thing and caused my stomach to cramp. So I was going to go right into the spider's web. "Jim, I'm sorry how I reacted… it's just-"

"It's okay, I understand. I'll be round in half hour."

I hung up, sat thinking for a moment, daydreaming about going undercover. Then I realized I was a mess, hadn't showered for three days. In the little time I had, I did my best, whizzing around my apartment, jumping in for a quick shower. As I dried myself, I felt a sudden nausea. There it was in my stomach, building up to… I ran to the toilet and threw up, retching until there was nothing left. My punishment for pretend sickness, I thought, or just nerves over what I was going to do. Flushing the toilet, I stood and felt the sickness pass. I dressed in a plain white dress, pulled out a scarf from my only attempt at fashion and wrapped it around my head like some 1960's house wife. The large sunglasses finished the look perfectly. If I avoided talking to anyone, they wouldn't know who I really was and Clarissa could stay home sick. My heart jumped when the buzzer to my apartment went and I ran down to meet Jim.

**

The journey to the Regency was the complete opposite of last week. The atmosphere was much lighter and we talked the entire way. Jim was only a boy when I first met him. I strongly doubted he had any part of this craziness, and I had already decided to do a little digging on his Mom. Jim was having a hard time at work, slipping in that it didn't help not speaking with me. That made me blush, surprising myself as I thought our relationship had grown beyond such things. But I felt different around Jim. So hard to explain, but it was like I was another person. Perhaps it was just the headscarf and sunglasses disguise that made me act differently. Jim was dressed in a smart dark brown suit with matching shoes. Looked quite the handsome man and I found myself smiling. The smile faded when we pulled up at the Regency and reality came crashing down on me, drowning me in woe. This was work, the very centre of all my problems. And fate was once again pulling strings, placing me exactly where I needed to be and I couldn't help think I was a piece in a chess game.

Jim booked us in at the desk and I hung back in the shadows, my head turning away as familiar faces walked by. They didn't notice me, almost like I was invisible. Jim was taking an age to book in and I began to have second thoughts, had the urge to turn and walk out the building and never come back. But there was so much to learn here. I didn't know what I was looking for, but I had a feeling whilst being here, it would find me. Jim returned and led me to the elevator, taking me by the arm. The happy married couple look, I figured. We nearly made it from the reception incident free and I let myself relax until the elevator doors swung open and Joy stepped out. She looked up at us as she went by, gave a weak smile, a slight glimmer of recognition in her eyes. When she continued on without a glance back, I loosened up a little and stepped into the elevator with Jim.

"You've got to try and relax," Jim said. "You look like you're hiding something." He selected the floor where our room was and the doors slid shut. A moment later, the lift jolted into action.

"But I am hiding something," I whispered through gritted teeth. "Jim, maybe this isn't such a good idea. I work with these people; they know me. What if they recognize me? I'm supposed to be off work sick." As the elevator smoothed to a stop, my stomach turned over and I felt the sickness again, returning like an old friend. I gulped it back and stepped out into the corridor, leading Jim to room 426. We passed by the Devlin's favourite room as we went and I couldn't help but stare at the closed door, wondering what secrets went on behind there. "How much is this costing you, Jim?"

We got to our room and Jim swung the door open and led me in. "Right now it isn't costing me anything. Next month when my credit card bill comes in it'll probably sting, but I can clear it. You deserve the best."

I sighed. "Jim, I can't let you do this." I walked around the room, familiar to me from when I took a sneaky shower there, but not as a guest. My eyes were instantly drawn to the quality of the housekeeping, the slight crease of sheets on the double bed. I knew that this room was purposely kept empty. *How on earth had Jim booked it?*

Jim flopped down on the bed and stretched out. There was a smile spread across his face. "Well, if you're the heir to this vast fortune, I'm sure you could afford to pay off my credit card bill and then some."

"Ah, you want to be a kept man, then?" I flung myself on the bed next to him and cuddled up into his arms. He squeezed me in tight and in that instant I felt safe, protected. It wasn't long before I felt his lips traveling down my neck, his hand running up my leg. I felt giddy, like I was sinking into the bed. His love making was urgent, but I know that I at least met him halfway. I'd missed him, I realized. When we were finished, we lay dozing on the bed, my head resting on Jim's chest. His heart thumped beneath me and I listened to the calming beat. There were no words between us because the moment was total peace. I felt my eyes grow heavy and then I drifted into a sleep where I sank so deep that dreams couldn't even find me. They just floated somewhere near the surface and I hid from them. No dreams today, I thought, slipping out of sleep for a moment like I was coming up for air.

When I woke up again, Jim was gone and it was dark outside. There was a bedside lamp lit so I wasn't plunged into total darkness. Jim had written me a note, telling me he'd popped down to the bar for a drink, didn't want to disturb me and that it looked like I needed the sleep. *Was that a caring comment or an insult?* I couldn't work it out as the note was obviously toneless. I got up and began the hunt for scattered clothes around the room. I got dressed and wondered about my next move. He knew I could hardly saunter down there and join him. Something told me that Watts wasn't in the hotel. Call it women's intuition or just a regular old hunch. Maybe it was just fate waking me up again.

There was a knock on the door. Like a rabbit in the

headlights of a fast moving car, I froze with wide eyed terror. The second knock jolted me into action. *What if it was Jim and he'd forgotten his key? What if it was Watts himself, come to see his daughter and reveal everything?* Edging to the door, I called out, "Who is it?"

There was a pause. I could count the seconds of the silence. "Is that you, Clarissa?"

My heart sank. I'd been seen. But at least the voice was a friendly one and I opened the door a crack, and peered out at Joy. The corridor was empty and I pulled her in, glad to see her, but at the same time felt nervous about her presence. "I knew you recognized me when you came out of the elevator."

Joy, took hold of my arm. "You shouldn't be here," she whispered. For the first time in years, Joy looked serious. So fate had chosen another pawn and this time it was sweet Joy. At least my theory was correct, that things would happen if I just waited. I must be either the luckiest girl or the unluckiest depending on your perspective. I was one of those half empty glass kinda girls, so generally I felt unlucky. "What are you doing, Clarissa? Just having a romantic trip with your guy in the place you work? Was it the employee discount that attracted you here?"

"We get a discount?" That I genuinely didn't know. Maybe it would take the sting out of Jim's credit card bill that I felt so guilty about. I could tell that Joy wasn't her usual self and I thought back to her encounter with Creed. It brought me back to the reason why I was there. Maybe she knew where Creed was? "Look, something is going on in my life, something complicated that I can't explain. It's…." I went silent, stared down at the carpet. Suddenly I felt silly, like some amateur detective snooping where I shouldn't be. A thought struck me that I was Thelma and not the desirable attractive Daphne. Worse than that, I was Scooby Doo.

"I saw Jim in the bar too, half cut, Its not like him"

"You know Jim?" I threw out in annoyance. There was a flicker of hesitation before Joy responded.

"No of course not, I mean I recognize him, I saw you with him outside once, and from what you've said, he doesn't drink much." Joy spoke with such conviction I felt stupid for assuming.

"Joy, there's this man called Creed who told me something about my life that's a real game changer," I found myself pouring out recent events without a second breath. She listened intently as I told her everything I knew. It felt good unloading this to someone else, sharing the burden of the mystery. It didn't matter now, because the game was up. Joy would either cover for me or turn me in. This was a loyalty test and I was glad when I realized she had passed.

"You know about the briefcase?"

"The one Creed was carrying? I think it's just papers to link me to my heritage." I was slightly confused by Joy's question.

Joy looked around her, as though she knew that walls had ears. Her brow was knotted and there was a desperation in her eyes as they widened. She looked scared. "I should've told you sooner, but… we didn't want you involved, we agreed it was too dangerous for you. I needed the extra money, so I agreed to help… him. It was stupid really and if J…. if, anyone else knew I would be in serious trouble." She sat on the bed and I sat next to her. We sat in silence for a few moments. I didn't need to prompt Joy to go on.

"Creed wanted me to make an exchange of cases between him and Mr. Watts. He offered me a fair bit of money to do it. He told me there was important documents in the case, that he'd been attacked for the contents and he didn't feel safe keeping hold of them. It was like he wanted me to know how dangerous it was. For the kind of money he gave me, it had to be. He said that Lord and Lady Watts would kill for the information in the case. So here's the deal: he wanted me to hold onto the case and keep it safe until he had what he wanted from Mr. Watts. Once he had that, then he said I could go ahead and give the case to Mr. Watts. I informed Mr. Watts of the arrangement, but didn't tell him I had the case. He calmly told me he'd get the money tomorrow and for me not to talk about this to anyone."

Joy sighed. "You know, I'm pretty good with locks…"

"You looked to see what was inside?" I was on the edge of the bed, desperate to know what Joy had seen.

"It was mainly legal papers, but what caught my eye was a family chart of the Devlins. It looked wrong to me, like the branches ended with Mr. and Mrs. Devlin. You know they're not actually married? They're half brother and sister!"

I could feel the colour draining from my face. "Are you sure?"

Joy nodded. "In the files were newspaper articles from years ago about a scandal, how it rocked the Devlin family and tore them apart. Apparently there was an affair between two long lost half siblings. Then I found the letters between Mr. and Mrs. Devlin. They spoke of a child, a daughter. There was an adoption paper drawn up with your name on, Clarissa. I wasn't sure what it all meant, or what it had to do with the Watts and the Devlins, and you." She turned to me, held my hands. "Mr. Devlin had a child with his half sister. I don't think they knew at the time they were closely related, but they spoke about how it could shatter their family. They named her Violet and I think she's your mother. Of course, it seemed Violet started a relationship with a young Mr. Watts, according to a letter Lady Watts had written to Violet. She told her she wouldn't have her family line mixed with the product of incest. Lady Watts was too late: Violet was pregnant with a daughter. It was all in black and white, Clarissa, every bit of document to prove the affairs and the children's birth certificates, including yours."

Things began to fall in place now. A young woman in love, carrying the child of the future heir to the Watts fortune and it turned out that child was a product of incest. A child that was… wrong. Damaged by genetics. I didn't have to ask the name of the child because I knew it was me. Had always felt wrong my entire life growing up. All those doctors and therapists. Now I knew why I was broken. And of course the Watts didn't want that scandal coming out and my mother had fled, sending me for adoption. *Just how scared was mom that she had to do that? Were the Watts family that dangerous?* I knew the answer to that, and quickly realized that the real dangerous person was probably Lady Watts. It was her influence on Mr. Watts that had forced him to turn his back on his own daughter. *Or had he turned his back?* I was here, after all, where he could watch at a distance.

"And what about Creed?"

"Creed was blackmailing Watts, whether or not he was meant to, I don't know. I bet Watts would hate for this to get out, people knowing the mother of his child was such a freak." I leaned over and began to cry, a mixture of shock and disgust at who I really was. Sure, my genetics from my grandparents had been diluted by the Watts line, but I couldn't help but feel ruined. Dirty. No one would want me if they knew the truth, even if I was in line for a small fortune one day. *Would Jim still accept me for who I was? What would my own children be like?* At the thought, I felt my stomach suddenly lurch and I jumped up, ran to the bathroom and threw up. Joy came in, held my hair back as I began to retch uselessly, nothing more to bring up. It was the shock of finding out who I was that caused such a violent reaction. My head spun as I sat back on the cool tiles and rested my head against the wall.

When I felt my stomach calm, I looked to Joy. "So Watts has the briefcase?"

Joy shook her head. "No. Mrs. Devlin intercepted me, quizzed me on why I was speaking with Creed. At first I denied everything, but I could see how scared she was. We came into this room to talk and she told me how her daughter has been on the run from the Watts family. She said that the contents in the briefcase would keep the Watts family at bay so her daughter could come back again, and not be afraid. On one hand I felt like I was going against my word, but on the other I thought about you, how it wasn't fair that you should be some dirty little secret. I gave Mrs. Devlin the case."

I put my hand on Joy's shoulder. She had done it for me. Always thinking of others. But what danger had she put herself in by doing such a thing? Watts was not a man to mess with and I didn't think Creed would be, either. It was clear he had never received his money. Perhaps that was why he had made contact with me? But I remembered the words of my mother telling me that I should trust Creed. My head was spinning with questions as I tried to figure out who I could really trust. *Wasn't Creed helping Violet, my mother?*

"You really are sick, Clarissa. You should come and lay down for a bit."

"I'm fine, Joy. What will Mr. Watts do now he didn't get his briefcase? He's going to go after Creed. That's why I never saw him again."

Joy looked guilty, cast her eyes away from me. "Mr. Watts was angry, Clarissa. I've never seen him like that. He made me tell him that Mrs. Devlin had the briefcase. And now Mrs. Devlin is dead…" Her eyes filled with tears. "It's my fault.

143

All my fault."

It was my turn to comfort her. "I don't think that, Joy. I think..." What did I think. Closing my eyes, I calmed my mind and tried to piece things together, make a logical tapestry out of events as best I could see it. Going back in time, I saw Mr. Devlin with a briefcase. The same one that Mrs. Devlin felt the need to intercept. I opened my eyes, looked at Joy. "How did Creed get the letters and adoption certificates? Someone must've given them to him. What if Mr. Devlin did that, working independent of his half sister? Maybe it was him behind the blackmail and he'd told Creed who was linked with their family to act as a go between. Only Mrs. Devlin got involved, and ruined the plan. That's two people who would want her dead: Mr. Watts and Mr. Devlin for preventing the blackmail."

Joy got to her feet. "It sounds so complicated, but you can't prove anything. All I know is that you're in danger, Clarissa. You should leave, resign and get a job elsewhere. There are games being played between powerful people and you're getting dragged into it." She gripped my arm, gave it a tight squeeze. "Please, Clarissa! You have to leave. I'm getting out of here myself. I don't feel safe. With the money I got from Creed, I'm going away for a few weeks to let it all blow over." She spun round and went to leave, then pausing at the door she added, "Mr. Devlin has checked in today, usual room. I wouldn't want to be near him or Watts. As for Creed... the man scares me, too."

"It's a shame you didn't get copies of those files," I said.

"Well... I did take photos of the papers on my phone. I'll email them to you so you can see it all for yourself." With that she was gone and I listened to the click of the room door and I was alone again, feeling sick.

Getting up, I rinsed my mouth, then brushed my teeth. When I finished, the door opened and Jim walked in, his face flushed from a few drinks. I could smell it on his breath. His arms went around me, but I pulled away and looked at him.

"I think we need to leave," I said.

Jim rubbed at his temples. "Again? But the fun hasn't even started yet."

Taking a deep breath, I led Jim back to the bed and we sat down. I knew he deserved an explanation, but I wasn't sure if I should tell him the entire truth. *How would he react if I told him the truth about my heritage? He'd run*, I thought. But as I stared at Jim's concerned face, I knew that wasn't so. He loved me and I think I loved him. And as I wondered what to tell him, I felt the sickness again and realized there was something more important to address.

"Jim?"

"Yes?"

"I can't be one hundred percent sure, but…" *Here goes.* "I think I'm pregnant."

CHAPTER 16

Jim stared at me with a stunned look on his face. I felt my heart sink and my eyes well up with tears. In that spontaneous moment when I blurted out the realization that I might be pregnant, I still hoped that he would respond favorably. I wanted him to continue being my knight in shining armor, and make everything okay.

"Uh, let's get going before it gets any later," he responded, starting to put the few things they had brought with them back in their overnight bags. I could feel a shift in his mood and that only added to my already frazzled nerves. I sat down on the edge of the bed and placed my head in my hands. I felt like a twig about to snap under the weight of an elephant. As Jim worked quietly, I toyed with my grandmother's locket that dangled freely from my neck. I started to feel some of the anxiety ebbing away, and wondered if my mother had felt the same way when she told Mr. Watts she was pregnant. Jim's mother had a dislike for me that was unexplainable. Hatred had radiated off of her in waves. If Violet had felt the same way, how did she cope?

"Okay, let's go."

146

Jim opened the door and looked towards me. I pulled myself off the bed and took a final glance at the room as I made my way to the door. My eyes were pinned to the ground as I crossed the threshold, unable to look up at Jim and risk burning him with a glare of disappointment, I bumped into what felt like a wall knocking me back a few steps. I gasped when I saw Mr. Creed.

"What the hell man?"

Jim pulled me back into the room and stood in my line of vision, blocking my view. I grabbed him by the arm and moved to stand in front of Mr. Creed. He looked up and down the hallway nervously, working his hat between his hands. I leaned towards him, nodding my head slowly to encourage the man to speak. Jim's nearness was obvious and I sensed his restlessness as he shifted back and forth on his feet.

"Clarissa, do you have a minute to speak with me?"

I straightened up and cleared my throat. I glanced at Jim, whose eyebrows were bunched up in confusion. He stepped aside so that Mr. Creed could enter.

"You're alive! I don't think its safe for you here. I don't think I should even be here. Everything is getting out of hand." I said with remarkable calmness.

His eyes darted around the room cautiously. He put his hat down on the chair and proceeded to look underneath the desk, then inspected the alarm clock sitting next to the lamp. Jim and I exchanged glances as he made his way around the room picking up random objects to inspect them, removing the dresser mirror and looking behind it like he was searching for a lost treasure.

"What's this all about, Mr. Creed?" Jim barked. I put a reassuring hand on his arm, to gesture that I needed a moment.

"Why didn't you come back to our hotel in Montauk?"

"Wait, he was at our hotel?" Jim sounded more than just

147

surprised. Like he was frustrated he had missed some big event.

"Yes Jim, I didn't mention it at the time as I just needed to process what Creed had told me about my family."

Mr. Creed placed the remote he had taken apart back together on the night stand. He sat down on the edge of the bed and rubbed his face.

"I'm sorry, but you must understand and be very aware of the danger you are in. I'm just making sure that there aren't any recording devices planted," he stated as a matter of fact whilst looking directly into my eyes, totally ignoring Jim. I pulled the fancy desk chair out from under the mahogany crafted desk and placed it in front of Mr. Creed. It felt dramatic and poignant, but I intended to regain some composure and concentrate on what this man had to say. My thoughts were getting so intertwined, like a knotted necklace, and my tiredness was weighing me down. I truly felt like I was in a suspense movie and I was the top billing actress.

"Why am I in danger Mr. Creed?"

I figured being direct was the only avenue left on this twisted path through the twilight zone. Mr. Creed gave me a weak smile and started to respond when there came an angry banging on the room door. All of us jumped in spite of ourselves, and Mr. Creed was wide eyed in alarm. Jim moved cautiously towards the door.

"Don't!" yelled Mr. Creed, reaching his arm towards the door as he heaved his towering frame across the room with more haste than I thought possible. Jim looked at him with a blank expression.

"Let me get it …" he said slyly. I was dumbfounded. I could not believe how bizarre the entire situation was. Maybe Mr. Creed was right, I felt comforted that he was here.

Mr. Creed slowly turned the knob; he looked back at me

and Jim with an insidious smile. He swung the door open aggressively and three men ran in with bags and rope.

"What the hell are you doing?" Jim screamed. He grabbed me, pushing me roughly towards the bathroom. Mr. Creed ordered one of the men to pull me back towards him. The largest of the three men swung at Jim. The punch was stopped in mid-air as Jim kicked him in the kneecap, bringing him down to the floor.

Mr. Creed screamed for one of the men to charge at Jim, while the smaller of the two took hold of my arms, pinning them to my sides. I started to shriek in terror, but the goon's gloved hand clamped down over my mouth. I struggled against him, even though he wasn't much taller, his muscle mass made him a suit of steel armor compared to my meager strength. Jim was grabbed and thrown against the wall, breaking the desk lamp and leaving a gaping hole. He sunk to the floor unconscious. I struggled against the goon's grip but slowly felt my energy depleting as waves of nausea rose from my gut. *Where is our help?* I knew that with all the noise, the guests on the floor would have reported a disturbance to the front desk; surely security should have arrived by now.

"Enough, Pervis," screamed Mr. Creed at my captor, his eyes ablaze and mouth twisted into a ghastly snarl. The biggest goon rolled around on the floor groaning, holding his knee to his chest.

"Move her, we're done here." he snapped. My panic kicked into high gear when Mr. Creed turned to face the goon that had assaulted Jim.

"Wallace, cover their eyes." he instructed.

With the last of my fading free will, I looked over at Jim, with mascara tears staining my fancy dress. He was still out cold, laying slumped against the wall and as the blindfold gripped my head tightly, I squeezed my eyes shut, afraid to strain against the material, knowing it would only add to my panic. I felt like I was on a cliff teetering precariously on the edge, and was about to fall off into oblivion at any minute. My mind raced, wondering what caused all this insanity that seemed to surround me. I think I trusted Mr. Creed, then in just a single moment I was back to feeling alone. That familiar feeling that had served me well, until I started to let people in again. I was frantic with panic; I worried about Jim, yet was still angry at his lack of reaction to our situation. My feelings conflicted with every pulse of my blood. I concentrated on my foot as it twitched rhythmically, trying to hold it together.

"Clarissa," I felt the name invade my mind, the voice that I recognized to be my mothers. It was crystal clear as if it had come from inside the room. My bound eyes searched frantically for the source. Mr. Creed continued to order his men around, and I heard a suitcase click as the clasps were released one at a time. There was no prior warning before the needle penetrated my upper arm. The liquid quickly did what it was designed to, and I felt my head spin as I drifted into darkness.

CHAPTER 17

I couldn't believe how fast I ran down the stairs! I kept running and running like a madwoman. I even pushed somebody aside on my way down without apologizing or caring one bit. A bright flash of light hit me. Those white lights were everywhere. Or were they yellow? The cold wind was passing right through me as I kept going. People shouldn't be leaving their windows open at night. *Was it really that cold or was I in a state of shock?* My - my breath! I was unable to catch my breath. But I had to go on. Just one more floor left. Damn it, I nearly sprained my foot on that final step! *Why had I not taken the elevator down? Would they get to me? Were they close?*

Another white flash. Somebody had left the main door open. *Who would do such a thing?* I sprang right through. I made it outside! I stood there for a moment, just a moment, looking around and making sure nobody else was there. Clouds of moist breath were coming out of my mouth in quick succession. I sniffed back the loosened phlegm, knowing I was unlikely to fight off the cold that was invading me. I was blinded by the headlights of an ancient car. So bright and sudden that my eyes watered. It's engine was making such a loud noise. So loud. A thousand swarming bees buzzing inside my head.

Yes, the lights were white, alright. They had always been white ever since the first day I stepped into that place. But... there was this other noise in the background. A constant piercing noise echoing nearby. It was coming from a barking dog, I was sure of it. *Bullseye, is that you?* He was watching me. It was as if he was trying to tell me to do it. I started running again. Running in circles.

I had to find the right place. I was running out of time! Yes, that was it! Right there, in the ground! I fell to my knees and started digging with my hands as fast as I could. There was no time, I had to hurry! At first it seemed as though I was going nowhere with it. As if the ground was unwilling to surrender to my intentions. But I was on fire! I kept digging even when the tiniest of rocks was stinging the insides of my fingernails. Even when I started to bleed. *Would that be deep enough?* I took the object out of my pocket and placed it inside. With no time to lose; I quickly started covering it, first with big handfuls then with frantic swoops. *Had I done it right?* I got up and shook all the dirt off my clothes. Suddenly more lights, bright enough to light the whole area entered my field of vision. Blue and red. *Was somebody calling my name?* Oh, another flash! Only, I couldn't take it anymore. I could feel the taste of bile in my mouth. I was going to be sick.

***

My eyes opened wide, shocking me out of my nightmare, then I felt a teardrop run down my cheek. I hadn't felt like crying at all, I was too consumed with a strange mixture of rage and fear. Some kind of fog, much like a white web of a mist, was very slowly dissolving around me. A stale odor hung in the dusty

152

air, yet smelled alarmingly familiar. My heart was racing despite the fact I was sitting with my back against a comfortable leather armchair. The room was dark and I could hardly see anything, but I could sense I was alone in the room.

I traced the sore spot on my arm, where the needle had stung me, and I strained my mind to remember what had happened. *Where was Jim? Where was everyone? Where had the bastards taken me?* I tried to call out Jim's name but my voice was redundant, my mouth ached for water. I needed to hydrate my lifeless self. With my head spinning, I placed a hand on my abdomen, a meaningless effort to protect the life that was growing inside me from whatever it was they had injected me with. Upon realizing I was no longer bound, I jumped up. Still dizzy, I stumbled into a writing desk, similar to the ones every high-end room at the Regency had. Flipping the switch on the desk lamp did nothing. I reached out and felt papers scattered across the desk. I randomly took a page, folded it several times, and then put it in my pocket.

As much as I didn't want to believe it, Creed had betrayed us. He had warned us about being in danger, yet he and his goons had become that danger. I wondered if they had drugged Jim too or if it hadn't been necessary, since he had hit the wall so hard. Feeling weak and still a bit disoriented, I dragged my legs back to the armchair I had woken up in. I fumbled around on the floor for the blindfold, but couldn't find it. They must have taken it with them.

My eyes could finally make out objects across the dark room. I could see the outline of furniture and where the door was. The windows were covered with what felt like heavy curtains, but I didn't have the strength to tear them down. There was not an inch of light coming from the windows. It must be nighttime. Just like inside, the darkness was overwhelming. I wanted to find the lights, but was afraid to draw attention to myself. Perhaps it was a good thing the desk lamp hadn't turned on and that I hadn't been able to call out for Jim. What if they were waiting for me outside the door, only to knock me out again, if not worse.

I pushed myself to walk back to the desk and fumbled around for a pen, prepared to use it as a weapon if I had to. I needed to get out of here as soon as possible. I brought my hand up to my neck, a habit I had recently picked up, but found the gold locket was gone. They must've taken it from me, or it could've broken off during the fight.

With quiet slow steps I made my way to the door. I held the pen with a weakened hand, unlikely to do much damage, but the motivation was there. The door opened without a sound. Still, something didn't feel right and it was more than the eerie silence. The darkness continued, and my eyes strained to make out the dimensions of the hallway. I closed the door behind me as quietly as I could. I still couldn't shake off the feeling that I had been there before; so many times, in fact, that it had almost become a second home to me.

Not seeing any immediate danger, I wanted to go back inside and search the room properly. The fog of the knock-out drug was fading, and I could feel myself getting stronger. Maybe I could find something useful, if nothing else, at least a better weapon to defend myself with. To my surprise, the door wouldn't open, no matter how much I yanked its handle. Like a typical hotel room, it required a key to open. I looked up at the door and I couldn't believe my own eyes. To confirm what I was seeing, I traced my fingers over the brass numbers. I now knew that this was the room I had been wondering about for months. The mysterious room the Devlin's had been staying in week in and week out. All this time I had been in room 427.

MR. LIONEL WATTS

"Every time I walk past the empty desks to my office, it reminds me how isolated I have become. My parents took from me the little trust I had acquired growing up in high society, when trust could land you broke. I was jaded, and hoped to bring a bit of heart back to the Watts empire. That was until March 16th 1994, a day etched in my memory. It was the day I learned that I would become your father in just six short months, and the day I lost the best thing that had ever happened to me; your mom Violet."

He scrunched up the paper and started again.

"I have tried to write this letter so many times, but the pain of what occurred makes it difficult. I wanted desperately to tell you who you are, and where you are from, but I have hardened over the years and have found it hard to even contemplate opening up to you."

"Why can't I write this damn letter?" Lionel stood from his desk and walked to his office window, looking out over the bustling Madison Square Gardens. He liked to sit down there sometimes and watch happy families spend their day together, wondering how his life could have been had he not been born into wealth. Lionel found no fulfillment in being a wealthy heir, it had brought nothing but sadness and misery. He didn't want that for Clarissa, and hoped to get to know her before deciding on the fate of his fortune.

Lionel knew there was something special about Clarissa the day she walked into the hotel and sat down in the cafe to observe everything. She stood out, not because she was undoubtedly beautiful, but more because of the small freckle on her temple, above her left eye, that was identical to Lionel's late grandmother's. It may seem like something forgettable, but Grandma June was responsible for some of Lionel's best memories.

Seeing Clarissa had felt like an omen, like a message from beyond the grave. Lionel couldn't believe he was finally seeing her up close, and spontaneously thought that if he hired her, it would bring back some of that lost Watts energy that he desperately needed. It was only during her interview that he realized what his Grandmother's message really was. This girl *was* a Watts, and it was about time he got to know her a little. He couldn't fathom how she could just walk into his life so easily, but she resembled the pictures he had seen, and the birth date on her application confirmed it. Lionel had gawked at her with fascination. *"She really was exquisite,"* he thought. She was his greatest achievement, and neither Watts nor Clarissa had any idea what that meant.

Lionel was always careful to ensure Clarissa's shift didn't coincide with a visit from his parents, and he tried hard not to treat her any differently than the other staff. Then things got complicated.

Mr. and Mrs. Devlin shared his loss when Violet had taken off. The years had made the pain more bearable, and through the sadness they formed an unlikely relationship. Watts looked out for them, motivated by guilt at the damage his parents had dealt. He knew about their questionable dealings, allowed them privacy at the hotel, and hoped that he would know if Violet ever returned. He never imagined that he would find Violet himself. The private detectives did a great job locating her at the New York Presbyterian facility in White Plains. Seeing her in there like that was painful for him. The woman he had known was now a distant memory, but he couldn't help but love her still. She was delighted to know he was watching over Clarissa, and despite her state she was sharp, and Watts agreed to take out an injunction against her, so no one would realize their connection. When Watts found out that the Devlins knew where Violet was all along, his trust in them was broken. He would not tell them what he knew of Clarissa before researching the people who may have a part in his daughter's future.

He was stupid to think they wouldn't eventually notice Clarissa's uncanny resemblance to Violet. If only he had known the danger he had put her in by hiring her. That was his first mistake, and the mistakes that followed were unforgivable. Lionel knew he would do everything in his power to protect his little girl, no matter the price.

He began writing again.

"You come from two dysfunctional families. One blinded by wealth and one blinded by scandal. You have to know that Violet never expected that bringing you into this world would expose our families' true colors. This is not your fault. You were helplessly thrown into the mix, solely because Violet refused to do anything but give you life and love you. She thought you would be the best of all of us. It sounds terrible, but I never got the chance to love you. My parents saw to that before you were even born."

"No, no, no. What am I saying? Why hadn't I just talked to her when I had the chance." He threw the scrunched up page across the room, adding to the balls of scrap paper scattered on the floor. He caught his reflection in the antique mirror hanging on the south facing wall of his large office. It reflected the majestic gaze of the early winter sun through the window behind him, highlighting his tired withdrawn features. Lionel hadn't shaved this morning, and his stubble grew fast. Lionel dragged his fingers over his chin and sighed. He still hadn't figured out how to fix any of this, and time was not on his side. Things had escalated in a way he never anticipated. He had to scold himself for being so stupid, felt responsible for not preventing this mess in the first place, and now he was about to do the unthinkable. It was a last resort. His next act was very carefully planned, but would bring great pain to the people he loved.

Like Violet, he had been naive for a second too long, just enough time for the vultures to close in. There was something good about Clarissa, something that made it easy for him to forget the rest of the world and see life with a long forgotten sweetness. He wished with all his heart that Clarissa would never be involved in all this wickedness, yet he already feared that she would never trust him. She already didn't trust easily, so how would he get through to her when the time came? Deep down, he knew she still needed him now. Out of all the uncertainties, only one thing was for certain. Clarissa would have a much better life than he was ever given, no matter the cost.

CHAPTER 18

I felt panic creep over me. I was more vulnerable here in the hallway, with no idea what to do next. I was in a familiar place but I was scared. I looked to my left, towards room 426. Last time I was here, Jim and I had some fun in that room. *How things change so quickly.* I needed to find Jim. *What had they done with him? Why had I woken up safe, but without Jim?* I reached the elevator and pressed for the lobby.

My knees shook. I had no idea how safe I was, and I'd really like to sit down with a cold glass of water, and a fluffy blanket. The elevator doors opened with a 'ding'. I lurched forward and slumped against the far wall. The door closed, and I felt more secure in the confines of the Regency elevator that was quickly delivering me to the safety of the lobby. Maybe it was whatever they'd drugged me with, or maybe I was just losing it, but when I took a moment to rest my eyes, I suddenly saw myself, sitting at a table with a plastic 'Happy Birthday' table cloth and a cake with no candles in the middle. Jim stood on the other side of the table next to a bright pink highchair with a baby in it. She smiled at me and I knew – this was Rose, our baby girl.

I wanted to go to her, but someone had glued me to my chair. Jim picked up a needlessly sharp knife and raised it above the cake. I wanted to warn him that he was doing something dangerous, but my lips won't part. He cut into the cake, and blood gushed out, covering all the birthday decorations and presents in the bright red fluid. All the while, Jim and Rose smiled at me. He offered me a slice and said, "Don't you trust me?"

The elevator ride seemed to last forever. As the doors parted, I was met with a grateful vision of a bustling lobby. Joy was at the concierge desk. A few patrons walked out the main door, and many more hovered around the seating area, awaiting to be escorted into the main dining room. It looked like there was a special function on, and I was certainly glad of the presence. I crossed the lobby and there was no screaming, no gun shots, no hooded figures darting out of the shadows. When I approached, Joy held up a finger. She was on the phone.

"I'm sorry to hear Mr. Watts didn't take your call," Joy said. "Would you like me to take a message?"

I tried to speak, but my voice was still caught on something, and Joy was looking down at the notepad – not writing anything, just looking at it as she listened to whoever had a complaint for Mr. Watts. She didn't seem surprised to see me, or even alarmed by my haggard state. I couldn't wait any longer. I walked around the desk and grabbed her staff key card, then went back to the elevator. I pressed floor 2 and sucked up enough courage to face Watts. The floor was vacant, but the desks looked different. There were loose papers and pens around, but the place looked like a ghost town. I knew that no one had worked in this area for many years, so it seemed unusual that there had been any activity of late.

160

The light from Watts' office beckoned me in, then I saw him and realized why he hadn't been taking calls. I clutched the door frame to steady myself. A letter opener was sticking out of his neck. A few splotches of blood ruined his sport coat, and a larger stain ran down his dress shirt. I fell to my knees, and gagged on vomit as I fought against it's hasty exit from my mouth.

Who had done this? I thought I was the one in danger, not him. I felt strangely detached, and still doubted my vision as the drugs I was given had run amok around my system.

I grabbed the phone on Mr. Watts' desk. I meant to call the police, but my fingers dialed Jim's number. I was worried, even more so now that Mr. Watts had been murdered. The phone rang. I heard something buzz. I'd call the police just as soon as I knew Jim was okay. The phone rang. I heard the buzz again. I walked around Mr. Watts' desk and saw a cell phone buzzing on the floor. I picked it up. It was Jim's.

"Mr. Watts," called Joy from the doorway. "Why – aaah!" She screamed a gunshot of a scream. It went on and on at 50 miles per hour and taking no prisoners. I dropped the receiver and scrunched up into the corner, clutching Jim's cell phone. I looked down to see I was sitting in a pile of scrunched up papers.

Where was Jim? Who killed Mr. Watts? ... Did Jim kill Mr. Watts?

Joy stopped screaming. I looked up to see other hotel staff had joined Joy at the doorway. There were a few more screams, but none to equal Joy's. Someone said they'd call the police. I looked closer at Jim's cell phone. There was a smudge of red on the screen. I tucked the phone into my pocket. I didn't know what any of this meant yet. The new guy from Security ushered everyone out of the doorway, then yelled something at me. He probably wanted me to leave. I dropped my hands to push myself up and saw my name on one of the crumpled up papers. The Security guy walked into Mr. Watts' office and yelled at me again. I nodded, still unsure of my voice, and grabbed the crumpled paper. As I stood I swung my arm behind my back and slipped it into my waistband. He pulled me out into the large office, and directed me to go downstairs and gather with the other staff members in the conference room.

With the crumpled paper from Mr. Watts' office, Jim's cell phone, and a paper from room 427 hidden on my person, I didn't think it would be a good idea to meet with the police. I went to the lift as directed, but instead of pressing lobby, I headed back up to floor 3 then hurried down the fire escape stairway. The exit led me to the west side of the lobby, nearer to the front doors than the elevator would have taken me. I bolted, without looking back. The main door swung wide as I charged through. The crisp night air refreshed my senses. I turned left and sprinted – well, it felt like I was sprinting. I realized at the corner that my sprint had been more of a jog. While my head was clear, it was likely the sedative was still affecting my legs.

I finally dared to look back. No one was following me and none of the pedestrians had cared that a woman jogged by on the sidewalk. I didn't care if someone had seen me leave, I didn't care that the police would soon be looking for me. I was clearly deeply involved in this huge mess, and I had never trusted the police and was not about to start now. The walk signal illuminated. I crossed the road at standard walking pace, though even that felt like a workout. I needed a place to think, to look at the evidence I'd found, to get my legs back in working order. I wish I still had my phone on me, my hands needed its comforting distraction. If I wasn't working, that damn phone barely left my hands. I couldn't help myself, and started to scroll through Jim's texts. One stood out from an unknown number. Jim hadn't saved the number as a contact, and I didn't recognize it. The text was an address, not to far from here. *I have to try. For Jim!* I gave myself ample encouragement, knowing I had already decided to go there.

I kept to the inside of the sidewalk and restricted myself to looking over my shoulder no more than twice a block. A bit of luck led me down a tight alley to a door that was barely hanging onto its hinges. This opened out onto the road I had been looking for. My memory flicked back to a place my mother had taken me once, a sitting room through the back of a thrift shop. I was surprised I was able to recall it. The thrift shop was still there, but it was closed. There didn't appear to be much going on, so if Jim wasn't there, I could at least lay low and rest for a while. 'R hsc d & C ed' had been painted with drippy strokes above the door. Half the letters had worn away. I twisted the knob and it broke off the door. I looked at the jagged metal bauble and was sad. Nothing was working out like it should. The door fell open. The top hinge had let go entirely and the middle hinge made a sad little bridge between the door and it's frame.

"Hello?" I called out, pleased to hear my voice had recovered. No one answered. I walked into the shop. Strange outlines and twisted shadows lined the walls. Half a cup of tea sat next to the register. It was stone cold. Past double stuffed shelves and loose piles of knickknacks, I saw a door leading to a cozy sitting room. I walked inside and the memory snuggled next to my heart. Several armchairs of various decades were gathered around a circular wooden table. The carpet was a nasty orange and green patchwork. The corner caught my attention most of all. I felt certain I had sat there many times before, perhaps with a doll or a juice box. I sat in the corner and felt safer than I had in months. I laid out the evidence on the carpet. A folded paper I had taken from room 427, a crumpled paper from Mr. Watts' office and Jim's cell phone.

I unfolded the page from 427. It was a ledger. It had columns for the date, amount, reason, and recipient. Mr. Creed's name filled up half the boxes in the 'recipient' column. I ran my finger down the rows with his name. The reason was always a number of hours between ten and twenty. The amount of money was 100 times the number of hours. And the date was the first of each month, five years ago.

Who aside from Violet, would pay Mr. Creed $100 an hour, and for what?

I picked up the cell phone next and scrolled through the recent call list. They were all from me, and Mr. Creed. My head spun with wild theories and heart-wrenching accusations. I scrolled even further down the list. Still the only callers were myself and Mr. Creed. That couldn't be right. I'd seen Jim take calls from his mother and there should be at least a few calls from co-workers, old friends, and misdials. Someone must be trying to set Jim up. I didn't know what to do about that yet, but I felt relieved. I had been right to trust him. There is no way I could believe he would kill Watts, my father. But one thing worried me. Either Jim had been in Watts office, or whoever had Jim had been there. And if this person was capable of killing a man with a letter opener, what chance did Jim have? I knew panicking was not an option, so I cleared my head and returned to the evidence at hand. I uncrumpled the page from Mr. Watts' floor;

'Clarissa, I have tried to write this letter so many times, but the pain of what occurred makes it difficult. I wanted desperately to tell you who you are, and where you are from, but I have hardened over the years and have found it hard to even contemplate opening up to you'

CHAPTER 19

I woke up with a horrible headache and no idea of where I was. It was dim, and it smelled like dust and mold. My mouth was so parched that it hurt. The crazed events from before I passed out started to come back to me in jagged fragments, and I realized that I was in big trouble. I had run away from a crime scene, I had disrupted the crime scene, I had stolen evidence... I looked at the partially written letter that was now streaked and muddied with blood. I still held it in my hand, and some reality started to jar into place for me. Whatever sort of man my father had been, he was dead now and his blood was on my hands. There had been too many bodies, too many deaths, I had been drugged and maybe I had been drugged because they wanted me dead too. That seemed more than a little likely. With Jim gone I had exactly zero allies on my side. This had gone far enough, I needed help. I took out the cell phone and dialed 911. A reassuringly earthy voice answered the phone but when I tried to speak I could barely make my throat crack. It was like the worst hangover ever. I forced my voice out of my throat, "I need help."

CWC – The Concierge

It seemed like forever before the ambulance arrived. They were taking my blood pressure when two plain clothes detectives walked in. They didn't smile when they saw me, and their grim faces were a reminder of the blood on my hands.

"Are you Clarissa Banks?"

I nodded, it was still hard to speak. The paramedics had started an I.V. for me and it had instantly made me feel less like I was dying, as the cool fluid flooded into my veins. The dark faced man nodded in satisfaction, "I'm Detective Ren and this is Detective Edwards, we've been looking for you, Miss Banks."

I felt fear at the dreaded words, but more than anything else I felt relief that this wasn't my problem anymore. Even if they thought I was the murderer at least I wasn't the only person now trying to unravel this mystery. Ren's partner was a smooth faced Latin man whose voice was as soothing as the formers had been harsh, "Are you alright, Ms. Banks? Are you injured at all?" "I'm not injured ... but I'm so thirsty, it's hard to talk."

Edwards turned to the medics and asked if I could have something to drink. "She needs to see the doctor first, can you talk to her at the hospital? We're taking her to Angel of Mercy."

I had about an hour to think about the police and what I could possibly say to them. I wanted Jim more than anything else but he wasn't here, and that fact hurt me more than the fact that my father had been murdered. My head was still pounding, but the doctor ordered bloods and urine and then gave me painkillers and told me food would be coming. She gave me a white plastic cup filled with ginger ale and let the detectives into the room. Edwards smiled a little at me this time. Despite my brave words, I did care if they thought I was a murderer. I couldn't help the cool wash of relief that spread down my limbs from that one glance that showed he knew I was a human being, and maybe he didn't think I was some murdering monster.

166

A lady officer in uniform came into the room right behind them.

"We have a few questions to ask you, if you don't mind, Miss Banks."

"Yes, I want to tell you everything, I'm so tired of doing this on my own."

Edwards and Ren exchanged a look. "Tired of what, Miss Banks?"

"Well, at the moment, I'm tired of being called Miss Banks. Please call me Clarissa."

Edwards pulled up a chair beside the bed and sat down. He seemed friendly and I thought his eyes were kind, even though I could see that behind the kindness was a sort of constant measuring and gauging going on. He was not a foolish man.

"Alright, Clarissa it is. Can you start by telling us why you were in the second hand store?"

"I don't remember why. I was drugged."

Ren snapped open a notepad. "Why do you say you were drugged?"

"Because I had never felt like that before ... I couldn't walk, or think very well."

"Do you have any idea who would want to drug you?"

"Yes, I know who drugged me. I was kidnapped by Mr. Creed."

"Mr. Creed..." Ren flipped through his notes. "How does he fit into all this? Nobody has been able to find him."

"He worked for Mr. Watts, or Mr. Devlin, well - I'm not entirely sure."

I handed Edwards the note that I had been clutching in my fist, "I took this from the crime scene. I'm sorry."

It sounded trite to apologize, but I had been out of my mind at the time and I didn't know what else to say. Edwards handed the note to Ren, who took it with a tissue and got the lady officer's help to put it in an evidence bag. I had washed the blood off of my hands when I had given my urine sample and I was happy that I had at least that shame removed before I had to face all of this head on.

"Why would Mr. Creed want to kidnap you?"

"I don't know. I never knew whether to trust him. When I first met him I was very young, but my mother told me to trust him and so I tried to. He's always been very menacing and peculiar to my mind."

After that it was easy to spill my story. I told the officers everything that I knew, about the briefcases and about Creed being on the payroll, about Montauk and about the night Mrs. Devlin died. When it came to the kidnapping, I couldn't help the tears, and Edwards handed me the box of tissues that I clutched to me. Hearing the words that came out of my mouth and the reactions Edwards and Ren had to them, I realized that Creed was a very suspicious character to them as well. They interrupted enough to try to get the story straight, but otherwise they let me just tell them all about it.

I remembered the cell phone and gave that to them as well, the nurse had left it on the table beside the bed. It wasn't until I was exhausted for words and had nothing else to say, that they asked the first question that I didn't know how to answer.

"How does Jim Roth fit into all this?"

"Jim ... he's my boyfriend. I've known him for about 6 months. At first we were just friends, I used to visit MacDonald's quite often, then things progressed about 3 months ago. He's been sweet."

"Are you aware that he has received several paychecks from Lionel Watts over the lasts few months at least?"

"What? No, he works at MacDonald's. Are you sure?"

"Very sure."

"How do you know this?"

"We've been watching him, and anyone else in contact with the hotel since Mrs. Devlin was murdered there. We've been trying to find you to talk to you as well, but you and Mr. Roth have been remarkably hard to get a hold of."

I had watched enough police shows to know that Edwards and Ren were suspicious of Jim. Ren's next words confirmed this for me.

"Do you know any reason why Jim would have been coming out of Lionel Watts' office while you were allegedly being held by Mr. Creed?"

I flinched at the word 'allegedly'. It was a modifier that hinted at disbelief, and highlighted that all I had going for me was my word, and a story that didn't make sense, even to me. Then the impact of the question Ren had just asked hit me. "Jim was in Mr. Watts office?"

"Yes, we have the security footage, and he left the office about twenty minutes before you came down the hallway and went in to find the body. We know that you didn't kill your birth father, Clarissa. The time doesn't match up, but we need your help to find Jim. Do you have any idea where we might find him?"

I shook my head. The movement and trying to picture Jim stabbing Mr. Watts in the neck made my headache flair up again. Edwards smiled sympathetically and handed me a business card, a phone number was written on it by hand in black ink.

"That's my personal cell number, do us all a favor and contact me if Jim gets in touch with you."

I found it hard to agree with him about that. I looked down at the white sheet and felt tears well up in my swollen eyes. Edwards took my hand in his and looked at me with large, soulful brown eyes that I found myself trusting despite my bond to Jim.

"I'll call," I promised. Edwards squeezed my hand and glanced at Ren, who's nod signified they were ready to leave.

"Thank you, Clarissa. They're running a 'tox report' to try and find out what you were drugged with. If you have anything that you think of, don't hesitate to call me, day or night."

"I will." I whispered. They were words that I feared were laden with betrayal for Jim.

How could I think I was betraying Jim by speaking to the police? There must be some reasonable explanation for why he was in Watts' office. Maybe he was looking for me and found the body before I did, but that didn't explain the paychecks he had been getting.

What was he being paid for?

There was more to this than I knew, and I was worried that the explanation was as dark as Edwards and Ren had hinted at, or worse. There was a killer or killers on the loose after all and Jim had been so nice, so understanding of everything, taking me where I needed to go, so easy going about missing work and helping me ... *did he have an ulterior motive?*

I had nearly drowsed off to sleep when I heard the door open. I didn't open my eyes until I felt a familiar warm hand on my forehead. My eyes flashed open. "Jim!"

He smiled down at me. It was a sad, strange smile. I realized that I had learned very little about the man I had fallen in love with, and come to trust above all else.

CHAPTER 20

I squeezed my eyes tightly shut. I had so many questions but the sadness on Jim's face was hard to look at. A shiver of something cold ran down my spine, almost a feeling of déjà vu. I saw a million moments with him pass before my eyes in that instant before I opened them again. Jim stood there, motionless, with that same strange, sad smile on his face, his hand still on my forehead. He leaned close to me and softly whispered that he had to go. I tried valiantly to sit up, but he held me and with gentle pressure he pushed me back and tenderly brushed my lips. I almost melted with the tenderness he showed me, but I was still confused and afraid. Speaking softly, he tried to tuck me in but I lashed out at him. I felt like I was in someone else's life, outside of myself, the panic began to crawl into my belly, and try as I might I couldn't stop it. I no longer cared.

I heard myself shouting at him, "Jim, I have to know! What were you doing in Mr. Watts' office? Why were you taking money from him? What is ...?"

"Shhh," I heard him whisper as he began to nervously

glance around at my raised voice. He took my hand and sat beside me on the bed and put it tenderly to his lips. It calmed me down; I let him keep my hand, my nerves soothed somewhat by his slow, calm movements. He measured his words carefully, and I watched his face as he told me that he had been working for my father. He was looking straight into my eyes, his own asking for an impossible absolution as he began telling me that he had been guarding me, watching and keeping me safe.

"I wasn't supposed to fall in love with you Clarissa, but I did."

I felt wooden. A lie ...was everything a lie? This could not be happening. I remembered our first passionate kiss, and all the promises it held. I remembered too much. I couldn't speak, I felt the blood leave my face and I knew Jim had seen it too. My eyes looked at him accusingly, as diverse emotion played silently across my face. Jim began telling me quickly that he loved me, over and over but I was too far gone to read his eyes, or to care. I knew I was on the verge of hysteria as I heard Jim describe his true feelings for me, how he had searched in vain for me when he had awoken. He finished with the last words I would coherently understand in this conversation ... "I had to come and see you. I had to make sure for myself that you were alright, and the baby," he finished.

"Oh my God, the baby?" I just whimpered.

I couldn't breathe, it sounded like a rasping noise as I fought to draw in air. My hands flew to my body and I felt helpless, hot frustratingly fearful tears begin to slip down my face. I didn't even care, I heard myself moan from a distance and I began to sob. The dam had burst; I was shaking all over and felt like I was choking. I tried to speak but the thoughts raced through my mind like the blood raced through my ravaged body. I began to shake. I was so cold, what was happening to me? Fear clouded my eyes and pain shot through my chest making it even harder to breathe. I tried to sit up again, struggling even harder for every difficult breath.

I felt Jim's arms tight around me, but I could take no comfort from him. I didn't even know him anymore. The shaking intensified and I tried to push against him while I heard his soft voice from very far away, begging for my understanding. How could I understand? I couldn't think, I couldn't even breathe.

I was dazed and could not hear clearly, but I knew Jim was screaming for the nurses. I could hear the desperation in his voice and that frightened me even more. Soon the room filled with medical uniforms and I felt the prick of needles and the oxygen mask, none too gently pasted to my face. I was disoriented but I could see Jim in the periphery of my vision. His eyes, his entire body language begged my forgiveness for the duplicity. I remembered the letter from Mr. Watts, Lionel Watts my father, who had loved me. My voice was weak, but I had to ask. I had to know,

"Did you kill him, Jim … did you kill my father?"

I saw genuine shock register in his features, as my eyelids began to droop and then I knew nothing. It was dark when I woke. Before I even opened my eyes I could sense an unwelcome presence. I was sure it was Mr. Creed. I felt apprehensive, but I still couldn't move. My limbs were heavy, I stirred but I was sore, tired and too drowsy from what they had given me. I could not even cry out for help and slipped quietly back into the welcoming fold of slumber.

When I opened my eyes, the lights were on in the room and a familiar nurse with beautiful brown eyes was struggling to fasten a blood pressure cuff around my arm. I guess I had been resisting her. She stuck a thermometer in my mouth that was joined to a box in her hand.

"Good morning, Clarissa. It's good to see you finally awake," she said pertly.

She noted the numbers on a paper which she put in her pocket and strode to the window and pulled the drapes. She was small and her white nurse's uniform was becoming with the light sweater hanging off her shoulders. The brighter light hurt my head.

"I have to go to the restroom," I croaked out. My throat felt dry and painful. Then I remembered the baby.

"I need to know if I'm pregnant," the words rushed out of me. She looked at me with surprise and said, "I see no reference to pregnancy here Clarissa." The nurse's badge was blank except for the Angel of Mercy logo, and that made me uncomfortable for some reason. I must be losing it, so much in my life now was never what it seemed to be.

"Will you see if they've done a test please?" I asked her, as I sat up on the edge of the bed.

My head swam and I kind of shook it to clear the fog. I was still weak and trembling. She watched me.

"Are you alright honey, do you need some help?"

I felt dizzy and realized for the first time that all I had on was one of those open backed hospital gowns.

"I ... I think I'm alright, I'll just take it slow. Could you check that test for me please?"

She watched me get unsteadily to my feet and take a wobbly step or two hanging onto the IV tree for dear life. She took my arm under the elbow and helped me to the small, very bright bathroom, then considerately closed the door.

"I'll be right back," she called.

The nurse didn't return. I was very weak so I pulled the cord beside me. I could stand alright, but I didn't think I would be able to make it back to the bed. I certainly didn't need to fall whilst connected to all these contraptions. A nurse came into the room and I called to her. She quickly opened the door of the restroom and as she helped me to the bed, she admonished me for getting up without assistance.

"I had help from the nurse who took my blood pressure and temperature," I told her.

She looked at me quickly, the concern evident on her face. "We wouldn't have to take your temperature and blood pressure Clarissa. It's monitored from the cuff attached to your left arm. She reached across and showed it to me.

"Right here above your IV."

We were at the bed now and I sat down heavily. "She was here," I said, a hint of alarm in my voice.

"She helped me to the restroom and she was going to check and see if a pregnancy test had been done."

"Let me check your chart, this may be a misunderstanding," she said, as she quickly stepped from the room. She was back in a moment with a thick bundle.

"No one was in here since 3:00 AM Clarissa."

I began to feel the panic spreading again and I looked directly into her face. She was short and appeared capable. Her brown hair just touched her shoulders and her sparkling blue eyes were brightened by the sky blue color of her scrubs. Her name tag said Ivy. She was calm and assured of what she was saying. I began to cry,

"Someone was here," I said through my tears. "She was dressed in a white dress with a sweater, she told me good morning and she helped me to the restroom. She took my blood pressure and temperature, and drew the drapes... I stopped and swallowed hard as I involuntarily glanced at the closed drapes.

"She had blonde hair and pretty brown eyes, she was here, I know she was." The nurse smiled and handed me a tissue.

175

"Calm down dear, we'll call the doctor and see what he has planned for you today. Here, you need to get some of this ice water down you." I drank, small sips. It hurt to swallow.

"You had such a stressful day yesterday; maybe it was just a realistic dream. Nurses don't dress like that anymore and the drapes are not drawn Clarissa, you see that for yourself. It was just a vivid dream, nothing to be upset about."

I glanced again at the drapes that were not drawn, as I used the tissue and blew my nose. I took another swallow of the water; it hurt a little less. I felt so bad, I just gave in and lay back down, determined to try and rest.

The nurse stuck her head back in the door and smiled.

"By the way, there was a pregnancy test ordered. It is routine at your age when the patient is unable to give information. The result of the test was negative. I hope that helps to ease your mind," she smiled again as she quietly closed the door.

I felt a wave of gratitude colliding with the same size wave of disappointment. I was too tired to sort it all out. I needed sleep. When I woke up again, there was a wonderful scent wafting through my room. I turned my head to find a large vase of yellow roses on the stand beside my bed and Ivy smiling down at me.

"You seem to have an admirer," she said as she bent to inhale the scent. "There was no name on the card, but they're lovely."

I smiled at her and said nothing. I was torn knowing the flowers were from Jim, but it made me not feel so alone. I didn't even know how to reach him. The police now have his phone.

"Are you ready to get cleaned up?" Ivy asked. "A package arrived with the flowers, filled with toiletries and a soft, green cotton gown and slippers."

I sighed. That was wonderful news. "Thank you Jim," I said under my breath.

I didn't want to think of anything yet as Ivy helped me clean up and get dressed. I crawled back into clean sheets feeling much, much better, but exhausted. My hair felt glorious, clean and soft. I sighed deeply and finished my third glass of water. My stomach told me I might be ready for some solid food, but before I could ask, the door opened and the doctor arrived. He was tall, distinguished looking and in a hurry. He cursorily listened to my heart and looked in my eyes and my throat.

He checked the chart and then listened to my heart again, and was obviously satisfied. He pulled the cover back up over my legs, and took one more look at the chart as he began to speak. Not looking in my eyes, he told me I had been drugged with one of the Benzodiazepines for at least two days. Stopping them suddenly was possibly to blame for my uncontrolled hysteria yesterday and that unfortunate side effect could last for a few days. I had been seriously dehydrated and my blood levels of potassium were very low. That accounted for my weakness and confusion. He was giving me IV fluids with electrolytes, and sodium chloride with some glucose to combat the dehydration and he would begin an extra infusion of potassium every six hours until my levels returned to normal.

"It's time to begin eating and drinking as you feel you can tolerate it. Be prepared to spend at least 3 more days with us Clarissa … Banks," he said, looking for my name.

"I'll see you again tomorrow," he said as he left the room quickly. I thought he was an odd fellow. He never gave me a chance to ask a question, or asked me anything about what had happened to me.

I lay there quietly feeling clean and refreshed, sad, alone and more confused than I had ever been. Mr. Watts' partial letter had told me how much he loved my mother, and me. Now, I would never be able to talk to him or to completely understand the past. My mother had told me to trust Mr. Creed, but he had drugged me. I sat bolt upright and the motion made my head reel and my stomach feel a little sick. I remember thinking he was in here last night, but I was too lethargic to open my eyes. Maybe that was a dream too. I remembered the nurse from this morning. She was still vivid in my mind and the thought that I knew her had been nagging at me all day. I was so tired, but Ivy came through the door with something that smelled heavenly and my stomach growled on cue. We both laughed and I smiled at her as she set down the tray and placed the bed table where I could reach the food.

"I'll be leaving you now Clarissa, but I'll see you in the morning," she said. "Here take these." She handed me two little blue pills in a small paper cup. I swallowed them with the last of my water. I had lost count of how many glasses of water I had put away.

"The doctor told the officers they could speak with you now, so you'll probably see them tomorrow as well," she finished.

"Ugh," I groaned with a mouthful of something not quite recognizable, but delicious all the same. Ivy laughed at the face I made and said goodnight. I was thankful for her company today. I only got down a little of the food, but I felt much better and in moments, very tired. I wondered as I lay back if the little blue pills had been something to help me relax.

My last thought before sleep, was of Jim. I had trusted him so completely. I wondered where he was, and what he really had to do with all of this. Jim's face swam in my dreams. I watched him sneak into my apartment. I saw Mrs. Devlin again and heard her screaming, "OH NO, NOT YOU!" I saw again, her

178

broken body and the blood on Mr. Creed's silver briefcase. I saw Bullseye again sitting at my feet as if he wished he could talk. I tossed, half awake and half asleep in the visions that plagued my rest. I was eight years old running to my mother all shining and yellow. She seemed to be surrounded by the sunshine, and I jolted awake. My mother, Violet Devlin had been the nurse this morning! I was certain of it. The tears came unbidden, and I didn't fight them.

     I had no fight left in me.

MR. JAMES ROTHSCHILD

Jim sat polishing off his third beer. Joy and Eduardo were his best investigators, but Joy had taken off recently, saying she needed a break. Jim knew all too well how stressful this job could be, especially when you get close to the subjects, but as Eduardo, who had been working as a bellhop at the Regency, was busy keeping an eye on Clarissa at the hospital, he knew he could relax somewhat.

Detectives Ren and Edwards were on their way. Jim laughed to himself. They had him pegged for the murders of Rosemary Devlin and Lionel Watts. They would change their minds shortly though. *I don't want them bothering Clarissa any more*, he thought.

"She doesn't know anything, and they were certainly in for a surprise!" Jim smiled as he rose and went to the large filing cabinet on the back wall. He withdrew his contract with the late Lionel Watts, leaving the fat research and surveillance files in their place. Each bore a name tag beginning with Lionel Watts, Violet Devlin, Patrick and Rosemary Devlin, and Carlisle Creed.

The last...his Clarissa. He knew that she was the only innocent one in this mess.

Jim sighed, shook his head at the closed files of Rita and Jonathan Banks, then gently closed the drawer. Rosemary had hidden the truth of Clarissa's parentage, the DNA test that Lionel Watts had ordered secretly to make absolutely certain that his Last Will and Testament would stand up in court. At the request of his old friend, Jim also had the originals of both documents under lock and key. Lionel had recently decided that he wanted Clarissa to have it all. Lord and Lady Watts would have no say, nor would the Devlins.

Clarissa will be fine, whether or not she can forgive me, Jim thought. It was Lionel's final wish, and he would ensure it was honored.

Jim remembered the day three years ago when Lionel had walked through the double maple doors of the Rothschild and Lind Investigation Agency. Jim had heard him arguing with the receptionist and hurried to the front. Lionel immediately recognized him and offered his hand. "I must apologize for my behavior, Mr. Rothschild, but I have something that requires your personal attention."

That was the day it began. Lionel had been searching for Clarissa for years before asking for help. It took time to find out that she was still in New York. Then everything stepped up a gear when Jim reported that not only had he found her, but her parents had been killed. He suspected that Violet had a hand in their demise, but couldn't be sure. Fearing for Clarissa's emotional health, her parents had refused Violet access to the girl for so many years.

Poor Violet. The innocent product of incest was never emotionally stable. That evening when Lady Watts had dropped her bomb shell and Violet learned the truth of her parentage, something in her had broken, unwinding her already fragile mental state. Lionel secretly supported Violet through Creed, but Creed was careful, and Lionel hadn't been able to get anywhere near her. He didn't even know how she was doing, but he did know they were not capable of raising their precious child. The pain of those early years, dealing with the separation and giving up Clarissa, damaged any hope they both had of reuniting their family, until they heard she was alone again. It wasn't the happy ending Watts had hoped for, though he had always loved her. The only good thing they had created in this life was Clarissa, wide eyed and unspoiled. Lionel had never before experienced love like that, and was more than forthright when sharing with Jim his story.

'Maybe someday I'll be able to tell her everything, but right now she is still in danger,' Jim recalled his old friends words. He studied the contract that laid out the job duties and description of services for which he had been hired.

Jim wistfully thought of the first time he laid eyes on the boss's daughter. He had seen her meandering around the city, looking for jobs. Eighteen years old, she was the most lost-looking thing he had ever seen. 'Fragile' was the first word that came to his mind. Beautifully fragile. Her deep brown eyes sucked in everything around her. Her pale skin accentuated light brown hair that framed her face and those inquisitive eyes. He had courted her at first to keep an eye on her, but he had fallen fast and hard for both her innocence and determination.

Jim was only twenty six himself at the time, but his upbringing had given him certain advantages that she did not have. Clarissa was impressionable but determined. She suddenly started spending time in the Regency cafe in hopes of getting a job there. She was persistent and strong, and Jim admired her from the start. He knew he should have discouraged her

182

somehow, it was too close to 'home' but he reckoned she was a force that could not be stopped. He had spent a lot of time watching her, and was pleased on that particular day when Lionel recognized his own daughter in the flesh. Jim saw the glee in the man's eye at finally seeing her, the confirmation Jim needed that he was working for the right man. He trusted Watts' good intentions, and that made his job worthwhile.

Clarissa's confession that she might be pregnant had surprised him, but he was secretly overjoyed. He would have loved nothing more than to spend the rest of his life with Clarissa Banks. Watts did not yet know that their relationship was genuine, and that the feelings they shared were true. Yet Jim was confident he would have had the man's approval.

The buzzer brought Jim from his reverie. Jane Adams, Jim's secretary, showed the detectives into his office, where he sat behind his large mahogany desk. Jim shook Detective Ren's hand first and then Edwards', offering them a seat. Jane inquired if they would like coffee, but both understandably declined. Jim recognized the puzzled expressions on both faces.

"I will get right to it, Detectives. My name is James Rothschild. I am a private investigator, and this is my company. I have been working for Lionel Watts for over seven years. This is his file." The detectives took a moment to read the file together.

"Do you know what is going on here, Mr. Rothschild?"

Jim stood and walked around the desk. "I know more than anyone except Lionel Watts."

Detective Edwards stood. "You'll have to come with us, James. We need to question you at the station and determine your involvement in this case."

"Are you arresting me?"

"Not unless we have to, Mr. Rothschild!"

CHAPTER 21

When it was time to leave hospital and return home, I'd expected to be picked up by Jim. When two uniformed police officers turned up, my heart sank. They were the silent sort, ones who were there to do a job and didn't particularly care. Guiltily I thought about my own job and the apathy I often felt towards it. The younger cop held back, and I noticed how he would avoid direct eye contact with me. I felt as though I was too disgusting to look at, but the older cop had a kinder face, his cool blue eyes holding my gaze. He must've been at least fifty, maybe not that far off from retirement. If you could get through to retirement in this city, they said you were lucky. That's what I'd heard. But I doubted their life was as dangerous as mine was right now and the prospect of me seeing each day through seemed pretty slim.

"I'm officer Hants," the older cop said, taking his hat from his head. "You need to come with us, Ma'am."\
I should have been upset, maybe even scared, but I'd been through so much that this seemed to pale in comparison with everything that had come before.

184

"Am I under arrest?" *Had they decided that I was the killer, and working my way through everyone to get to the fortune I could potentially inherit from my father?*

Hants shook his head. "No, it's not that at all. But it's important you come with us and do exactly what we say. Your life maybe in danger."

Something inside snapped, like I'd been held together with fine glue and tape. Now I was finally breaking. Instead of tears, I laughed, unable to take anything seriously. Aware that I must look totally insane, I controlled myself, though inside I could hear the laughter continuing, like the distant rumble of thunder within my thoughts.

"You're only just beginning to think that? I've been kidnapped, drugged and found my employer who is apparently my father, stabbed in his office. On a risk scale, I must be rated pretty highly, don't you think?"

Hants rested his hand on my shoulder. I flinched from him, turned away and stared from the hospital window down to the busy city below.

"Miss, there's been some developments in the case, that's all I can tell you."

"Where are we going?" I asked, watching the world go by outside. My mind was drifting away and it was difficult to focus on anything. Yet I clung to reality, imagining my nails digging into it. *If I closed my eyes, would it all go away? Would I wake within the safety of my own bed and find this was all a bad dream?*

"We need to take you down to the station. Detective Edwards believes he knows who kidnapped you and who killed Mr. Watts and Mrs. Devlin." His tone turned gruffer, the impatience surfacing as his eyes narrowed. "I can't tell you much more beyond that lady, because I don't know a damn thing

185

myself. We're just the drones, sent out to do a job. Personally, I don't really care, 'cause I get paid anyway." He gave a half smile, then added, "But it would be a shame if anything happened to that pretty face." The younger cop behind him sniggered, which faded fast when he saw my glare.

"Ah, the caring attitude of a cop that's been on the streets too long."

I could tell Hants didn't like my remark, but I didn't care. There was no mistaking his cynical nature. *What was the point in making things difficult for me?* If they knew who was behind this, then I wanted to know. There'd been too many people killed over this, too many people involved. There was a spider that was spinning a web. It grew larger until more people fell into it, waiting for the spider to come out from the centre. I had thought that spider was Watts, my father, but he was dead. So it had to be Creed. As I followed the cops from the hospital and into their cruiser parked in an ambulance space, I wondered just what Creed's angle was. *So he'd been paid by Watts, seemed to be working for my mother, too.* I still couldn't get why he'd seemed to turn on me, drugged me. Had he killed Mr. Watts too?

My mind raced as the police cruiser headed through morning rush hour. In the back seat, a protective plastic sheet sat between me and the front, I felt like a prisoner. In a way I guessed I was, imprisoned by my own fate that was now leading me down paths darker than I cared to imagine. The world was moving on as normal outside and here in this bubble in the back of a cop car, I was floating in darkness, drowning in confusion and horror. I felt numb against it all.

Nothing could surprise me, nothing could hurt me. There was only the thought of Jim, and the baby that I thought I was having. They'd said the test was negative, but I wasn't so sure because I could feel something inside me, something growing.

I'd dreamt of a daughter, and even thought I would call her Rose. In a future life, I saw myself as a family with Jim, but it was all coming apart. Maybe I'd drifted between alternative universes where in one I was pregnant and everything made sense and then there was this one where I had entered Crazy Ville.

What's real? Am I just a dreamer floating through events and unable to influence them?

We slowed down at a red light. Couldn't cop cars skip the lights? I just wanted to get it over with. A sudden loss of patience made me grit my teeth and clench my fists until I felt my nails dig in. Looking behind, I noticed a car driven by a woman in dark glasses and realized she'd been there for the last couple of blocks. She looked away from me when she caught my glare and when we pulled away, her car followed right with us. The two cops were oblivious, throwing banter back and forth about the latest Super Bowl game. Another turn left and the woman followed, keeping the same distance. I stopped looking, sure I was being paranoid.

When we pulled into the police station, I could feel tears that were hiding suddenly surface, telling the world that I was in pain. Luckily, I managed to control myself as I got out of the car and followed the cops into the station. I glanced behind and the woman in dark glasses was nowhere to be seen. She had probably gone by. As we entered the station, I caught the black ford parked a few cars down, away from the cop cruiser. I shuddered.

I was led through the front office, out back to where the real action happened. We passed a line of desperate looking people waiting to be booked in by arresting cops and the air was filled with curses and threats from both sides. They led me through the mad circus of reality, up a flight of stairs to an office with the door wide open. Hants told me to go right in, probably relieved to be free of his responsibility of me now.

"I don't care what you think," Detective Edwards barked into the phone, "I need those files sent over right away. We're on the same side here, so do we really need a data protection form?" He paused, looked up and saw me then waved me in. On entering, he pointed to a seat in front of his desk, motioning for me to sit. Like an obedient dog, I sat. "That's great, email me. It's quicker than fax."

He hung up, sat back in his own chair and breathed a long sigh of relief. "Damn forms and authorization. It's like having a hand tied behind your back."

I sat there, just looking at Edwards, wondering why he'd brought me here. I liked the man, felt like he believed me and he had already gained my trust. Perhaps I was too free with my trust lately, too quick to fall in love. Immediately I thought of Jim.

"What's going on, Detective? Why did you send for me? Is it Jim?"

Edwards shook his head. "Jim has been helping us with inquiries into the death of Watts. He's quite safe for the moment and I want to keep it that way. For both of you."

"You spoke to Jim?" I asked, sitting upright.

Edwards regarded me in silence, like he was studying my reactions, looking for a clue from my body language. I'd read that cops did that and I folded my arms, wondering what he'd make from that. He smiled and a little warmth returned to his face.

"What do you know about Violet Devlin?"

My heart thumped wildly at the mention of my mother's name. "Not a lot … I think she's my birth mother and you pretty much know the rest by now." I'd gone through most of what I already knew with him in the hospital, and was wondering where this was going.

"I've been doing a little digging. It seems Violet had a

188

troubled past, in and out of therapy, moving constantly around since giving you up for adoption. She was quite a difficult woman to track down until I found her trail that led to a mental health institution. She was committed there three years ago. Her police record reads as a violent schizophrenic. Unstable. I was just on the phone to where she was being held until about six months ago."

"*Was* being held?"

"She'd pleaded insanity to a GBH a few years back, beat a woman unconscious. It was either there or prison. She eventually escaped, badly injuring a member of staff in the process. A few weeks ago a woman matching her description was stopped in this city by a patrol officer. She attacked him and made off. We've got a warrant out on her, but she's kept a low profile. I think this Creed character must be working for her, but I'm not sure what she's after."

I looked down at the floor. It was obvious who she was after and I think that Edwards also knew.

"She's after me, isn't she?"

Edwards put his fingers together in a steeple. "We think she came here looking for you. Just before she escaped her confinement, a man we believe to be Watts visited her. Could be he told her about you, that he was going to tell you everything. Something tipped her over the edge and she didn't want that." He opened a file on his desk, flipped through some printouts.

"We suspect she killed her own mom, Mrs. Devlin, who may also have been trying to help you, then went after Mr. Watts. There's motive for both. Mrs. Devlin, your grandmother, wanted to keep you detached from the Watts association, and we think she knew that Lionel Watts had decided to put you in his will as the sole heir. Although your father Mr. Watts wanted you to inherit everything, we think he realized Violet could be a

189

problem, so he had an injunction taken out a few months ago against her, ordering her to keep away. I'm sure she didn't like that."

"You've no evidence she murdered those people beyond assumption," I said, desperate to defend my mother, although I didn't really know anything about her. I had no idea she'd been committed.

"You'll not convict someone with that evidence."

Edwards closed the file, looked back at me. "We've gone through the CCTV and it shows an unknown woman entering Mr. Watts office shortly before he dies. The rest of the footage has been wiped, but lucky for us the person who did this got their times muddled leaving us that snippet. It's quite possible you were drugged and held in that room to protect you. I believe Creed is working with Violet, maybe out of some loyalty to the family or a share in the money. Your money. Perhaps both."

"What do you mean, my money? I don't have any money."

"I can't confirm at this time, but we have it on good authority that Watts had already amended his will, and his entire fortune will be rightfully yours. I'm sure this whole investigation will delay the judges ruling on that, but an astute private detective had been hired to ensure all the required documents could be provided when needed."

I was stunned into silence. Rather than be excited by the prospect of being wealthy, I was terrified. I never knew what having money felt like and I couldn't help but think that actually having money would only make the target on my back bigger.

"There was a nurse in my room," I said, my voice distant. "But no one knew who she was. I think it was Violet. She didn't seem to want to cause me any harm, and really she didn't even seem unstable."

190

Suddenly seeing my mother as a murderer was like getting a cold hard slap: too much to take in. I thought back to my past, looking for answers. My adoptive parents were killed in a car accident. How much of an accident was it? Had Violet been involved in that? It was like she was the spider in that ever growing web of lies and deceit. Killing people one by one who were close to me, so that one day she could be there, have me all to herself. Have me and the fortune I would inherit now from the Watts fortune as sole heir.

"I want to post a uniform unit to watch your apartment," Edwards said. "Maybe she'll surface, try and get to you."

"So you want to use me as the worm on the end of a string? I'm bait, right?"

Edwards shrugged, but didn't say anything. He didn't need to. Violet was out there somewhere, waiting for her chance.

CHAPTER 22

The never-ending noise of the city floated through the open window. Fall was quickly turning into winter, and the empty trees created blank silhouettes against the grey skies. The window let an icy breeze into my bedroom, but being in the police station all day had made me feel claustrophobic. As soon as I returned home I opened all of my windows, despite the protests of the young police officer who was sent to accompany me.

It was dusk by the time the police car had dropped me off, and after finding a bagel in the cupboard – I realized I hadn't eaten all day. I shooed the trainee officer out of my building to wait in his car across the street. He tried to insist that he should stay with me, but the dark rings under my usually bright eyes, and the grey tone of my already pale skin helped to convince him that I needed to sleep. He knew I would be going straight to bed. I watched from the bedroom window as he walked to his car and got in, pulling a sandwich from a bag on the back seat and reclining the driver's seat to settle down for the night. The street lamps on the block started to light up as darkness fell over the neighbourhood. Would I still be alive to see the sunset over Queens tomorrow? Or could this be my last night on earth? Events were moving so quickly; it was hard to keep up. I'd been living on adrenaline these last few days – weeks, even – and it seemed as if it was never going to end.

I ran a bath while I waited for tiredness to creep in. I didn't want to go to bed and lie awake, listening to the creaks of the apartment and wondering if it was someone coming for me. I lay in the water with my iPod playing my favourite classical tracks in the background - soothing melodies which my adopted parents had played to me as a child. I tried to relax and make sense of what had happened. *My own mother was after me?* But she wouldn't hurt me, not if she knew that I was due to inherit Watts' fortune – if that was even the case. I could only take other people's word for it. My father was dead. The truth suddenly sank in as I lay still in the warm water. Gazing at the tiled wall in front of me, I tried to piece all of the puzzle together, like tiles in a jigsaw. My grandmother, Mrs. Devlin was dead. Now my father was too. My mother was believed to be a schizophrenic nutcase and she was after me. *What about Creed? Would he come back?* And then there was Mr. Devlin. It was hard to believe that the wealthy gentleman was really my grandfather. He hadn't stayed at the hotel for weeks since his wife had died. *Could he have been responsible?* In the centre of the five tiles I pictured Jim. The others all represented my past, but he could be my future. The words of the nurse who gave me the results of my negative pregnancy test rang in my memory. I wasn't carrying his child. But that didn't mean I never would. *Did he really love me?* Right now it felt like he was the only person I could trust. Plunging my head under the water, I shut my eyes tight and breathed out. *When was this nightmare going to end?*

193

I drained the tub and wrapped a large duck-egg blue towel around me, squeezing the water from my dripping hair. It felt good to scrub off the grime of the day, like starting anew with a clean body and mind.

In the silence between my classical tracks, my ears heard a creak on the other side of the door. The relaxed state of mind shut off in an instant and the adrenaline rushed back through my veins. There was someone in my apartment. Silently opening the medicine cabinet on the wall, I scrambled to find a pair of nail scissors. It was unlikely they would do much good but I needed something in my hand to make me feel less vulnerable. I was naked and I had nowhere to hide! The floor outside creaked again, and I heard footsteps walking away, into the bedroom.

Taking one last look in the fogged-up mirror above the sink, I stared into my wide brown eyes. If this was the last moment I had on earth, then I wasn't going to go easily. I would go down fighting. I gripped the door handle tight and took a deep breath. It was now or never. I opened the door, and cried out: "I'm not scared of you!"

I was actually surprised that my voice sounded steady as a rock. My heart thumped in my chest as my breathing quickened. I could see that the door to the fire escape was open. I'd left it ajar to let some air into the apartment and I must have forgotten to close it when I went into the bathroom. There was silence. No-one had answered my call. Maybe it was just a cat that had slipped in.

I softly padded on my bare feet across the living room to my bedroom door. It was closed. Gripping the handle I flung the door open so hard that it hit the wardrobe behind it. As the impact made a loud crash which filled the room, I screamed.

A woman was sitting on the opposite side of my bed, facing out of the open window with her back to me. She was tiny, her matchstick arms hung out of the grey woolen dress that she wore, and her shoulders were hunched over. A shimmering mass of golden hair hung down her back as her only identifying feature.

"Violet?" I whispered, clutching the towel tightly around me.

She exhaled as if she had been holding her breath, and putting one hand on the bed behind her, she slowly turned to face me. Her heart-shaped face was the same as the nurse I had seen in the hospital, framed with strands of her honey-blonde hair and long bangs. But it was her eyes which startled me the most. I hadn't noticed them in the hospital, but the brown irises gazed at me now with a questioning expression. They were exactly the same as my eyes, flecked with almost indistinguishable dots of green and violet which reflected the light.

She patted the bed next to her. "Don't be afraid Clarissa, I'm not going to hurt you." Her tone was gentle and calm, not at all like the frenzied person I'd heard on the phone all those weeks ago.

"Here," she handed me my soft blue robe which was lying on a chair in the corner of my room. "Put this on, it's cold in here. I'll make you some tea."

I took the robe uncertainly, but I couldn't help but follow this woman's instructions. She left the room and I heard the kettle boiling in the kitchen. I shut the window, closed the drapes and wrapped the robe tightly around myself, pulling my long damp hair up into a clip so that it wasn't wet around my shoulders. My mother was here, in my apartment. I had so much to say to her, but I didn't know where to start.

Violet came back into my bedroom carrying two mugs of chamomile tea. "I thought this would be calming after the day you've had," she said, handing one to me. "Will you sit with me?"

I sat on the edge of my bed and wrapped the robe around my bare legs, clutching my mug of tea to warm me. Even after the hot bath, I was now shivering as I took in the situation. Violet rested in the chair opposite me and placed her mug on top of my bookshelves, next to a picture of me as a little girl at the Long Island fair, one of the only reminders I had of my childhood.

"You were a beautiful child," she began, looking at the photograph. "I don't expect you know it, but I was always watching you from afar."

Her eyes caught mine but I didn't speak. I didn't know what to say. I'd waited years to properly meet my birth mother, and I didn't want to miss the opportunity to hear her story. My questions could wait.

"I know these last few weeks have been confusing for you, Clarissa, but it's become essential that you know what has happened, where you came from and the silly silly game you've been caught up in.

"I'm sorry about your father. I didn't kill him, you know that. I still loved Lionel after all these years" ... she trailed off. "You know about my parents, don't you?" I nodded. "I'm sorry that you have that stain on your family. But I've learned not to feel guilty. Their love – however wrong it was – was not my fault and I can't carry their guilt with me. You shouldn't either."

She leaned forward in the chair towards me and fixed me with her eyes which mirrored mine.

"There is nothing wrong with you Clarissa, you know that don't you?" I looked down, ashamed that I had ever felt guilty about my lineage. "My parents are the ones who did the wrong thing, but they fell in love, and that's the only crime they committed. I did the same, when I met your father. It was love at first sight, although that sounds corny. I first saw him on the first

196

day I was working for his mother, your grandmother. Lady Watts was good to me, at the beginning, and she had me follow her around so that I could see what she needed me to do as her personal assistant. In her dressing room that morning, I saw a photo of a handsome man on her boudoir table. His bright blue eyes stared out at me. I knew if I ever saw that man I'd fall in love with him right then and there." Violet smiled, staring above my head as if she was reliving the memory.

"Later that day Lady Watts sent me to fetch her son for dinner. He'd just got back from college that afternoon. As I approached his room, I felt sick, there were butterflies in my stomach as if I knew what was about to happen! Then I saw him, sitting there, tying his shoelaces and as he looked up at me under his blonde bangs, I knew he loved me too. It was hard of course, all the sneaking around while I was working for his mother, and knowing that Lord and Lady Watts would be horrified if they ever found out, but we loved each other Clarissa, we really did, and I want you to know that."

Tears started falling from my eyes as I listened to this stranger talk. The love story sounded like it belonged to someone else. *Were my parents really ever in love?* I had always felt so out of place, so unwanted, that it seemed unreal to me that I could ever have been the product of such true love.

"But as you know, things weren't easy after Lionel's parents found out about our love affair. Or my parents for that matter. It's been … difficult ever since," she broke off, tears streaming down her face, holding her hands to her head.

I sat there awkwardly, not knowing what to do. This was my mother, but I didn't feel any connection to her. I could see that I looked like her, and I pitied this woman sitting in front of me, but it just didn't seem real.

"I never saw my mother again after Creed saved me one

day. Lionel made sure that I was looked after, albeit from a distance. He paid Creed to ensure that I had everything I wanted, but I'm starting to suspect Creed was also working for … him, I think."

"Who?" I finally spoke. I couldn't believe that the thin man I'd seen hanging around the hotel had been capable of killing Mrs. Devlin.

"My father, Mr. Devlin. He's behind all of this. He was the one behind my mothers death. I don't know how he did it, but years ago he found me and had some woman attack me. He knew I wouldn't just take it, and I defended myself. It was too late though, he had a psychologist certify me as schizophrenic. Strangely that was also when I found out I did have difficulties, and whilst I was relieved to finally know why I wasn't coping, I didn't want to be locked up. I spent two and a half years in that hell hole before I figured out a plan. I got help from some of the other inmates – I mean, patients. Now you have to help me Clarissa. I'm the only person you can trust. And you're the only family I have left. Will you help me?"

I looked at her. I didn't know what to think. Could she be telling the truth? She certainly didn't sound insane, and she'd coped for all those years and only ever been kind to me. But what would she ask me to do?

"I need time to think," I said finally. Violet got up and walked over to my lamp to switch it off. In darkness she crept over to the window and pulled back the drapes.

"You don't have time," she whispered. "He's here."

MR. PATRICK DEVLIN

Patrick Devlin leaned back in his chair and exhaled a deep a thick cloud from the Padrón Series 1962 Cuban cigar he was smoking. Being without Rosemary had been more problematic for him than he believed it could be, and he was agitated. He slammed his feet onto the floor as he rose from the chair, poured himself a straight scotch, and paced.

When Violet had found herself pregnant by the very wealthy Watts, Patrick Devlin had seen a vision of the future. But Lord and Lady Watts had absolutely put an end to any hope the young couple may have had for a life together when they turned Violet out into the world, broken and alone.

Devlin had set his sights on Lionel Watts many years ago, patiently and painstakingly carrying out his plans. He had to wait only for opportunity. In the meantime, he and Rosemary stayed close to Watts by using the weekly rendezvous at the hotelier's hospitality. That particular location had actually come in handy many times through the years. It seemed to intimidate the less fortunate, giving credence and power to Patrick Devlin's demands. He and Rosemary had a lucrative arrangement for many years, both compounding and making money from the misfortune, or the *indiscretion* of others.

Patrick had not always been up front with Rosemary. As Clarissa came of age, it had cost him a fortune to quietly put Violet away. That and recruiting Creed to their service with the promise that he would eventually be reunited with the woman. Creed did not care about anything in life but Violet Devlin. She was all that drove him forward into another day.

Devlin had begun to collect the pieces with which he would bring down all the Watts. Two years ago, he had a guy "fix" Jonathan Banks' car, resulting in the fatal accident that left Clarissa on her own. Then Devlin convinced Lionel that someone meant Clarissa harm. He intimated it was Violet, driven insane by her private torment. Lionel had half believed him in the beginning, and had already hired the young detective to find Clarissa. The man never had any idea that the only danger to his daughter was welcomed under his very roof.

Devlin sat slowly and heavily in the broad wing-back chair again, as if the wind had gone out of him. He had not realized how much he would miss Rosemary. The poor woman always had a soft spot for Violet, and in turn Clarissa, whose eyes mirrored her mother's soul. Since discovering the truth, he had no such compulsion; they were simply the means to an end for him.

Opportunity had come knocking when the young, wide eyed Clarissa appeared at the concierge desk. It was clear that Lionel Watts wanted to spare her any entanglement with her past, the painful knowledge of her mother's insanity, and their ugly life history. Lionel had been passionate about that, protecting Clarissa from that emotional upheaval. Devlin huffed as he downed the last of the scotch and rose to pour another.

They had set it up so carefully, Creed and him. Devlin had acquired, at great expense, the genuine signature of Lionel Watts and had it incorporated into the will. This gave Clarissa's grandparents the right to manage her fortune. They had never shown the girl any deference, had never given Lionel a clue that they recognized her. But seeing their granddaughter regularly had proven too much for dear Rosemary. She began to question Patrick, to keep things from him. And then, to find out what Lionel had unearthed! He could no longer tolerate it.

He was livid when Rosemary began demanding answers, even after telling him about the test. But she had stood her ground and Patrick was wholly unprepared for that unpleasant turn of events. Rosemary had been devoted to him and had always been very malleable. His anger with her had been swift and bitter. She had seen through him in his fury and betrayed him. In turn, she had warned both Lionel and Violet. She had stolen the sapphire worth a small fortune from the silver briefcase, procured from what turned out to be their last joint venture. And the will, Rosemary had taken that also. She knew he would dispose of Lionel, and then Clarissa would be the only thing standing between him and the Watts Legacy. She had given her life to prevent that from happening.

Devlin had sent Creed to fetch her home, but she fought him violently. Her resistance produced the blow to her head that killed her. It had worked to their advantage though, and as leverage against Lionel, Creed set up the entire *"murder"* farce in Clarissa's apartment to involve her. Patrick had helped with that one himself. They had searched everywhere, but never found the stone or the papers.

Lionel had given Clarissa paid time off which she spent with the detective, while Creed kept a watchful eye on the pair. Lionel was on to Devlin now, and he and Violet had schemed to drug Clarissa and her young lover to keep them from Devlin's grasp. And Creed always followed Violet like the lovesick fool he was! Watts really had no clue that Creed was so easily paid off, which had kept Patrick one step ahead.

Once that deed had been accomplished, and Clarissa was safely tucked away in Room 427, Creed went looking for Violet and found her in Lionel's arms. It had incensed him, made him sick, and he arrived at Devlin's door in a rage. Patrick did not know for certain, but after learning of Watts death, he believed that Creed had returned to the hotel to kill Lionel, forever putting an end to his competition for Violet's love. Either way he didn't care. He had the will signed already, and now just had to figure out what Rosemary did with it. He was also very grateful to Creed, for taking care of Watts so he didn't have to.

Patrick formed an arrogant smile. Violet did not care a whit for Creed and never would. He had been her lackey his entire life for nothing. Devlin assumed the man had planted Jim's cell phone in the room. Now the police and young detective were chasing their tails trying to situate all the pieces that they would never find! He normally would have found this turn of events amusing, but the missing will was tantamount in his mind now.

"Where the hell is Creed?" he shouted into the lonely air around him. The scotch splashed raggedly over his desk as he slammed down the almost empty glass. The phone rang. When he answered it, Creed's panicked voice met him at the other end.

"She's with Clarissa. I found her. She's with Clarissa!"

Patrick Devlin slammed the phone back into the cradle with a curse, and grabbed his coat.

"This has gone far enough!"

CHAPTER 23

The door slamming open was like a gunshot. In the dark abyss, footsteps heavily echoed throughout the room. Each move the intruder made twisted my stomach harder and harder. Shrinking into Violet's side, I anxiously moved my hand around in search of hers. When her fingers enveloped mine, my eyes slammed shut. I was not scared easily, if anything, I was tougher than I used to be. From Mrs. Devlin's death to Mr. Watts', it would have been nearly impossible to carry on without steeling myself, but in my cold apartment, surrounded only by the ominous, foreboding sounds of steps and labored breaths, I felt like a child, but for the first time, I could hold my mother's hand.

Unlike other children, I grew up quickly and not a day went by that I did not remember how that felt. Even though moving from house to house, job to job, was all I knew, I understood that it was not normal. There were days when I begged whatever God there may be to give me a family that would last. To prove that he existed by giving me a semblance of happiness. Was it so wrong to want to be the piece that completes a puzzle? To want to believe that parents out there were just waiting for me to enter their lives?

But while there were times that I sobbed and screamed, there were also days when I cursed out my birth parents, shouting into my pillow while clutching the stupid, beat up stuffed bear that came with me home to home. From the death of my adoptive parents to now, I dreamed of being removed from the inconsistency and insanity that surrounded my life. My heart could not handle any more breaks, yet here in the darkness, in my broken-into apartment, holding onto my birth mother whom I have not seen in over a decade, I felt safe.

"Violet, come out, come out," taunted a deep voice.

Approaching the bedroom, all movement halted as the door flung open and the lights sprang to life. Standing there, on the threshold of my room, was Mr. Devlin. He always carried himself above the rest, but as he stared at us with his pearly white smile and sinister eyes, he looked like a demon straight out of the deep depths of Hell. "Found you."

Quickly, Violet stood in front of me, her arms stretched out as a barrier. "One more step and I'll kill you, I swear."

"You'll kill me?" he laughed. "That's no way to treat your father, dear."

"Shut up, my father would never do something like this for petty revenge! You're just some monster that killed my mother."

"And you're a schizophrenic lunatic who killed your dear lover boy."

"Shut up, shut up! I would never hurt Lionel. Why are you saying that?" Violent pleaded, tears rushing down her face. "Why are you so determined to ruin your own daughters life?"

"Daughter?" he said as though it was a foreign

concept. "A while ago, Rosemary came from Watts's Hotel, crying because Lionel told her he knew the truth about Violet. Rosemary had always suspected, but she chose to ignore the possibility that I wasn't your father."

Violet gasped in shock.

"She spent all these years letting me live with the shame of a sordid family secret. You were the product of siblings, it was the final nail in the coffin that tore our family apart. But all along it was a lie. That stupid bitch tricked me into a living hell."

"You murdered my mother?" Violet screeched.

"No. She murdered your mother," he yelled, nodding his head my way. Tangling my hand in my hair, my lungs gasped for air. This was too much, too much was happening at once.

"If Watts hadn't arranged testing to confirm Clarissa's inheritance, we never would have found out. When we found you Clarissa, we believed we could be a family again, with the Watts empire in our hands. The plan was just so easy. All I had left to do was take care of Watts, then everything would naturally fall into place, but your stupid mother screwed everything up. She was furious at me, when she realized what I was doing, she thought by telling me the truth I would back off. How foolish. I put the time in, and I want what's rightfully mine."

Violet looked back at me, I could see the resolve fade, she looked scared. She had probably hoped that deep down he could never go through with hurting his own child, but evidently that was no longer the case. I eased in front of Violet as Mr. Devlin continued to talk. For his plan to work, he needed me alive, so I knew I had to protect Violet now.

"For a while, things seemed to be going smoothly, even after your mom died, but then that stupid girl who worked with you just had to stick her nose in where it didn't belong."

"Wait, Joy?" I asked, my voice cracking at the end.

Taking a step forward, he moved his left hand to reveal a gun. At the sight of the cocked weapon, my body froze. With all that had happened in my life lately, was this how it was all going to end? From the day I saw Creed to now, every moment I lived seemed to be taken straight out of a horror novel, some dramatic play that only was believable on stage. As he aimed the gun my way, I could see the curtain slowly falling. *This man was crazy. Surely he didn't think he could claim the inheritance without me?*

Slowly, he moved his arm so the gun was lined up with Violet.

"Why don't you tell her about Joy, sweetie?"

Turing around, I stared into her eyes. Everyone seemed to have answers except for me. Looking at me, her gaze softened before she whipped her eyes to Mr. Devlin, glaring.

"Joy works for Jim," Violet explained, eyes locked with the threatening man. "She's undercover."

"Joy worked for Jim? Wait, what? At McDonalds?"

"No Clarissa," Mr. Devlin interjected "You still don't know about Jim huh?"

"What are you talking about? I know Jim was paid to watch over me, he…he loves me!"

"Your lovely boyfriend Jim is a private investigator working for Watts. He was paid to *like* you Clarissa, and your dear friend Joy worked for him. So I guess you could say no one truly cares about you. You're just a pay check for everyone. Pathetic."

Churning at this new found information, I could feel my stomach pushing its contents upward. From the moment I began working at the Watts Regency Hotel, Joy had been my best friend. Even among all of the madness that began to take over my life, I could only think to myself how lucky I was to have her and

Jim as constants. The two people removed from the pure insanity that consumed my days. But no, they were working together.

It was a sick reality, the notion that they knew me before I even spoke to them. Jim must have planned his meeting with me, and I thought that I was so lucky to meet someone like him, that it must have been fate giving me a chance at a happily ever after. Working at a hotel that catered to the likes of the Devlin's, it is easy to feel insignificant, to feel the isolation and grandeur that is New York, but Joy was a reminder that we, as workers, existed as people and not as pawns moved from spot to spot.

"That girl just could not keep to her job, she had to go and dig through information that was not hers to have, and to top it all off she went and told you," he spat. "Her loyalties were skewed, always lying with you in the end, Clarissa."

Eyes locking with the old man, anger burned beneath my skin. I stood in front of the gun, arms limply at my sides.

"And what's wrong with that?" I whispered. "What's wrong with siding with a friend?"

Violet's hand touched my shoulder.

"Clarissa, nothing is wrong ..." Violet started.

"Everything!" shouted Mr. Devlin, his arms wildly thrown out to the sides. It was in that moment, in the second of relief that followed when the gun was moved away from my face that his threatening veneer vanished. His thinning hair was disheveled, his shirt untucked from his pants, his eyes darted around the room. Even the designer labels that adorned him from head to toe could not disguise his frantic and anxious disposition.

Patrick Devlin was unfolding.

"In this world, no one can trust anyone. Everyone is always looking to stab someone else in the back to climb higher. Not a single person gives a damn about who has to fall in order to rise," he said, his eyes dancing with pain. Rosemary had deeply hurt him.

"Violet, you never understood this because you *loved* the Watts boy, but all that served to do was dig up your heritage, and look where that got you, locked up in a hospital."

"You were the one who put me there," Violet screamed.

"I may have given the order, but you did that to yourself. This world is dangerous, and anyone who poses as a threat is removed. Your poor admirer did not understand that, idiotically acting on his own and evidently killing Lionel. Creed made himself a liability by showing how deep his loyalty to you runs."

Giving Violet a hard look, Mr. Devlin moved the gun back into my face.

"He should be dead around now."

Hearing a violent cry escape from behind me, I gave him the dirtiest glare I could muster.

"You're sick."

"No, I'm realistic. You're sick if you think everyone can live happily ever after. You probably somehow think Rosemary is innocent in all this, yet it was me who was fooled. Believe it or not Violet, I loved you. you were *my* princess. Everything Lionel has done for you Clarissa, has torn the little family you had to shreds. Look at us now," he yelled. The pain of his words stung in his throat.

Everything seemed to pass in slow motion. His right arm raised to join his left in holding the gun. Violet threw me to the side. My head collided with my bedpost. Shadows appeared behind Mr. Devlin.

A bang sounded. A body fell.

CHAPTER 24

He just lay there as Rosemary had, on my living room floor. I just stared at what seemed like some strange warped version of Romeo and Juliet's Shakespearean tragedy. Only no one would mourn this protagonist. The only movement in the room was the blood seeping from his body and the only noise that I heard was the painful silence.

"Let's go Clarissa. Quick - pack a bag, we need to get out of here!"

Raising my head I could feel the pain setting in where I had knocked the bedpost. I expected to see blood when I moved my hand away, but the only blood in the room was pooling around Patrick's body. I looked to the doorway to see Creed standing there, urging us to hurry up. He had shot Mr. Devlin, without so much as an ounce of regret on his face. Yet this man was clearly no threat to us. Maybe it was Violet's presence, but I felt inclined to trust him again. He was more caring with Violet than her own father had been. But then again, if Mr. Devlin wasn't Violet's real father, and my grandfather, then who was?

"Clarissa come on, we must go, you can't be found here with another dead body."

"Go where? What is happening here? I'm so confused."

Violet walked over to me and reached for my hand. I gave it grudgingly. All I could think of is Jim. I hoped his affection for me had become genuine. I needed someone to hold me and squeeze all this pain away. With everyone dropping dead at this rate, I was sure to be alone again soon. Despite the craziness of late, I couldn't deny that I felt alive, possibly for the first time ever.

"Please Clarissa. I know this is hard for you," she reached for my hand again. "Clarissa, you need to trust me. I'm your mother, and you are the only important thing in this world to me now that Lionel is gone."

She looked deep into my eyes. "I promise you're safe if you stay with me."

"But Mr. Devlin said Creed had killed Watts, and he kidnapped me Violet, he hurt Jim; yet you still trust him?" I yelled, angry at the lack of sense with which any of this made.

"There is more that needs to be explained. There is a lot of greed in the world, but Creed as you call him, would never have killed your father; I'm pretty certain of it. I was behind your kidnapping honey, but it was for your safety, I'll have to explain later, I'm sorry. We have to get out of here, get a bag packed and we'll go. Trust me"

Violet spoke with persuasive conviction, and although panic and realization rushed through me, I agreed to go. A body lay on the floor, motionless. I had welcomed Mr. Devlin at the hotel so many times, but to see him like this, lifeless in the same place his wife had died was surreal. It was almost like fate had brought him and Rosemary back together. I wondered how much love they truly had for each other throughout their tortured

210

relationship. I should have been angry that he wanted to hurt us, but he seemed so totally lost in those last moments. I really could relate to that feeling of desperation.

"Where are we going to go?"

"Somewhere familiar. You'll know it once we get there."

Closing the door behind us, Violet spun around like the karate kid, and high kicked the door handle. I was stunned at her strength. How could such a small framed woman have so much impact?

"What? We need to make it look like he broke into the apartment. Now come on."

"What about the police, they are watching my apartment?"

"Don't worry, I made sure that cop wouldn't wake up anytime soon."

Instinctively we grabbed each other's hand, and ran along the hallway towards the stairwell. As we reached the bottom step, Justin turned the corner with Bullseye who started going nuts. Violet was stunned. Nothing had shocked her to date, but that tiny dog stopped her dead in her tracks.

"It's ok. He's a sweet dog, Violet. Just wait a second. Hey Justin, can you let Bullseye off the leash? I feel like he's trying to tell me something." The Pit Bull raced up to me and sat by my legs, looking up at me.

"What does that usually signal Justin?" I asked.

Justin scratched his head. "Well, it's hard to say really, we've been working on a few things. He usually sits still like that when he signals to me he's found something."

"Ok, good. Maybe that's what he's telling me. He did this last time, Violet. I think it's important."

"Clarissa, we really have to go … now."

"Bullseye, go find."

At my command, he darted off. We all gave chase as he led us to the overgrown thorn bushes in one of the abandoned flower beds. He started digging frantically, but after a shallow attempt, returned to my side. Justin looked embarrassed.

"I'm sorry Clarissa. I'm really not sure why he's acting so strange. It's probably an old bone or something stupid like that."

I had a hunch that he had found something, but I let Justin put Bullseye back on his leash and take him home.

"Clarissa, this is silly, I really must insist we leave."

"I grabbed a small flat stone, and used it to dig as fast as I could. It didn't take long before I could hear the rustle of plastic. Violet got down on her knees to help, surprised there was anything there at all. I hoped with all my heart that this wasn't another body, or part of one, as I unearthed the edges of a wooden box wrapped in one of my old neck scarves, then covered with an old yellow Shoprite plastic bag.

"What is it?" Violet asked impatiently.

"I removed the box, and unlatched the tiny clasp. Both myself and Violet gasped at the contents.

"The stone. It's true!"

"What's true?" I asked.

"Mom told me that she and Patrick had come across this stone on one of their endeavors. She chose not to be more specific, so I thought it was just a stupid story to give me hope. She said she would ensure it was kept safe for you, so no matter what happened with Watts, you would have something that would ensure you would always be ok. Clarissa, this stone is worth more than you can imagine."

"What are these papers?" Violet unraveled the folded pages, and gasped again.

"These are probably what got your father killed. Lionel was determined to make sure his legacy was handed over to you.

We didn't think he had managed to get the paperwork done before he was killed, but look at the date. Clarissa, he signed this will months ago."

I looked closely at the date. He had signed them just a month after I started working for him. And all along I thought he didn't even like me. I felt overwhelmed and began to cry. I didn't want to be holding on to this piece of paper with his signature on, I wanted him. I wanted to know the man who appeared to love me.

Suddenly Creed was behind us.

"Don't waste your time staring at that, now the Devlins are dead it's redundant. Now come on, lets go." He pulled us up, and urged us towards the parked Malibu. These cars were a dime a dozen, so if anyone was looking for us, we wouldn't stand out.

As we pulled off, Violet asked about Bullseye, and how he could possibly have known that box was meant for me. I really had no idea, but suspected that Rosemary had buried that there before she was killed that night.

"It must have been the scarf. He knew it was mine, I wore it so many times when I played with him. Do you think Rosemary planned that?"

"It's possible Clarissa, your Grandma was a smart woman. That's one special dog!"

I smiled at the innocence of Bullseye before drifting off into an exhausted nap. The car jolted to a stop outside an old store. Violet was right, I recognized it instantly. I came here that night, exhausted. The rickety sign still read 'R hsc d & C ed'

"What is this place?" I asked curiously.

"Ah, Rothschild & Creed. This place was my life, my sanctuary. Like you I felt like I had no family after everything that happened. I couldn't have you, I couldn't have Lionel, but Creed and Mrs. Rothschild became my family. They looked after

213

me."

"Did you live here?"

No, this was like a second home. I spent so much time here. It made me feel close to Lionel and you, and I felt normal when I helped out. Creed went into business with Mrs. Rothschild, and the store was just a front really, but it was popular. I loved looking through the old trinkets and imagining where things came from."

"So who is Rothschild?" That name didn't ring any bells to me, but if what Violet said is true, they sounded nice.

Brenda Rothschild, you will meet her soon enough I'm sure. I haven't seen her for so long actually but I can't wait to introduce you. She knows a lot about you, but I think someone else should tell you the rest of that story first."

I had become accustomed to riddles and couldn't be bothered probing further. I had so many questions for Violet I hardly knew where to start.

"Violet, why did you spend time in an institution?"

She looked sad when I asked, like she was drawing on a dark memory she had tried hard to erase.

"Honestly, it was probably best for me. Patrick arranged it when he got wind of the fact I was making plans to reunite with Lionel. My plan to be a family again became erratic, and I was out of control. The time spent inside did me good. It gave me time to take stock and focus on what was important. My dad didn't see it though. He just wanted me to be safe, or so I thought. I always thought Lionel's family was the threat, not my own."

Violet sighed heavily, then started to speak again. "Only recently Rosemary - my mom, told me she didn't trust Patrick anymore, and she wanted to tell me more about my father. I assumed she meant Patrick but it wasn't him after all. At least if what he said last night was true. We agreed to meet the next morning but she never turned up. She was found dead in your apartment."

A sad moment fell between us. A tribute to Rosemary my brave grandmother. She deserved that at the very least. Our tribute was broken by the creaking of the old front door.

"There's someone coming," I said frantically.

"Ah, he's here sooner than I thought," Violet said calmly.

We moved from the comfort of the living area to the shop front. The sun shone behind him as he walked through the open doorway, still decorated with broken 'police' tape after my last visit here. The light framed his strong, tall physique. He greeted Violet affectionately, like old friends would.

"Hello Clarissa. I guess I have some explaining to do." Jim confessed.

CHAPTER 25

Jim walked towards me. Taking my elbow he guided me to one of the chairs and eased me down into it before dragging another chair closer so he was sitting facing me. Taking both my hands in his, he nervously looked at Violet. She came and put a hand on his shoulder and gave it a squeeze to reassure him.

"Jim," I began. "Just start from the beginning," I whispered hoarsely.

"I have just come from meeting the detectives, Clarissa." I fought back tears as he continued.

"Don't worry," Jim said as he caught one of my tears with his thumb as it tried to escape down my cheek. "I've told them everything I know and before you ask, I didn't kill anyone!"

"I've wanted to tell you the truth for so long; I never expected to fall in love with you. When your father, Mr. Watts came through my door and hired me to find you, and make sure you were safe, I had no idea you were that little girl Clara from so long ago, until you recognized my father in the picture. I started to see my encounter with Watts as fate, bringing you back

216

into my life."

Jim saw my puzzled expression, so he began again:

"I am James Rothschild, I have a detective agency. Joy and Eduardo also work for me. I needed people close to you when I couldn't be, especially at the Hotel. Your father Mr. Watts was unaware he was harboring each month, the very snake who was trying to take the hotel and all its worth from under him and ultimately away from you. Mr. Devlin has been after the Watts Empire for quite some time, and has delved to levels I can't quite believe. Mrs. Devlin, who God rest her soul after such a long time of being manipulated by him, had finally seen him for who he really was and it ultimately cost her, her life."

I looked at Violet and motioned for her to come and sit beside me. I could see the sadness in her eyes; we had all lost someone who we were only just reconnecting with.

Jim continued. "Once the Lord and Lady Watts exposed the Devlins long kept secret, they were cast aside by high society and left to fend for themselves, which pushed them into the illegal trade of black market stones. I have a feeling Mr. Devlin never forgave Violet for becoming involved with your father, and he has been scheming for years to get revenge, seeing you working at the Hotel was the final piece of leverage he needed."

"What is it"? Jim searched my face.

"Mr. Devlin, is no longer alive. We had an incident at my apartment …" my voice trailed off.

Violet continued for me, and filled Jim in on the events of the last few hours. I glanced nervously over at Creed. He was leaning by the doorway connecting the front and back of the shop. He seemed to be keeping an eye on us and an eye on the front door.

With everything that had happened with this man, my trust was firmly on reserve. *How could he convincingly play for*

217

both teams? What was in it for him I wondered? I felt Violet touch my hand bringing me back into the moment.

"And after following Bullseye to the disused garden bed, we dug up these that she had buried for Clarissa."

Violet opened her bag producing the small wooden box and passed it to Jim. Opening the lid gingerly, Jim looked shocked by the contents.

"I can't believe how beautiful it is," he said as he held the huge Sapphire up to the light. The titanium and iron in the gem's crystal lattice structure, was mesmerizing. "I've only ever heard of these. I've never seen one in real life. No wonder Devlin was so angry at Rosemary, this is worth a small fortune."

"Plus we also have this Will, signed and dated. Creed says its no good." Violet gave Jim the Will to peruse.

"When I saw him that last time at the Hotel, he led me to believe that he had still not made a final decision. Then I had a document delivered to my office, containing the correct will. I have that kept somewhere secure. I guess after everything we'd been through over the years, he didn't trust me enough to tell me had finally decided, and I get that. I wouldn't trust me either, not after all that's happened."

Violet briefly looked over to Creed and sighed. "I am really sorry that it had to be like this Clarissa, I only ever wanted you to have everything you deserve in this life, it just wasn't meant to happen like this."

I squeezed her hand again. "It's ok Mom, I'm here with you now and that's what matters the most. We found each other, albeit in not the most usual of circumstances, but we did. It can only get better from here."

"Would you like me to take care of these Clarissa? I'll put them in my office safe until you need them. They'll be secure there, I promise. I need to let the detectives know what has happened with Devlin, let me make a quick phone call and I'll be back." Jim stood and bent down to kiss me gently on the forehead, "I love you Clarissa, remember that."

Jim then looked at Violet. "I have some news for you as well. I've found your biological father."

"What?" we both said in unison, "I can't believe it," Violet said. "How? … When? How did you know about that?"

"Watts had known for some time, he asked me to look into it. Let me just make this call and I'll fill you in on all the details. He's actually on his way to New York as we speak."

Jim made his way to the front of the shop, nodding at Creed as he walked past before quietly slipping out the door. I hugged Violet hard.

"I can't believe he's found your real father. It's the positive news we needed after all this mess. You must have slight trepidations though in meeting him as well."

Violet stood and paced around the room. "Sorry, force of habit," she said. "It's what I do to calm myself down, it helps get rid of the anxiety. I'm not sure what I think. I never had a true connection with my father. He was always aloof, pre-occupied with things on his mind, and maybe he knew deep down I was never his daughter. I always felt he was happy to pass me over to Lord and Lady Watts before I got involved with Lionel." Violet seemed to shudder as she spoke their names.

"I know you never got to truly know your father Clarissa, but believe me when I tell you, he was nothing like his parents, nothing."

With that she headed for the small kitchenette to the back of the room.

"Let me see if there's anything here to make us a cup of tea."

I thought about the crumpled letter I had found that day

beside my fathers body. It would be the closest I would ever get to hearing how he truly felt about me. The fact he was trying to express his feelings, meant more to me than a finished letter. Suddenly I heard tires skidding to a halt outside the shop, then car doors opening. We all raced to the front of the store pulling apart the plastic blinds to get a better look at what was happening.

"Help him!" I screamed at Creed.

Creed took his gun from its holster, positioning himself near the front door.

"Open the door for me Clarissa, on 1, 2, 3."

With my right shoulder to the door, I opened it for Creed to swivel out of, his arms locked as he fired off two shots before pulling back inside. The driver of the vehicle slammed the car into reverse before tearing off down the street. Creed flung himself out the door again firing off another four shots. I followed him out onto the street. Thick tire smoke dispersed in the air around me, and all that remained was Jim's new cell phone that he must have dropped in the tussle with the four men all dressed in black. Their faces were covered by hooded sweatshirts, making it hard to get a good look at them.

"Did you get the license plate of the car?" Violet said to Creed.

"I got the make and model, it's a black Dodge Durango. I know some of those shots hit the car, so I'll ring around and get my guys onto the chop shops. Whoever owns that car will want to dump it as quickly as they can, but we have something else a little bigger to deal with right now."

Hearing footsteps on the road behind me, I slowly turned around, not knowing what to expect. Violet rushed ahead of me and embraced a figure. As she moved away, Jim's mom stood before me.

"Everyone get inside now. Hurry up. Quickly," she ordered.

We all gathered back inside the shop. Creed positioned himself near the front windows, scanning the street through the slit in the blind. Violet paced nervously back and forth, whilst I slumped into a chair. I felt as though my life was literally being sucked from me. When will this madness stop? I thought to myself, just when it all started to make sense, Jim had been taken.

Jim's mom cleared her throat as she walked back into the room after checking the back door. I felt so nervous around her, I instinctively sat up straight in the chair, waiting for the impeding wrath to come.

"Hello Clarissa. We meet again under not so ideal circumstances I must say. I am sure your mom has told you who I am and where you are. We can get to know each other later but for now I need you to tell me what the hell has just happened here?"

Both Violet and I took turns filling her in with the details of the last 15 minutes. Jim's mom stood with her arms folded the whole time, slowly rocking back and forth on her heels as she took in all the details. At the end, she circled around the room, taking a deep breath and slowly letting it out between her pursed lips. Once she had released it all, she faced Violet.

"I thought they would try to take Clarissa, not Jim," she sighed. "I knew it was only a matter of time before they came to stake their claim."

I looked at Violet and she looked as puzzled as myself.

"So you thought they would take me, and you were just going to let that happen?" I stuttered.

"Clarissa!" Violet was unaware of mine and Mrs. Rothschild's previous meeting. This woman didn't like me then, so it was clear to me she probably didn't like me now either.

"Clarissa, our only goal has been to protect you, I assure you of that. Jim carries tracking tabs. As soon as he got here he would have put one on you or one of your belongings. Do you have a phone?"

"The box!" Violet and I said in unison. "If you're right, Jim most likely put one on the box containing the Will and the Sapphire."

Mrs. Rothschild's eyes narrowed in thought. "I didn't realize you had those, but yes, you're right. That's exactly what Jim would have done. Damn them!"

"Who?"

"You didn't honestly think that Patrick Devlin was the only person who wished to seek vengeance on your father? And now they have the stone and the Will, they have no use for Jim."

The meaning of her words stung deep in the pit of my stomach. I couldn't loose one more person. We had to get Jim back. The sudden ring of Creed's mobile phone made us all leap into the air.

"Yes?" He barked.

"Keep an eye on them, I'll get back to you."

As Jim's mom finally sat down flustered, Creed turned to her. "The tracker is active, it's picked up a car that's just pulled into the underground car park of the hotel. We can only assume that they have Jim with them."

"I should have known they would take him back to the Hotel," she said.

As I opened my mouth to ask who 'them' was, my pocket started vibrating. Jim's phone was ringing. I looked at the screen, it was Detective Edwards.

Jim's mom turned and stretched her arm out. "Hand me the phone Clarissa."

"Hello, this is Jim Rothschild's mother speaking ... certainly Detective, as soon as I see him, I'll pass on the message."

"Why would you do that?" I screamed at her. "We need them, they can help us get Jim back."

"Clarissa," she barked. "If there's one thing 35 years in the detective business has taught me, it's to never trust anyone, even if they're wearing a badge."

I lay my pounding head in my mother's lap as she stroked my temples softly whilst humming an old tune under her breath. I had been longing to see Jim for so long, but barely had ten minutes with him before he was gone again. My heart ached in so many places, I couldn't figure out how I was still breathing. I believed Jim when he told me he loved me. I longed to be held by him. I didn't care about the sapphire or any version of the Will, I just wanted to enjoy this feeling of love forever. I needed Jim to be safe.

CHAPTER 26

It had been twenty four hours since Jim had gone missing and there was still no word from his kidnappers about a ransom or any other demands.

Brenda Rothschild swept in and took control of everything. At first, that had been relieving despite the fact that she considered me to be a non-sequitur in his disappearance, and in the rest of his life. Now, a day later and being no further ahead, her presence seemed more and more like an invasion rather than assistance. I was too emotionally raw and weary to deal with the realization that I hated the woman who had given birth to the man I loved.

My mother was getting tense and started to pace. Her rising anxiety was playing off my own nerves.

"Mom, could you sit down?" I tried to keep the tension out of my voice but I could hear the irritability in it. Violet reacted like I had slapped her. She was too sensitive and I was too worried about Jim. It didn't seem fair that for the first time I had my mother and I was the one who was forced to act like the adult with her. She sat down, rocking, with the occasional whimper leaving her mouth. I began to wonder how much of her 'togetherness' had come from the medication she had been on. Brenda's presence also seemed to upset her and I saw her looking at the large woman with a surprising amount of malice. She had insisted this woman was pretty special. I wondered what had changed.

There were too many things to keep lined up in my mind. I couldn't deal with my mother, Brenda or everything else. All I wanted to do was to find Jim. I stood up abruptly. Brenda and Creed both stared at me. I took my mom's hand and she stood close behind me.

"I'm going to go for a walk with Mom. We're not helping anything just sitting here."

"Well, going out and getting yourself kidnapped or lost, or God knows what, isn't going to be helpful, either."

I decided to ignore her sniping and just walk away. We found a park bench and sat down together under a young oak tree. The air seemed fresh after the oppression and tension in the room we had just left. Mom seemed dazed and I was worried about her. I could not imagine how she was managing at all without having any medication with her. I hugged her to me; she was so quiet and limp. I had always wondered what it would be like to have my mother in my life, but I never imagined this. Even my brief memories of her had been of a smiling, happy and carefree young mother.

'Never trust anybody...' Brenda's words repeated themselves to me as clearly as though she were sitting beside me. I realized that I had been nearly dozing off and jumped at the sight of someone crouching down in front of me. I looked down to see a familiar face.

"Eduardo? What is it? Did something happen?" His gaze

was shifty and nervous. He came close to me and spoke in a low voice.

"I know where he is, come with us."

"Jim? You know where Jim is?"

He nodded and grabbed my hand to pull me off the park bench. I wondered if it was safe, or if he really knew where Jim was. *Why hadn't he told Brenda or the police? Why was he acting this way?*

"Please, come with me. You're the only one we can trust." I found myself rising to follow him. Mom was awake now and she seemed calmer even though she still clutched her purse like it was a teddy bear.

"Let's go with him, Clarissa, we need to find Jim."

Eduardo led us to a dark colored van. Joy was behind the wheel and Eduardo gently pushed me and Violet into the van and slammed the door behind us. I felt panicked, but Violet seemed content.

"Joy you came back!"

"I made a mistake Clarissa, but of course I'm here, Jim is family to me, as are you now."

"Where are we going?"

"Were going to get Jim." Said Eduardo with more determination than a junkie looking for a hit. "Jim is our boss but Brenda's not; I wouldn't work for her if it wasn't for Jim. You understand what I'm saying?"

"No, I don't. Isn't it the same thing, I thought they owned the agency together?"

"No, it isn't the same thing at all."

Joy seemed like a different person as a private eye than she did when we worked together. I marveled at the life that filled her voice as she quickly navigated the busy streets and explained the situation to me.

"Brenda shouldn't have a PI license. She can hardly keep the rules straight, and that's when she wants to follow the rules. She's not ethical. Eduardo and I have a real problem with that and we always have, but we never caught her on the wrong side of the fence, so to speak, until now. We have it all on tape and it's bad, it's real bad."

"You better start at the beginning, or at least near it. It's a lot to take in." Eduardo smiled at me sympathetically and I felt relief that I had found some people who not only had an idea of what was going on but also the inclination to tell me what was happening.

"Jim called Violet's real father to come and meet him. That was a huge mistake. Jim didn't know his mom was involved with this guy, and chose not to tell him about Violet over the phone. He came to town alright, and he also arranged to abduct Jim. He's run out of patience with waiting for Brenda to get hold of the Watt's fortune, and he's tired of having his plans interfered with."

"What?!"

"Violet's real father is named Richard Dane. He's deep into the mob and he has a lot of aliases but usually you'll hear him just called 'Dicky Dane.'

"Oh my god, I've heard of Dicky Dane on the news about a mob hit. I thought he was in prison."

"He was for quite a while, for witness tampering, that's all they could nail him for, but he's out now on 'good behavior', and it couldn't have come at a better time for Brenda. She loves Jim like a regular mama bear, and you're getting in her way. So is Jim. More than that, she has been under the delusion for years that she and Dicky were meant to be together. She'll stop at nothing to keep Dicky and Jim both to herself."

"But I love Jim."

227

"That's the thing. You're the problem and too many people have died." Eduardo's voice was earnest and I felt a shiver go over me.

"We gained access to the video surveillance that Brenda put in place at your apartment..."

"What surveillance?"

"She didn't tell anyone that she had put up cameras, and she believes she is the only one that can access the footage. We intercepted the line though, and found she even captured the murder of Rosemary Devlin."

Joy could see the alarm on my face, and quickly filled in the gaps. "Creed, the heartless son of a bitch, obediently murdered her, then dumped her body in your living room."

"It doesn't make any sense. I didn't see any cameras. And why was there dirt in my room?"

"The cameras were removed by Brenda. She must have realized that Creed had been bought, as he wasn't acting on her behalf. She got there just after Creed left that night. She's smart; she didn't want the police to find anything.

I blushed knowing I had been so easily fooled. "It explains how she knew I was at Jim's that day he was at work. I guess she wanted to see the client she planned to double cross up close and personal. What a bitch."

"We also found other footage Brenda kept when we were searching her place for clues about Jim's kidnapping. We knew she was involved, it's just her style. That's when we realized that Brenda isn't just the sort of woman who you hate to work for; she's also up to her neck in crime."

"Can we take this information to the police?"

Eduardo nodded, "We can, and we probably should... But time is an issue and we need to get to Jim fast. Brenda thinks Dicky Dane obeys her every command and trusts that Jim will be safe while his goons hold him captive, but we aren't that confident."

"He's been growing increasingly suspicious of his mother's 'sources' and he's been conducting investigations of his own. This is what led us to start looking a bit closer to home. Our theory is that his mama doesn't know about the investigations, but Dicky does. He's paranoid and doesn't have any reason to protect Jim but every reason to not want to go back to prison."

"If they can frame him for anything, like say, a murder that even you were beginning to suspect him of, then killing him will cast doubts on all his investigations. It would be all the better if they can shut him up for good, too. Brenda has no idea the sort of danger she's put her only son in by authorizing his kidnapping."

"Are you certain Dicky doesn't know about Violet?"

"We're pretty sure. Brenda learned of Dicky Dane through Watts all those years ago. Watts knew that Rosemary had an encounter with Dicky. I hate to say this Violet, but it may not have even been consensual, that's why Rosemary buried it inside her. Rosemary only knew for certain after Lionel showed her the paternity results. From all accounts, she was pretty furious at him. I guess not knowing was easier for her."

Mom took a bottle out of her bag and took a swig of it. She had been quietly listening this whole time. Her breath smelled like bourbon. I grabbed the bottle from her, "Mom! What are you doing?"

I looked at her in shock. Eduardo took the bottle from me and sniffed it and then handed it back to Violet.

"What are you doing? That's the last thing she needs right now! She's not well."

Eduardo smiled at me grimly. "Yes, I know. I've worked with people in her situation before; it's very common for schizophrenics to self-medicate. Unless you have a bottle of pills from her doctor handy I would suggest you let her do whatever she needs to do until we can get her back to the doctor."

"I'm sorry, sweetheart, you must be so disappointed in me." Violet was no longer the strong woman I had become accustomed to. I longed to help her, but knew better than to take control of something I knew nothing about.

I just shook my head. I couldn't speak from the tears that were stuck in my throat. Through all this, the one thing that stood out clearly was that Jim really did love me and that he hadn't killed anyone. My heart was right and I regretted ever doubting him, even for a second. I also regretted trusting Creed. He really was a snake, and seemed to be playing to the tune of his own fiddle nowadays.

"So tell my why Creed put dirt in my bed. It doesn't make sense."

"It doesn't make sense because it wasn't him, it was Rosemary."

"What do you mean?"

"Rosemary came into your apartment erratically. She looked frightened. Creed was close behind. I guess she thought he hadn't seen her, and she got into your bed pretending to be you asleep."

"But I was there that night, how could I not have known."

"You were probably drugged earlier that evening, by either Creed or Rosemary, one to protect you and one to indict you." My crazy visions must have been real, my mind was lost but pieced together what I had seen. It all suddenly made sense.

"Creed quickly found her and dragged her out. She was covered in dirt already, so she must have gotten it into your bed. We don't know why Rosemary was so dirty, and you really don't want to know the rest of that story."

"I know why she was dirty. We found a will from Mr. Watts buried with a sapphire in the small rose bed downstairs. She must have realized her husband was onto her, and rather than leave it somewhere he could find it, she buried it. My neighbors' dog knew it was there and eventually alerted me to it."

Violet was shaking. Hearing what happened to her mom was a lot to take in when she had no meds in hand. She was killed by the person she had trusted most. That level of betrayal was unfathomable. "Eduardo, please, how do I help her?"

"Her delicate state makes it difficult for everything to make sense in her world. Sometimes her actions seem bizarre to us, but she is trying to patch together her own fractured reality however she best can. Once she gets her meds, she will be ok, I promise you."

My head was spinning as all this new information dawned on me. "I thought *my* family was messed up - how is Jim going to feel when he realizes what his mom has done? How could she do this to her own son?"

"Power. Jim isn't easy for her to control and the only thing that kept her in his life was that he worked too hard to ever pursue romance. You've changed that for him and after what we've seen, we don't think Brenda will stop at anything to make sure that she stays in the agency's driver's seat and the number one lady in Jim's life."

"What about Mr. Creed? How could he turn on Violet like that?"

"Maybe a long time ago his true allegiance was to you, Violet, but you rejected him and he turned on you. He works for Brenda, but more importantly, he appears to be out for himself now. With everyone wanting a piece of the money pie, it was inevitable Creed would start feeling he deserved it more than anyone"

Tears welled up in Violet's eyes. "I didn't reject him."

"You didn't even notice how much he loved you. He did the things he did for you because he was smitten with you. You thought of him as a friend, but he thought of you as a lot more."

I was rapidly waking up to the ramifications of Violet's schizophrenia. She wasn't reliable. I had been sure she was the one who had called and told me to get away from Mr. Watts and that he couldn't be trusted, but everything I have heard since indicates that she trusted him implicitly. I knew that had been her voice, she must have been confused, I was sure of it.

The van came to a stop. We were outside of a warehouse.

"Creed said Jim was at the hotel, why are we here?"

"I told you, you can't trust Creed. Jim is here, and we're dammed if we're leaving without him."

I felt energized by Eduardo's words. "I'm in; whatever you need me to do."

"You just stay here, with Violet. She needs to be watched right now. We just want to make sure that you two don't get captured or killed while we do this. We have everything we need, so just stay here and if anyone comes near the van," Joy tossed me a gun lightly, "Shoot them."

They locked the doors behind them as I clutched my mom in the backseat of the van hoping to hell that the two of them knew what they were doing.

CHAPTER 27

As I watched the shadows of the old warehouse swallow up the figures of Joy and Eduardo, I wondered how long it would be before I saw them, and Jim, again – if at all.

My head was spinning. Nothing was as I'd thought it was. Joy and Eduardo were far from the humble hotel employees I'd believed they were. They were highly trained security professionals and I was now certain that despite her seemingly sunny disposition, Joy would have no hesitation in shooting to kill if she had to. I didn't know for sure who to trust, but something in my gut told me they were on my side.

Let's face it, I didn't have much choice.

And then there's Jim. Good old reliable, no unpleasant surprises Jim. Well, at least I had thought. I certainly swallowed that fairy tale hook, line and sinker. I guess I just wanted to - needed to - believe in the possible happy ending. And there's no bigger fool than the one who wants to believe, is there? Yet, deep inside me, I knew it wasn't all a lie. I might have been wrong about the facts, but the love, the tenderness and the passion had been real. That much I knew.

And now, I didn't know if I'd ever see him again.

I shook myself violently, and forced myself out of my thoughts. I had to focus on here and now if my long-lost mother and I were going to get out of this alive.

I turned to Violet, who was staring blankly at a crumpled paper tissue in her hands, whimpering softly as she slowly but methodically shredded it into dozens of tiny, equally-sized pieces.

"Mom?" I said softly. No response but the light rip-rip-rip of the soft paper.

"Mom!" I repeated, louder and more urgently. She looked up as if I'd just appeared, with a question in her eyes. "What is it, sweetheart? Can I get you something? Some milk and cookies, perhaps? That always makes everything alright, doesn't it?"

She reached for the car door handle but I halted the movement by grabbing her wrist hard and pulling her round to face me.

"No!" I hissed through my teeth, with tears of frustration stinging at the corners of my eyes. "What I need is for you to get your act together!"

"The man I love, and whom I'm pretty sure loves me, is in there and his life is in danger. I'm not going to give him up without a struggle, and I'm not going to let you sink back into madness after all these years of missing you. You've got to pull yourself together!"

The harshness of my voice cut through her confusion like a hot knife through ripe brie. She dropped the tissue and for the first time looked steadily and resolutely into my eyes: "I'm sorry. I'm here, really I am."

She wiped her nose with the back of her hand, like a scolded ten-year-old, and then tucked a stray hair behind her ear.

"So what do we do now? Just wait and see?"

"I suppose so," I replied.

She eyed the gun on the seat between us. "Will you use it if you have to?" She asked.

"I don't want to, but if I have to, then I will." I edged the pistol a little closer to me, still not completely convinced that my mother was fully sane right now. Violet watched the movement then looked at me with a clear-eyed look dripping with meaning.

"You don't have to worry about me right now. I needed telling off and that's exactly what you gave me. For now, at least, I'm OK and I will be for as long as I need to be to get us through this. I just lost it all for a moment – it's not being off my meds that's to blame, it's just all been too much to take in."

She too had been shocked to her core. One of the few people she thought she could trust, her old school friend and confidante Brenda, has been revealed as a manipulative, socio-pathological snake with no more concern for her friend of 25 years than she would have for a fly in a spider's web.

"It was Brenda and Frank I went to when I first found out I was pregnant, though I now realize Brenda was the one who told Lady Watts before I had the chance to do so. I suppose she was hoping for some reward or a way to squirm her way up through high society. I thought she was my friend. I certainly knew her husband Frank would help; he was the most decent fella in the world. Funny though, she always seemed angry and disappointed with him. He gave her a good life, but it wasn't the high life she always hankered after."

I realized that she was talking about Jim's father. What she said agreed with what he had told me about him, and the hazy, happy memories of my brief stay with the Roth (or should I say Rothschild?) family.

"I knew that Frank had taken you in," she went on. "It

made me feel happy, knowing you would be loved, giving me the freedom to move away and try and find out how to be me, so I could come back and be a mom to you one day. I know you stayed with them for a while as a foster child, but I don't think Brenda knew your were mine. I had no idea she'd sent you back in the blink of an eye, I'm sure if she'd known who you were she would have adjusted to having you around."

I strongly doubted that, but could see that Violet wanted to believe there was some integrity in their friendship.

"I guessed the welfare department mixed things up after that, someone wrote your name down wrong, and when I asked them about 'Clarissa' and they had no-one in their records of that name. I wonder if Frank changed your name to protect you?"

So, that's where 'Clara' had come from.

"You know, we always think that we have one friend who will always be there for us no matter what, for all our lives, come what may. Just goes to show that was yet another fairy tale."

I shrugged. I wouldn't know. I'd never really spent long enough in one place to form that kind of bond with anyone.

Violet certainly seemed clearer and calmer right now. That, at least, was a relief. I was about to ask her if she really hadn't realized that creepy Creed had been infatuated with her all these years when a cacophony of bangs, shrieks and tinny gunshots exploded from the dark warehouse. Shouts, three abrupt flashes of light and then… silence.

Stunned, we stared at one another then turned to look at the building for signs of life. Nothing. Everything was quiet – way too quiet. Nothing stirred.

It seemed like an eternity before we could rip our gaze away from the dark shape silhouetted against the dying light of the day. A lump of apprehension was stuck in my throat and I could hear the whooshing of the blood in my veins as I strained to hear something, anything, from the warehouse.

The discreet ticking of my cheap wristwatch seemed like a deafening death watch, until Violet broke the silence with a shocked and wavering "What do we do now?"

"I don't know." I looked at my watch and suggested we wait to see. Five minutes passed, ten, twenty.

Somewhere in the distance a dog barked, and a clatter of upset dustbins shattered the quiet of the evening air. After half an hour, there was still no sign of life from the warehouse.

Resolve shot through me. I had to know, one way or another. I couldn't just be a spectator any more. Whatever had happened would have a direct impact on my life and it was time for me to take control.

I opened the van door. The fading daylight poured in and highlighted a battered old toolbox. I rummaged through and found a torch. I took it in my left hand, gripped the gun in my right and looked inquiringly at my mother.

"I'm coming," she said and opened the door.

Slowly and oh-so-carefully, we made our way through the broken gate to the warehouse. It was partially hanging off its hinge and we had to inch around the jagged edges to get past. Our footsteps seemed to echo like distant thunder through the cooling evening air. Before us was a loading bay, gaping wide open and inviting us into the darkness and whatever hid inside. I clicked on the torch and offered a silent prayer of thanks when it produced a ray of yellowish light before we gingerly made our way through the doorway. I swept the walls with the torchlight for a clue of what had happened, but they revealed nothing. Crumbled concrete and old fast food wrappers (McDonalds, I noticed with a wry grin) scrunched under our feet as we made our way deeper into the building.

The place smelled of neglect, mingled with damp and

dust. But there was something else. A faint metallic tinge to the air. Something I couldn't quite place.

The main warehouse was lined with lanes of shelves where the goods had once been stacked. As we rounded the corner of the third aisle, I heard the faintest moan and swung the torch to face the source of the sound. It fell on the figure of a man, slumped against the wall and bleeding heavily from his shoulder. It was Jim. He was alive, but injured. He squirmed in the light and held his good arm over his eyes as he peered into the dark to see who was behind it.

"Who's there?" He croaked. "If you've come to finish the job, just get on with it, will you?"

Trembling, I turned the glow of the torch to show my face.

"Clarissa. Oh thank God!"

I rushed to him with a flood of emotion. He winced as I took him in my arms, accidentally crushing his injured shoulder. He was weak and limp, probably from loss of blood, but the bullet looked like it had passed through his shoulder and missed any vital organs.

A quiet bleep from the shadows reminded me of Violet's presence. She had taken Jim's cell phone from my jacket pocket that I had draped over her earlier, and was calling for help. I breathed a sigh of relief. It looked like she was indeed keeping her act together for as long as she needed to, after all.

Shaking, I tried to shift Jim into a more comfortable position and slumped down next to him with my back against the wall. I swept the torchlight around the room. A sharp intake of shock made me catch my breath and tears pricked my eyes as I saw Eduardo lying in a pool of blood. I knew he could not possibly have survived loosing that much blood. If we had not waited, we might have been in time to save him, but after 30 minutes or more, the man I'd first met as a happy-go-lucky hotel bellhop was beyond help.

Behind him was Joy. I scrambled up and went to her. She was spattered with blood – probably Eduardo's. It looked like he had tried to shield her and she now lay unconscious on the floor. She was still breathing steadily and calmly. My instincts told me she was going to make it.

Distant sirens wailed in the night, and flashing lights illuminated the sky outside. To my left, I heard a strange, soft creak, regular as a clock pendulum. My gaze followed the sound. Starkly outlined against the red and blue lights was the figure of a man; A spare, slight, sinewy man, swaying gently as he dangled at the end of a rope. Creed.

Violet ran to the spot, and looked up at the lifeless figure. Tears streamed down her face as she tried in vain to lift the dead weight and stop the rope's stranglehold. Too late, of course, as evidenced by the protruding tongue, bulging eyes and blue tinge to his lips. Already his limbs had started to stiffen like the branches of a long-dead tree.

I ran to her, wrapped her in my arms and pulled her away from Creed, cooing reassuring noises in her ear like you would a distraught toddler. She crumpled in my arms and I gently sat down on the ground and cradled her, rocking her softly as sobs shuddered through her body.

As I did, I spotted a ragged piece of paper beneath the suspended body. Surprisingly neat and rounded handwriting was clearly visible, even in the dim light. It read:

"I'm sorry. I've done terrible things. I did them all for love, but there was no love for me. I hope you can forgive me.

Violet, I will always be yours, body and soul. Goodbye and find peace."

At the corner of the paper, holding it firmly in place was a

239

familiar wooden box, still streaked with dirt from the flower bed. The box was empty.

I heard Jim groan again, and pulled a reluctant Violet to where he was sitting.

"Creed's dead Jim"

"I know, I know, I think that's the only reason I'm alive. Creed sneaked in and went for the sapphire Dicky took off me. I'm sorry Clarissa, I didn't see this coming."

I scoffed at his words, sickened by the knowledge that Jim may not have known, but his Mom sure did.

"Eduardo and Joy were the perfect distraction and Creed must have held back, looking for an opportunity to get what he came for. They got to him though Clarissa. I saw it all. Creed didn't flinch when they hauled him up there. He didn't squirm or fight; it's like he accepted what was coming. They pulled that note out of his pocket, and left it with the empty box. Dicky yelled as he left. 'Tell Brenda thanks.' Did my mom do something to stop them from killing me?"

"I don't know Jim." My heart ached for this honest, wounded man who had no idea what kind of woman his mom was. "Help is here, let's get you and Joy straightened out, that's the most important thing."

Being back in the hospital seemed to have happened too soon, despite being on the other side of the looking glass this time. Joy cried for Eduardo, and Jim asked for his mom. I wondered where my own mom was, she wandered off to get coffee and hours later there was still no sign of her.

Whilst Jim rested, I headed for a quick bathroom break. As I quietly closed the door behind me, I turned to find Lord and Lady Watts standing there. They looked out of place in their starched attire. Their faces stung with distaste as they discreetly gawped at their surroundings. They looked directly at me; clearly

I was who they were looking for.

"Hello Clarissa."

Words failed me. I looked down the hall in both directions, wishing for an easy escape.

"I don't have the time or energy to deal with you right now."

"Well you better make the time Clarissa, because we're here to offer you a deal." Lord Watts did not make the statement sound attractive. As much as they didn't want to be here, they also didn't want to give me anything. His words were laced with reservation, and Lady Watts sighed heavily whilst he spoke.

CHAPTER 28

"What sort of a deal?" I asked, looking around in hopes of seeing somebody that I knew who could help me out of the deep, dark waters I felt myself treading in.

"We've been doing a great deal of thinking and we think that perhaps an amicable solution can be found to all this-" Lady Watts waved her hand with distaste towards the door that hid Jim from public view.

"All this, as you call it, are lives of people, real people that have been wrecked and ruined. If it takes 'all this' to wake you two up enough to decide to act like human beings, well, then I'm glad I've gone my entire life without ever knowing the two of you."

"Please, child-" She started.

I whirled around and hissed at her through clenched teeth, "You will never ever have a right to call me 'child', and Lady Watts, you ain't no lady."

"Be reasonable Clarissa. We are ready to be, surely you can do the same, to prevent more bloodshed." His words were bland but his eyes were threatening. There were sharks in these waters I was treading. I couldn't let them see any sign of weakness, that would be blood in the water to them.

"I'll be reasonable with you both when I have my lawyer present." I turned on my heel and walked away, my heart pounding in my chest. I didn't have a lawyer of course, that was absurd, but finding out what I had to do to get one would at least give me some time to imagine being face to face with the two of them again.

I went into Jim's room and locked the door behind me. He was sleeping and his arm and shoulder were held up in traction. It looked like he was stuck in a stationary wave. I pulled up a chair beside the bed and held his good hand and rested my head on his chest. I could hear the sound of his heart underneath the beeping of his heart monitor, steady and regular. I sighed and it turned into a deep wrenching sob. I felt Jim's hand squeeze mine back and I started to cry harder.

"I'm alright, hey, don't cry." He tried to put his arm around me but his cast made it awkward and we both started to laugh. The laughter released something else in me and I kissed him, half lying on the hospital bed to reach his lips. I felt so safe and sure as I looked deeply into his eyes and spoke the truth, of the knowledge of what one surreptitious trip to the bathroom with a test the nurse had given me had provided. Apparently the stress and drugs that had invaded my system of late offered some explanation to the false negative test I'd had.

"Jim, we really are going to have a baby."

His good hand had been resting in the small of my back and I felt it tense against me. I tensed in response, my eyes imploring him to be happy, to be kind... like the crashing breaking of a tsunami, relief flooded to me when I saw his eyes smiling even before his lips. He laughed out loud and kissed my lips hard, crushing my body against him.

A week later, Jim was out of traction and was allowed to go home. He was in good spirits but there was something in the air that sucked the happiness from us and made our laughter echo hollowly. Worry was eating away at both of us. We had 24 hour police protection and despite being together at last, we both knew we weren't safe.

I had turned away Lord and Lady Watts at the hospital but the phone calls from them and their attorneys had been unceasing. I had reluctantly gone to stay at the little bungalow where Brenda lived. It was sandwiched between two brownstones that dwarfed the dark blue house and made the slightly unkempt grass look wild next to their austere dowdy faces. They were like disapproving matrons keeping an eye on us. However Jim and I felt their presence far less than the ever constant presence of Brenda.

Joy and I agreed to Detective Ren's plan. Jim was not to be told about Brenda's involvement in everything, and I was to keep it to myself until the police could deal with it. They didn't think taking Brenda out of the equation would help much at this stage, there was still so much uncertainty.

She wouldn't leave Jim and I alone for a minute and it was only Jim threatening to take me to a hotel that finally got her to quit 'accidentally' forgetting to knock on Jim's door. My apartment was a no-go zone. Between the Watts and their lawyers calling at all hours and pounding on the door and the cloud of reporters who had materialized like black flies by the side of a highway, there would be no peace for us there. Brenda insisted on letting us know every time someone tried to get a hold of Jim or myself, each time protesting that 'they said it was really important', and shattering our peace. It was after yet another interruption that we lay side by side on Jim's bed, as chastely dressed as teenagers that he turned to me and said,

"So, what do you want to do now?"

"To do? You mean other than murder your mother?" I would soon regret having made my glib remark as things became a bit too real, but for now I snuggled against Jim's chest and enjoyed the illusion of safety it provided.

"I don't know what to do, Clarissa. This was my home since I was a child and I have a lot of memories here. I had always imagined if I had kids that I would raise them where I was brought up. My dad worked hard to keep our little lot from being developed and this place means something to me, but I'm not stupid, I see how hard my Mom makes it for you to be here and I know that you want to get a place where Violet can come and live with us." He sighed heavily, "I'm glad my dads doing okay, I just wish he was still here. I had no idea he and my mom had problems"

Problems was an understatement. Jim had no inkling that his mother had made life more than just hard; and not just for me but everyone, even those she claimed to love. I desperately wanted to confide in the man I loved, but at the same time had such a strong urge to protect him. If anyone would eventually understand that my deception was for the best, Jim would. After all, it was his deceptions that brought us together in the first place, so I knew we could handle this.

"My moms doing a lot better now, I think that having people care makes a big difference. I'm glad she checked herself back into a clinic. Seeing her acting so erratically was hard, I think she realized the burden she would be. She's finally getting the right balance of meds and I can't wait to really get to know her. Your mom on the other hand, well that's a different kind of mental altogether."

"She's... well, she's sometimes difficult. She doesn't

245

understand how important you are to me and she's being selfish. She's jealous and probably upset that my dad left, she just seems so angry."

I knew just how angry she was, and Jim would too soon enough.

"If she knew that you were Clara, the little abandoned girl who stayed with us, maybe she would warm up to you a bit?"

Jim had no idea that his mom had tossed me out like old trash. He must have assumed the authorities re-placed me.

We both looked up, hearing a gasp of realization from the now open door. It seemed that Brenda had forgotten once more that she was supposed to knock before entering.

"You're Clara? I knew it, I knew it all along. Damn Frank, he always knew didn't he? Violet always had a way of getting to people. I should have known. I was right to get rid of you then, and I'll do it again!" She took a step forward with her arm upraised, and I didn't know if she was going to come at me. Jim stood up and stepped in between us.

"What are you talking about?" He demanded.

She shook her head, her eyes still glaring venom at me. "Nothing, I didn't mean anything, I was coming to tell you there is someone in the living room... someone you will want to see."

Brenda seemed paler than a Japanese geisha, and I wondered if that was solely due to her new found knowledge, or for some other reason? She turned and left, Jim took my hands in his, "I don't know what part she's played in all of this, but I don't trust her, I'm not blind to the strangeness in her."

I felt relieved that Jim was seeing her unfold. The truth wouldn't sting so hard if he was eased into it. "We will go see who she's let in and then we will talk, talk about our future, what we want to do, and if you would like me to put a ring on your finger?"

He kissed my third finger quickly and smiled at me. I started to say something, I didn't know what, but I felt my lips move. He pulled me into the living room in his wake before I had a chance to respond. I saw quickly why Brenda had let someone into the house despite Jim's specific directive not too: she had let in a ghost.

The man I saw sitting there was dead. He had been dead, I had seen his body. To my further surprise he smiled and awkwardly embraced me. He sat down, gesturing for me to do the same. Jim and I exchanged nervous looks, this man, he had been my boss, I had been warned that he intended me some sort of harm, he had been killed... and now, he was back and I felt like I was at a séance.

"I realize that this must be somewhat uncomfortable, there has been quite a bit of inveigling and obfuscation on my part, and I've come to confess all to you." I sat down on the far end of the couch from him, my spine rigid and my nerves shot.

"I'm sorry, Clarissa... I would like to apologize. I'm not very good at apologies, but I would like to say I'm sorry. For everything really, faking my death and all the mountains of lies... I should have claimed you as my own when I found out Violet was pregnant... I should have, but I didn't, and the only excuse I have is that I was a coward."

I thought he was very brave to say all this to me, but at the same time, I didn't want to let him know I was impressed and I also wanted to make sure he was really sorry. Leopards don't change their spots, or so I had been told. Then I saw that there were unshed tears in his eyes - eyes that held so much pain like mine, and I felt my heart open just a little towards him.

"Why did you do it? I don't understand, I saw that you were dead."

"You saw some very good acting on my part. With help

247

from the best stage make up artists I could find. The police were in on it, detective Ren has been an incredible ally. Once I knew the extent of the problem surrounding your inheritance, I realized it was more than myself and James could handle. Sorry James, I have never doubted your skills, but I had to do this."

"Everybody thought you were dead... your parents have been looking for the will..."

"Yes, I've been aware of the situation. It isn't everyday you get a chance to see what will happen if you were dead. I used the opportunity to find out if I had done right in the writing of my will or not, I've had a few things changed now that I've seen my grandparents were completely correct in their assessment of my parents."

"I'm so confused. What does this have to do with anything?"

"It has to do with everything. Did you ever stop to wonder why my parents were so eager to get an inheritance from me? Unusual for parents to be looking for that in their child, don't you think?"

"I... I had never really thought about it."

"Fortunately for me, and for you, my grandparents were canny people and they saw that their son Lionel Watts the third, was a man who was not to be trusted, when they died, their entire fortune skipped my father and mother and instead went to myself, Lionel Watts the fourth, at only age fifteen."

"At fifteen! I think I had less than $100 to my name, and I was pleased with that." Lionel laughed at my quick remark.

"My father always saw this as a great injustice. He had always taken for granted that the family fortune would be his. It was that expectation that probably caused him to loose sight of his humanity. He's not a nice man Clarissa. I did feel bad for my father's loss of the hotel, not badly enough to give it to him, of course. Until I was 21 I didn't have full control, but strict measures were put in place by my grandparents to ensure my parents couldn't intervene. It killed the little relationship we already had. I suspected my parents only had me to ensure their future, but when the inheritance skipped them, they really lost sight of what being a parent was all about."

Lionel could see the sadness in my eyes that mirrored his own, as I recalled my own heavy memories of longing to be wanted by my parents, and yet here was one of them, professing to have felt the same. I'm not sure if it made me feel more or less understanding of how they could have lost track of me. Thinking better of interrupting, I let him continue.

"I made sure that they had an involvement and that they always had a say on the board and things of that sort. It wasn't enough though. He wanted the hotel and I made the dire mistake of confessing to him one day that I knew about your proximity and that I thought you were hardworking and diligent. I told him that I intended to tell you the truth about your parentage and, if all went well, to one day give the hotel to you when I died."

"You... you really wanted to get to know me? You thought I was hardworking? I thought you didn't even know I existed.. You treated me like I was just another chambermaid!"

"Of course I wanted to know you, I still do." Lionel shifted awkwardly after making the most heartfelt statement I had ever heard. "I'm not very good at affection, besides... It seemed a safe way to make sure that you wouldn't become greedy or try to use me the way my father so often had. It wasn't fair to you, I'll acknowledge that, Clarissa, but I hope you'll understand that I've dealt with vipers and my own family wanting my money my whole life. I couldn't bear to tell you that you were my daughter only to have you do the same. Not only that, but I finally realized the lengths my parents were willing to go to, and

I knew I had to fix it. I unknowingly exposed you to so much danger, and for that I'm truly, truly sorry."

I saw Lionel Watts the Fourth then, for the first time. He wasn't my boss, he wasn't my estranged father, he was a little boy who had grown up in the shadow of a ruthless father. I knew that Lionel loved the hotel and that he was hardworking and mostly a fair boss and now I could see that he was also a human being. I took his hand in mine and when he didn't flinch away I leaned forward and hugged him.

To be hugging my father after all this time was an impossible dream. He put his arms around me with the same awkwardness that he had hugged me when he first came in. Jim stood in the doorway watching.

"Mr. Watts..."

"You'll have to call me Lionel now. I think it's a little late to try 'father' but Mr. Watts is an absurd thing to call your father."

"Lionel... I have to tell you, I hope you'll be happy for us, I'm going to have a baby... and I think Jim asked me to marry him."

He looked from one of us to the other, "A baby? I'm going to be a grandfather?.. Also what do you mean you 'think' he asked you to marry him, did he or didn't he?"

I looked to Jim, "I sure did sir. I'm still waiting for her answer."

"Yes, Jim, of course I'll marry you!"

Jim's arm was still in a sling but he put his other arm around me, his movement nearly obscured the movement by the kitchen doorway but I saw the flash of a gun barrel and screamed. Jim pulled me down and Lionel threw his briefcase at Brenda just at the muzzle flared. The gun jerked upward and instead of hitting me in the chest it went through the drywall ceiling instead.

Lionel and Jim tackled Brenda and in the commotion they didn't notice my grandparents and Dicky coming through the front door.

Brenda wasn't acting alone, it had been an ambush it seemed. Jim had his mother's gun and he shot Dicky as Dicky was pulling something out from his belt. Lionel the Third, my grandfather, yelled at Lionel, "This time we'll put you into the ground for good, you ungrateful bastard!"

He pulled out his gun and pointed it at my father who lay still on the floor. Jim pointed the gun that had just shot Dicky at his soon-to-be grandfather in law, "You do it and you're a dead man."

Lord Watts looked from Dicky's body, to his son on the floor, to Jim's gun. He paused and his finger twitched against the trigger. He dropped the gun onto the floor, it bounced harmlessly on the carpet. My father put his hands down and lay back down in relief. I darted forward and picked up the discarded gun while Jim held his aim on them.

"Call an ambulance, call the police." Jim said.

"Don't worry son, they're already here." Lionel announced. "About time detective."

The police descended on the house like a swarm of hungry bees. Detective Ren did not look pleased with how the encounter unfolded. He knelt down to check if Dicky was sill alive. He wasn't, but with everyone else in custody and enough evidence to ensure that they served some real time, he could finally put the case to bed knowing I would finally be safe. I felt the tension in my shoulders ease and enjoyed that settled feeling my gut had been so longing for.

JOY

Watching Rose grow into a toddler was an honour for me after everything her parents and I had been through together. Clarissa named her Rose in the spirit of her mother's flower name and in testament to all the lives that were recently lost. Rose was Clarissa's hope for a brighter future, that would finally break the circle of pain that was their family's strongest heirloom.

So many people had died over the legacy of a hotel and a sapphire that mattered nothing at all to those who had found that they couldn't take it with them past death's door. I had fought for Clarissa and Violet, but of course my loyalty lay all the while with Jim. He always had faith in me, and my ability as a P.I, but this last case left me with too much doubt. My placement in the hotel was fun, but I got to like Clarissa, and it pained me to see her fighting through so much confusion. I also admired her. If that had of been me, I'm not sure I would have held it together so well. Jim understood when I told him I could no longer continue. He didn't blame me for my indiscretions, in fact he empathized how our last target had truly gotten under everyone's skin, no one's more than his!

He repaid my loyalty by making me Rose's godmother, and that is a job I will always take very seriously, but for now, I was happy to be rewarded with a permanent position at the Watts Regency. Of course Jim instructed me to watch over Clarissa, but that girl didn't need anyone. She was extraordinarily resilient and I have nothing but admiration for my closest friend.

Mr. Watts naturally took Clarissa under his wing and trained her how to be a concierge. She insisted on learning the basics, but it wasn't long before she assisted with managing most of the hotel. I guess one day she or Rose will inherit it all. That isn't the important thing though, Clarissa isn't the type to care about that sort of money, she's just happy to have a place where she belongs. You can see the light in her face when she looks at her dad, she's so happy to have a family.

Violet stays at the hotel now too. She's doing a lot better and keeps pretty well balanced so long as there isn't too much stress in her life. She's careful to keep to her medication schedule and Mr. Watts, he takes good care of her. I suspect their old romance is brewing once again, of course they don't advertise it, but myself and Clarissa share the odd knowing glance when we see them together. Not only does it make Clarissa happy, but there is a tenderness to him that is new. I think he always needed Violet in his life, some connections are just that powerful.

Lord and Lady Watts are no longer associated with the Regency. They left and went to Europe, after the police had a hard time proving their association with Dicky. It was they who had initiated everything, drawing Brenda into the fold, and connecting Lionel to Jim. Lionel had been clueless to their underhanded plot to reclaim what they thought was rightfully theirs; and although their plan had failed, the one thing they did do right was to ensure that no path could lead back to them.

Brenda was another matter however. She is serving twenty-five to life at Bedford. She took Dicky's death pretty badly, and occasionally Clarissa visits her. Not to make her stay there more comfortable, but to remind her that her and Jim are happy, despite her best efforts to intervene. Jim refuses to go, and who could blame him.

The highlight of this last year was seeing Jim and Clarissa at their wedding. Clarissa's wedding dress gently obscured the bump that soon became my beautiful goddaughter Rose. As she repeated her vows, her hands trembled around the flowers of the same name. Her father paid for the lavish wedding, insisting they all needed a beautiful day to enjoy. This one time, Clarissa knew better than to argue with him, and we had so much fun picking out everything for the day.

There were so many tears, but they were all out of joy. Clarissa Rothschild stepped into her new life full of new challenges as she learned how to be a wife, a mother, and the best Concierge she could be.

THE END

CHAPTER 28.1.

I looked at Lord and Lady Watts, barely able to disguise my disgust, but still managed to chuck out a reasonably civil answer to their question.

"What can you possibly want from me, the illegitimate daughter of your son, when you have always refused to acknowledge me as your granddaughter?"

Watts replied, "We know we were wrong the way we treated your mother, but we didn't realize it would have such an impact on her life. We never wanted that. We just wanted the best for our son, and her parentage made her unsuitable. Brenda Rothschild told us what we now realize was nothing but lies, but we had no way of knowing that. Nor had we any idea what a manipulative woman she is."

"Well, it changes nothing. The fact is, my mother was sectioned and you are partly responsible."

"Yes, we know that," said Lady Watts. "But do you know that Violet attacked Brenda when she found out the woman had fostered you? Brenda named you Clara to make it difficult for

Violet to find you. Then Brenda's husband reported her when he finally saw how she mistreated you, and you were taken away from her."

I stood there, completely shocked by the information. I suddenly found myself remembering things that I had pushed away, things I didn't want to think about. Now these things were being dredged up, forcing my mind into undeniable knowledge. It dawned on me that my body was shaking, but my mind focused on the memories of repeated slaps to the face, the pain of being pulled by my hair, being dragged to a dark, cold place. I realized now that it was the cellar, where I knew no one would hear my screams.

Lord Watts' voice tore me away from the building terror. "Where is your mother now?"

I swallowed, forced myself to be still. "She went to get some coffee, but it's taking a bit long. What is it you want from me?"

"Well, Lady Watts and I want to offer our sincerest apologies, and we wish to make amends in whatever way we can."

"I don't see how that's possible," I said.

"My son created a Last Will and Testament," he continued, "of which his mother and I did not approve at the time. But he was adamant. He wanted everything to go to a single beneficiary, but knew that if he left anything to Violet, she would be vulnerable to the Devlins. By then he had discovered what kind of people they really were."

"What's all that got to do with me?" I asked. These people were crazy.

Lord Watts gave a tiny smile. "Clarissa, we were pleased to learn that you are an intelligent young woman with a high degree of integrity. We respect that very much."

"We decided that Lionel was right. Despite your youth, you are just the person to take The Watts Regency forward into the next phase of the hotel's history. That means we will not be contesting the Will."

"What are you talking about?"

"I am talking about the Will that was inside the box," Lady Watts said. "That surprise your neighbor's dog dug up. That Will names you as the sole beneficiary."

"The other document that the Devlins forged is now in the hands of our lawyers. They will discredit it, and there will be no legal challenge to our son's wishes." Mr. Watts seemed to straighten then, confident in their decision.

His wife sighed, her face softening in sympathy. "Brenda had been blackmailing the Devlins. Her…unsavory boyfriend had told her of their illegal activities with precious stones. She also knew they had forged Lionel's Will to their own benefit."

My mind raced, and all I could think about what whether or not Jim knew all of this. He was, after all, a Private Investigator. Was that the reason for his growing interest in me? I pushed such thoughts away, trying hard not to remind myself that Brenda was his mother.

Lord Watts must have read my mind before he spoke again. "You need not worry yourself about Mr. Rothschild. He has been a trusted employee of ours for quite some time, and is now in possession of the authentic Will.'

"Why would he go against his own mother?" I asked. I couldn't help myself.

"You were not the only child his mother mistreated, Clarissa. Brenda's husband discovered her affair with the gangster, and he divorced her and fought very hard to get his son home."

"Mr. Rothschild knows his mother for what she is," Lady

Watts added.

There was a long silence. I felt like a dying fish the way my mouth gaped open.

"I'm sure you need time to digest all of this, my dear," Lord Watts said kindly. "Once again, please accept our most sincere apologies."

"We only wanted the best for our son," his wife said. I wondered if the shine in her eyes was the beginning of a tear. "I hope that one day we can put all this behind us. At our age, time is of the essence, and we would like to end our days having done right by our son and his daughter. Goodbye, Clarissa." They both turned and walked away.

I watched them go without a word. It was too much work to both process their words and give a farewell. Besides, my mother had been gone for a really long time. I needed to find her. In her state of mind, it wasn't impossible that she would be wandering about without a clue as to where she was.

As I walked the corridors looking for my mother, I found myself in the Emergency Department just as an ambulance rolled up outside. The hospital doors burst open and two paramedics quickly wheeled in a stretcher. I heard shouts of "shooting," and "gunshot wound," and a panic struck me. I wouldn't have put it past my mother to get into this kind of trouble.

I strained to see onto the stretcher, and when it rolled passed I couldn't believe my eyes. The person bleeding profusely on the stretcher was Brenda!

No, not my mother, but I was already convinced that she had something to do with it. Had she actually shot Brenda? I couldn't remember what had happened to the gun. I had it when we got back into the van, I remembered putting it on the seat. But after that it had vanished from my memory.

Oh, dear God. I hope not, I thought. I had just *found*

Violet; I wasn't going to lose her again. I pushed my way through the main door and ran toward the parking lot. My heart raced faster than my legs. I had to find her!

The parking lot was huge, and I hadn't even gotten to the hospital's garages yet. I had thought I'd have more energy, but the entire day had drained more than just my emotions. Then I saw her in the distance. She was just shuffling around in lazy circles, confused and vacant and desperately in need of her medication.

Somehow I found the strength to run to her, and as she saw me a slow smile of recognition slid across her pale face.

"Hello. Would you like these? They're very pretty," she said, pushing a handful of dandelions into my hands.

"No, Mother. I want to know where you've been. You said you were going for coffee."

"I've been on a little trip. My friend Brenda took me for a ride in her car. Wasn't that kind?"

I swallowed the lump in my throat. "Where did she take you?"

"She took me to meet a man who she said was my father, but that wasn't true, was it?"

Her addled comments were more than irritating. I had to get some kind of information out of her before her memory got even worse. "What happened?'

"The man said they wanted me to play a part in a film. I never knew Brenda worked in the film industry, but they never got that far because they started shouting at each other. Then Brenda said, "This imbecile is your daughter, Dickie. Does she make you feel proud?" The man told her to shut her mouth, but she just wouldn't."

"Mother, do you know why they started shouting in the first place?"

Violet gave intense focus to the dandelion petals, which she plucked and flicked to the ground. "The man said something about her not keeping her end of the bargain, and something else about some boy."

"What boy?"

"A boy named Will."

Light crept through the shadows of my brain as I realized they had been talking about Mr. Watts' Will. And Dickie, that was...

"Violet...Mother...I think that man really was your father."

The twisted look of pain on her face was followed by an enthusiasm that surprised me. "No he's not, because Brenda shot him. She would have shot me too, but I had the gun from the van, so I shot her first. She was happy when she told me that she named you Clara so I couldn't find you. The worst thing was that she said she was going to put us *both* away in an asylum, lock us up." Her eyes bored holes in me now, pleading for understanding. "So I shot her first! There was a lot of blood thought. I was careful not to get it on my nice clean dress."

I wanted to fall apart right there. I knew I should tell the police, but I hadn't had enough time with this woman, the mother I'd just found. I decided to take her back to the hospital. Maybe I could get her some of her medication, and if the two detectives were still there too, so be it.

I didn't know how I was going to explain anything, but I had to find the words somehow. So I took hold of my mother's hand, as if she were the child and I the parent, and walked her back inside the hospital. I desperately wanted to see Jim, far more than I wanted to talk to the detectives, but there was little choice left. They were in the waiting room, looking bored and tired.

I quickly gave them a brief summary of my mother's hazy recounting, and they said they needed to bring her to the precinct for a more detailed interrogation. I offered to go with her, couldn't let myself abandon her, but she shook her head.

"No, I want to go on my own. I've never been in a police car before."

That settled it. I watched them leave with a lump in my throat. Violet excitement was so innocent, so childlike. She walked lightly alongside the detectives, completely unaware that she might face a murder charge.

Now I could see Jim. I had no idea as to the extent of his injuries, and I was a bit afraid of what I would find. But his dreadful mother would not be there, and that made me feel a little better. She was still in the Emergency Room, and as far as I was concerned, she could stay there. I had no sympathy for a woman who could put her own son's life in danger and then turn up with home-made chicken soup, to play the devoted mother for all the world to see.

The nurse I stopped in the hallway told me he was in room 23, four doors down, and I stalked the distance like my life depended on it. When I opened the door, I found him sitting up in bed, comfortable and alert.

"Clarissa," he said. He opened his arms and I ran to him. The strength of his embrace crushed me to him, and he kissed me hard on the lips like he was a man in the desert and I was his water. So much of the tension lifted from me, and I returned the kiss with as much passion as I could muster. Then I had to pull away slowly and look at him.

"Jim, I'm so sorry. Your mother is being treated in the Emergency Room...she was shot."

"I know," he said. "One of the nurses told me."

I breathed a sigh of relief. "Do you want to see her?"

261

"She can rot in hell, as far as I'm concerned. I can't forgive her for what she did to you." He brushed the hair away from my face, tucked it behind my ear.

The door opened and another nurse came in. "Mr. Rothschild, do you have a moment?" He nodded. She took a hesitant step forward and stood rigidly. "The doctors did everything they could for your mother, but she didn't make it through surgery. I am so sorry." Jim only stared at her. "Would you like to be taken down to see her?"

Jim frowned and slowly shook his head. "No. No, I don't want to see her."

The nurse blinked in surprise, gave a curt nod, then turned on her heel and left.

He looked at me, and I couldn't tell whether or not what I saw there was actually pain. "I can't stay long," I told him. "Violet was taken into custody, and I don't think she's lucid enough to answer questions. I need to be there with her. And I want to see how Joy's doing." Jim nodded when I spoke, but I saw the hurt on his face that had not been there at the news of his mother's death. I realized then how ridiculous it had been for me to doubt him at all. I thanked him, kissed him again, and walked out.

Joy was also in surprisingly better condition than I expected, sitting in bed and reading from a folder.

"Hi, Joy."

Startled, she looked up, and her face relaxed into a smile.

"How you doing, kiddo?" I asked. I hadn't realized how much I'd missed our joking banter.

"Kiddo! Cheeky beggar, I'm at least twice your age." Her smile broadened.

Reassured now that she actually was okay, my mind turned to more questions. "So, I know why Jim was involved in all this. But you, I don't understand."

"You haven't noticed the likeness, then?" The blank expression on my face must have been answer enough. "Rita Banks was my sister."

I gasped. "Oh, Joy. I'm so sorry. I never knew."

She nodded. "Before I joined Jim's outfit, I was a police officer in the UK. But something didn't seem right about this so-called "accident", so I came back."

"Rita was good to me," I said softly. "So was Jonathon. They were very kind people. They took in all the rejects, the ones nobody else would take. I was lucky enough to be one of them."

"Yes, well, I'm glad you were."

I put a hand over hers on the hospital bed. "I'm glad you're okay. I have to get back to Violet. She was taken into custody earlier, but I don't think she's going to be able to answer their questions."

"Go," she said, and waved her hand toward the door. "She needs you more than I do. Both Jim and I are being very well looked after. Go on." She adjusted the folder in her lap for reading again, and I took a deep breath, taking her smile with me.

Leaving Joy's room, I was stunned to see Violet and the two detectives walking toward me.

"Don't look so worried," the Hispanic detective said. "Your mother's account ties in perfectly with what we already had from a homeless man who called that warehouse home for a bit."

That explained all the McDonald's wrappers.

"Your mother just helped us fill in the gaps."

"So she's free to go?" I asked.

"She certainly is." The other officer looked incredibly relieved. "She hasn't stopped talking since we left."

"Oh, thank God," I said. Violet stepped forward and

enfolded me in an embrace that I couldn't help but return.

"Why aren't you with that young man friend of yours?" she asked me.

I stepped back and looked her in the eye. "I can't really leave you alone, can I?"

"Oh, I'm sure these men wouldn't mind keeping me company a little longer," she answered. Turning to the detectives, she asked, "Do you gentlemen have any other pressing engagements tonight?"

Their mock annoyance was betrayed by surrendering smiles. "We have to stay to speak to a few more people about the case. A lot of them will be here for a while." The detective who spoke looked at me. "She can wait with us." He didn't notice the look he got from his partner.

"Yes, and I'll get myself a coffee," Violet said, and glanced pointedly at the detectives. "They didn't offer me a drink. What is the world coming? They keep me talking so my mouth is as dry as a desert, and not so much as a glass of water in return."

"Violet, do you think you can stay here here while I go see Jim?"

"Don't worry," one detective said. "We'll be here for another couple hours. We'll look after her." He didn't notice the look he got from his partner.

"Yes, and I'll get myself a coffee," Victoria said, and glanced pointedly at the detectives. "They didn't offer me a drink. What is the world coming? They keep me talking so my mouth is as dry as a desert, and not so much as a glass of water in return. But I'll wait until you come back, shall I?"

"Okay," I answered, and with that I raced down the corridor to Jim's room. It had been a long and difficult journey but now, at last, I felt I could put my trust in someone. All the doubts and wondering what people's real motives were no longer troubled me. I was ready to love again!

CHAPTER 28.2.

"As I am sure you know, Clarissa, your father's Will is in our possession." Lord Watts spoke like a man who had rehearsed his words all too well. For a moment I wondered if he had ever spent a week without planning or discussing his every move with his consultants first, but the extravagant suit and tie underneath his heavy coat, the engraved family ring on his little finger, spoke for themselves.

"In our possession indeed," Lady Watts spat out, crossing the edges of her fur coat tightly around her at the height of her neck, as if to shield her heart from the greedy intentions she believed people like me always had. I wanted to send them both away, or at least tell them to respect the hospital environment. I would have done it had I not been interrupted by two nurses who passed between us, pushing an empty gurney down the hall. By the time we were alone again I had decided to keep my mouth shut and let them say their piece. Lord Watts continued uninterrupted.

"Yes, we were told about our late Lionel's paternity test.

Unfortunately for us, it is true that you are his daughter. Although, I see it comes as no surprise to you. Still, you must never fool yourself into believing you are a Watts'. You are not. You will never be a part of this family. Nevertheless, we must obey the law, no matter how much we disagree with it…" At that point Lord Watts took a worn and faded piece of paper from the front pocket of his coat and showed it to me from a distance. "The Will states that your grandparents have rights over your father's inheritance. Apparently, Lionel wanted to be kind to you and did not want to bother you with the burdens of an empire on your shoulders." He sneered and handed me the Will, which I skimmed calmly. "However, and this will show you that we are not the heartless people you imagine us to be, we offer to tear up this piece of paper as though it never existed."

I raised an eyebrow at my grandfather. He was only getting himself into more trouble with every word. So I let him talk.

"This Will is very suspicious, my dear girl. My lawyers insist that either the signature or the document, or perhaps even both, have been forged. We simply cannot let our future depend on this… thing. I am sure you agree." I let him place the document back into his pocket. "So, my suggestion is that we tear it up right here in this hospital and never mention it again. The Watts shall never bother you again. Of course, you can keep your job at the hotel, perhaps even become a staff manager in the very distant future if you so wish. Now, then, do you agree? Shall we forget everything that's happened and move on with our lives?"

Instead of an answer I took a piece of paper out of the inside pocket of my own coat and handed it to him. It was my turn to speak as Lord Watts tried to make sense of the document.

"First of all, Lady Watts, I'm glad that Mrs. Rothschild

told you about my mother's pregnancy. I'm glad you sent her away, because she didn't have to spend another day in the sick environment of your estate, or grow to be as poisonous as you people are. I was very lucky to be raised by real, decent people with beating hearts. Now, I'm certain that had I been raised by you, I'd have also ended up stone-cold and insignificant. Like you. So thank you for saving my life. And I thank *you*, Lord Watts, for recognizing the fact that my father didn't want me to go through what he went through in his life. It's true, he didn't want to give me everything he had. But that is for the simple reason being that his own fortune made him miserable. Maybe I didn't have enough time to learn much about him, but I know he was afraid you would never let me be."

"What is this?" Lord Watts asked, staring at the document in his hands and hardly even listening to me.

"As my father wrote in his *actual* Will, the very one you hold, Lord Watts, he didn't want me to be the heiress of an empire at first. He thought this kind of money would turn me into someone like you. But, you see, during the little time he did have to get to know me, he realized that that was impossible, that your schemes could never reach me."

The more I revealed about my father's Will, their faces lost all color as they bent over the document outstretched in Lord Watts' hand. I let my father reveal the rest through his own writing.

Lord and Lady Watts learned that Lionel left the hotel ownership to me and my children, should I have any at any point of my life, either of my own or adopted. This way, his future grandchildren wouldn't ever have to face the struggles I did because of the 'sins' of my grandparents. They also read there that half of Lionel's fortune was now Jim's; the young man whom my father had grown to love over the years like the son he never had. Lionel knew that Jim would use the money to help other parents find their own missing children, just like he had found his daughter. The Will ended with two wishes. First, no Watts would ever acquire anything he had earned or built by himself. Second, the other half of his fortune would be given to Violet, the least he could do after everything the woman he loved had been through.

As I expected, Lord Watts fiercely tore the document into many little pieces while his wife, standing a few feet behind him, covered her mouth with both hands. I removed an identical document from the same coat pocket and handed it to him.

"You don't need to worry about tearing that one up also," I told him. "It is only one of many more copies. It's a safety issue, you see, for everyone involved. I just don't feel right entrusting the original document to you." They stared at me with blank, pale faces. "As the soon to be owner of the Watts Regency Hotel, I bid you farewell. Grandmother. Grandfather." I tipped my head each of them, then turned to leave. I only allowed myself to smile once I had put a safe distance between us.

***

Weeks passed with no news from Violet. It had become very clear that my mother had abandoned me without a word. The warrant for her arrest really made no difference to me. She'd had the chance to say goodbye properly this time. As much as her abrupt disappearance pained me, I regained my own strength with both Jim's and Joy's gradual recoveries, visiting them as often as I was allowed. More often than not, I was the first visitor to arrive and the last to leave.

I admit that explaining to Jim why his mother had been arrested was not the easiest thing in the world, but it was better that he learned it from me. I did enjoy seeing Brenda behind bars though. I had never thought that seeing someone locked up

269

would satisfy me so much. The irony of her having been sent to a medium security prison right across the Chelsea Piers, not very far from the Regency, was almost too entertaining to bear.

Brenda looked almost cute in her one-size-too-large green-blue uniform as she walked down the corridor and into the visitor room to see me. It would take her a while to get used to those uniforms after all her fancy dresses and necklaces. At least now she would have the chance to watch plays, learn how to do her own laundry, and make new friends.

"They're about to sell this place, you know,' I said, gazing up at the ceiling. We sat face to face, but she only scowled at me. "I guess they think you're not worth the trouble of keeping in the heart of Manhattan. Not like all the other criminals in suits still walking around freely."

"What do you want?" she asked. I was surprised she had stayed for as long as she had, that she had consented to see me at all. The jumpsuit color agreed with her, and she had lost a little bit of weight. I didn't imagine she was a huge fan of the food. She'd be all right.

"Jim knows about you. He saw the recordings," I said. Again, there was no response. As much as I knew she hated me, I was her only visitor. It was going to stay that way until Jim wanted to see her again. If he'd ever want to see her again.

We talked for a while about Jim's recovery and Dicky's arrest, when he foolishly tried to sell the amethyst on the black market to flee the country. Dicky was bound to rot in some maximum security prison or other, but he would never find out the truth about Violet. I was determined to stay true to my mother's wishes, even if she had abandoned me again. I could tell by Brenda's response, or lack thereof, that she also wished Dicky the worst. It wasn't until I told her I was little Clara from the past that she gasped and swore until eventually she was

270

screaming. "I got rid of you once, I would do it again!" I let her ride her high horse until a guard joined us to remind her to either keep quiet. The added threat of revoking a month's worth of visitor privileges was an added bonus. I could help but remind her that I was all she had left, at least for the time being.

I then took the subway to Battery Park, where Jim and I had arranged to meet. It was a particularly cold winter evening, but once I reached the park, the orange glow of the fading sun reflected in the Hudson River made me feel warm inside. Small groups of people, some of them tourists, were still trying to get a final glimpse of the Statue of Liberty through binoculars before sundown. I joined them, looking towards the statue with half closed eyes. Then I saw Jim on a bench down the path, and went to him.

Jim knew I had gone to visit his mother, but had made it very clear that he didn't want to discuss her. Not yet. When I hugged him, carefully minding the arm brace, I had the sudden realization that he was grieving for his lost mother in very much the same way that I was. When we sat down with our fingers intertwined, I figured it was time to give him the good news that he desperately needed.

The day the doctors had told me that I wasn't pregnant had been a blur, something in my memory that felt both dream and nightmare. So after one of my visits with Jim in the hospital, I decided to take another pregnancy test. Just in case. I had thought then that if I was going to be told I was no longer pregnant, I wanted to hear it with a clear mind and a bit more drug free self-composure. So when I told Jim on that bench that the last test was positive, he grabbed me and held me against him so tightly that I had to stop talking.

I hadn't really known at all how much the baby had meant to him until then. He shed tears of joy and cheered like a

271

little kid, then finally gave me the chance to explain what had gone wrong with the first test. It turned out that between the fifth and seventh weeks of pregnancy, the natural rise of the HCG hormone can lead to a high number of false negatives in pregnancy tests, even when those tests are done in the hospital. I told him I couldn't remember the rest of what I had been told, but I was still pregnant and the details didn't matter.

Soon enough we were throwing around baby names, laughing and lost in our own world. I eventually suggested *Rose* if it was a girl, and that if we had a boy we could name him after Jim's father.

"How could I say no?" he asked. I had never seen him so happy. "So now we need to find a place to get married."

I frowned, and had to look down at our clasped hands, giving his a little squeeze. "We don't have to get married just because I'm pregnant, you know," I said. "I'd like a little time to live like normal people for a while, as much as we can with a new baby and a new inheritance. All this craziness is over, and we really don't have to add any more right now." I looked up at him, expecting his forlorn expression of disappointment that I remembered seeing before we'd ever started dating. Instead, his eyes were wide and dry, and his smile only spread wider.

"It's only a matter of time before you change your mind," he said. "I'm pretty sure I can wait that long." I laughed. "And I have news for you, too." He reached in his jacket pocket and handed me a small envelope.

I hesitated before grasping it with trembling hands. I slowly pulled the small page out of the envelope, taking a moment to admire the beautiful handwriting in smooth and rounded letters.

My Loving Daughter,

I'm going to be away for a while. Only for a while, and then I'll come back to you. I need time to process everything that has happened. Time to mourn the ones I've lost, but also time to celebrate everything I have gained. My precious daughter, I am leaving you in good hands. I only wish I had more time to explain.

We will meet again soon. I promise you that. Violet.

It was Jim's turn to wipe tears of joy off my face. He explained that Violet had left him with the envelope while he was still in the hospital before she disappeared. He had already read the letter, but had wanted to wait for the right time to give it to me. It was the right time then. Holding my birth mother's final letter in the safety of Jim's arms, I knew no sacrifice had been in vain.

JOY

Having taken a spur of the moment detour, I parked my old mustard yellow hatchback outside of the abandoned warehouse. Over a year had passed since the day Eduardo gave his life for me, shielding me from Dicky's gunfire. I had believed him. The cat and mouse with Creed had gone way beyond the average investigation, and at times I couldn't help but wonder if we had done absolutely everything in our power to do at the time.

It had taken me months and lots of physical therapy to recover. At one point I was even determined to get back in action, but it wasn't long before I hung up my role as a P.I. Yes, I was very good at my job, had loved it since day one. But too many good people had died too violently and too soon, and I didn't think I could handle any more sudden loss and grave failure. One of my biggest mistakes in that last case had been to let my emotions override my judgement. I had told Clarissa, now Mrs. Rothschild, much more than I should have. I chose to give her all those tiny details about who she was and where she came from, and I couldn't help but think that things would have turned out differently if I had just followed the instructions I'd been given. Even though everything turned out pretty well in the end, all things considered. But that mistake had been one too many, and I couldn't keep going.

I started the engine and drove for another hour until I reached the Rothschild and Lind Investigation Agency downtown. I parked in Jim's spot, knowing he had taken the subway to work that day. Clarissa had told me they were planning to change the agency's name, but I couldn't remember exactly what it would be. Was it Blooming Orchid? Amazing Azalea? Now that the agency's focus had been put on missing children, it made sense to call it something different.

Jim stepped outside then, standing back to take a look at the renovation on the front of the building. I smiled and waved. He motioned for me to come inside, but I shook my head no, tapping on my watch for emphasis. My ex-boss made one of his funny faces before heading back inside and I got back on the road.

Driving past the Regency reminded me of the soon-to-be newest addition of the Rothschild family. I had a feeling it was going to be another girl, although Jim's father had no doubt it would be a boy. Either way, I'd bought Clarissa that sunshine yellow dress for her little girl. Someday Violet would see her granddaughter wearing it. I truly believed that the woman had recently returned under another name and new disguise, but I'd never dare admit it to anyone. I'd learned my lesson.

My cell phone rang as I was about to get off the Brooklyn Bridge. I already knew who it was and why she was calling. I was pretty late.

As usual, Clarissa was worried about me, and I had to explain the detour. She told me how she had planted flowers –'Wild Violets' she called them – in the place where she'd found her father's Will and amethyst. I asked her to send me a photo, but she insisted I see it for myself.

"Well, I can't disagree with that," I said, and had to punch the car horn at the idiot who cut me off. "What did you say? I couldn't hear you."

"I said what are you up to these days? You sound different. Different in a good way."

"Oh, you know Joy. Now that I'm fine and healthy again I might travel a bit, learn new languages, take up extreme sports. I could check into a hotel and sleep for a week. Or do none of that." I paused and smiled to myself. "I've actually been thinking that I just might get a job as a real Concierge."

CHAPTER 28.3.

I was plainly exhausted, and all of a sudden tired of running. "Unfortunately for you, grandfather," I said, "I do not *have* to listen to anything you say. I don't care about your deal; I don't care about you at all. You have both hurt every single person that I have ever loved, and I want you to leave before I have you thrown out." I was breathing harshly by the time that words finished exploding from my mouth.

The color had left Lord Watts' face and he stood like a pale, furious statue. Lady Watts just stood there with her mouth gaping open, glancing around like she was afraid someone would hear us. "You will lis..." he began. I screamed.

"Security, help!" If looks could kill, Lord Watts would have been my murderer. He turned abruptly on his heel as a security guard loped toward us, eyeing Lord and Lady Watts. My grandmother looked like a small animal scurrying behind her husband. I told the guard that I was just exhausted, and that they had already decided to leave. But there had been no mistaking the quick flash of fear behind Lord Watts' eyes.

I suddenly had to turn for the bathroom, but hadn't taken three before Brenda Rothschild appeared in front of me. The guard had gone. Her face took on a scarlet hue with her heavy breathing, and her arms hung stiffly at her sides above clenched fists. She hissed unintelligible words at me, and I realized suddenly that she was angry at my refusal of the Watts' proposal. Of course, it was all about the money. Brenda was working with them and it had always been about the money. My mother had loved and trusted this woman. These people had ruined her entire life, and mine. Grief for my father stabbed me; so many lives ruined for nothing more than money!

"I don't have the energy for this, Brenda, but you can rest assured that the Detectives will!" The color drained from her face in seconds. I seemed to have a talent for making people pale.

I finally took my much-needed bathroom break, then grabbed my cell and fished out the card from Detective Edwards. I dialed the number marked cell and he answered on the second ring.

I began to cry as soon as I had identified myself to him. "I know who killed Rosemary Devlin, and I know what happened at the warehouse today. I know why... I know why so many people have died." I told him the disjointed story, unable now to keep back my tears.

"Clarissa, where are you?" I hadn't completely finished, but Detective Edwards' voice was calm and soothing.

"I'm at the hospital with Jim," I answered. I sounded like a goose with something wet stuck in its throat.

"I want you to stay right where you are. Don't leave and don't talk to anyone you don't know. Do you understand me?"

I began to cry again, but it was from relief. "Yes, I understand." I felt strangely defeated by his passionless tone.

"There is a detective at the hospital on standing watch,"

Edwards told me. "His name is Saunders. Stay near him and I will be there as soon as I can." I said good bye and pushed my phone back into my pocket.

I stood in front of the sink and splashed water on my face. Looking at my image in the mirror with shining water dripping from my nose and chin, I hardly recognized myself at all. But that had seemed to become my reality now.

Something moved in the mirror, and I turned as something swung dangerously close to my head. I jumped and ducked, then found myself staring at Brenda again. Her face was contorted into a mask of hatred, and I couldn't help myself. I pushed her. Hard. Then I jerked open the bathroom door and ran screaming into the hallway. I was surrounded by hospital personnel in moments. I knew that I was hysterical, that my story made no sense to anyone, but I had lost all ability to contain myself. Kind, competent faces looked at me like I was the crazy one! A nurse checked the now empty bathroom and then quietly suggested that I return to Jim's room and wait for him to wake up.

An out-of-uniform detective watched the commotion down the hall from outside Jim's room, put away his cell phone, and sauntered toward me. He caught my gaze and held it until he stood inches from me.

"I'm Detective Saunders," he told me in a low voice. "I'm here to keep an eye on Jim and Joy, and I'd like to ask you to return to the room where I can be with you also." I felt a cascading flood of relief. I swallowed, nodded, and let him lead me down the hallway in silence. "Can I get you something to drink?" the detective asked me kindly.

I looked at him closely for the first time. He must have been in his early fifties, and his grey eyes flickered, looking everywhere at once. Yet I felt that he was fully aware of me too, that I had most of his attention.

"I'll be fine with tap water," I said.

"All right. I'm going to be right outside if you need me." I returned his smile weakly as I entered the room and quietly closed the door.

Joy had been moved into Jim's room, a curtain separating their beds. She turned her head, smiled weakly at me, and held out her hand with visible effort. Tears stung my eyes. I thought of Eduardo lying in a pool of blood, and I covered the distance quickly to grasp Joy's outstretched hand.

"This is an awful mess," she said, and her watery eyes made me want to break down all over again. "We were ambushed today. Dicky had been waiting on us, and I think Brenda was involved too." Her eyes drooped, the drugs blurring her words. "When Jim wakes up, he's going to realize it too. It's going to be hard on him, Clarissa."

I could only smile and grasp her hand. "You need to rest, Joy."

"I can't. There's so much you don't know. Please sit with me." She struggled to sit up, and I obliged her by only sitting halfway on the edge of the hospital bed. "You're in trouble, Clarissa. We all are. Richard Dane, the one called Dicky, he's a small time mobster. Brenda brought him in a long time ago to help her steal the Watts fortune. But your father disinherited his parents. As the Watts heir, he took possession of the Watts Estate and fortune when he was twenty-five. He might have named his parents as the substantial beneficiaries in his Will, but he told us that Lord and Lady Watts never wanted him. He was an heir to them, not a son. No one ever loved him until your mother. When they did what they did to Violet, he cut them out entirely." She took a deep breath. "And the whole thing belongs to you. Every asset, every penny. Their home, even the clothes on their backs...

it's all yours. And they worked with Dicky, Brenda, and the Devlins to make sure that that never happened."

Her voice was barely audible by the time she finished. I didn't want to burden her with anything else, so I kept Brenda's attack to myself. She mumbled something for a few seconds, and then her eyes closed for good and her breathing fell quickly into a deep, even rhythm. I laid her hand on the bed and silently returned to the chair at Jim's bedside.

I didn't want to think about this at all. The Watts fortune had brought everyone who touched it misfortune. I wasn't truly sure that I wanted it anyway.

I watched Jim's face, noted that even in a drugged sleep his features were gentle, kind. A sudden longing for him coursed through me when I thought about how much I actually loved the man. I leaned the chair back carefully and tried to relax.

It had been less than a year since I sat in the little bistro on the bottom floor of the Regency Hotel, sipping my juice and wondering what the Hotel had to do with my adoption. So much had changed since then; it felt like a thousand years ago. I almost smiled remembering the way I'd mistaken my father's joy at seeing me for flirtation.

I searched my memories for pieces to this puzzle that had left such jagged holes in all our lives. I knew a DNA test had been performed with a sample, probably from my own glass that very first day. That was how they'd found out that Patrick Devlin was not Violet's father. Lionel Watts had taken no chances where my parentage was concerned. Jim had already described the way he'd procured samples from Violet, the Devlins, Lionel, and Lord and Lady Watts. There was no denying that I was the biological child of Violet Devlin and Lionel Watts.

Then Lionel had set Jim on Richard Dane's trail. The invitation had led to a videotape that Jim had not seen yet incriminating his own mother. Richard Dane was a mobster. He had been involved with Brenda Rothschild for years, he had also been in bed with the Watts, Patrick Devlin, and even Creed. A circle of treachery that had devastated so many lives had been right under everyone's noses. Tears burned my eyes, but another breakdown was interrupted by movement from Jim's bed.

I opened my eyes to find him watching me. I gingerly moved to his side and bent to kiss his fevered forehead.

"I love you, Clarissa," he whispered. His voice was weak and I was afraid that if I touched him too much he would break. I lowered my forehead to his and wept softly with relief. He put his uninjured arm around my shoulders and grasped the nape of my neck through my hair. We waited for the storm to pass together. "Everything is going to be all right. I need to speak with the police. Can you call them for me?"

I looked at him and felt my body go cold. He was too weak to handle the truth of his mother. His knowing eyes searched my face.

"What's wrong?" He'd forced his voice louder than a whisper this time.

I quickly made the decision that I wouldn't lie to him. Too much had been damaged already over lies. "I've already called them." Jim blinked. "Detective Saunders is standing watch outside the room, and Detective Edwards is on his way."

He smiled a sweet, sleepy smile, and I knew that I'd made the right choice. I rested my lips on his forehead.

"You are an extraordinary woman, Clarissa. You may have to come to work for me."

I smiled and stood. Nausea hit me like a fist to the stomach. I clenched both hands over my mouth and fled the room. I burst blindly through the door and collided with two struggling men. Limbs sprawled in all directions, and I landed hard on my knees. It was hopeless; I vomited violently in the hallway until there couldn't possibly have been anything left in my stomach. A nurse was at my side before I could move.

I sat back against the wall, and with a shudder recognized the man securely handcuffed now. He sat beside me with his back against the same wall while Detective Saunders spoke quietly into his cell phone. That same man had been in Room 426 when I was kidnapped. I thought his name was Pervis, but I wasn't sure. My bumbling distraction had given Detective Saunders a chance to gain the upper hand and the prisoner's eyes bored into me.

I looked away and dabbed at my face with the nurse's cold cloth. I didn't feel any better. The nurse still hovered near me while other hospital staff moved in and out of the room. I got up slowly, my knees still shaking. I went back into the room, embarrassed now that I hadn't thought to use the toilet there first. Somehow Joy was still sleeping, but Jim was sitting up in bed waiting for me. There was a doctor with him.

"I want you to have some blood work done," Jim said. There was no question in his voice. "You've been through so much recently. This could just be dehydration, but it could be something else entirely. It would make me feel better." He ended the request on the one note with which he knew I couldn't argue.

I sighed and sat down. "I'm just exhausted, Jim. I don't really need to have tests run, but I will. For you. I'll do it later though, okay?" The doctor cleared his throat.

"I'm Dr. Wells, Clarissa," he said, offering his hand. I shook it. "I'll have someone from the lab come draw some blood samples. That way you won't have to leave Jim at all."

"Thank you," I said. "How's he holding up?"

Dr. Wells smiled down at Jim. "Well, he's lost some blood, but it was a clean wound. Jim is strong as an ox. With antibiotics and rest, he'll be his old self in no time." He winked.

"No permanent injuries?"

The doctor smiled at me, "No dear. He'll be fine."

I actually got angry with myself this time when I felt myself start to cry again. The doctor said his goodbyes, and basically ordered me to sip the water I held. I had to smile, and caught Jim's eye. "Don't worry," I said. "I'm fine." And to prove it I took a small sip. He smiled and shook his head.

A nurse entered shortly after with a cot and clean blankets. I helped Jim lay back to rest, slipped off my shoes, and lay down on my makeshift bed. My bones felt like they had all settled to the bottom, I was so tired. But the thought of Detective Edwards got me on my feet again. Where was he? I padded in my socks to the door and opened it carefully, making sure the path was clear this time before stepping through. Pervis was gone, and another officer in uniform sat outside the door with Detective Saunders. They smiled at my cautious exit. "Is Detective Edwards still coming?" I asked, returning their smiles.

"He'll be here," Saunders answered. "It might take a while, though. He and Ren are questioning Pervis at the station."

I thanked him, closed the door softly and returned to my waiting bed. I think I must have been asleep before my eyes closed. It was bliss until I was softly wakened by a small woman in scrubs. She had wheeled in a skinny tray of vials and syringes, and I sat up, still desperately wanting to hold on to sleep, to let her take the blood samples.

When she left, Jim whispered without opening his eyes. "Thank you." I smiled into my pillow as I drifted off to sleep.

I dreamed that I was very young and that I was afraid. My heart pounded, and I wanted to run but didn't know why. I saw a much younger Brenda Rothschild with a vaguely familiar man. They argued violently, and when I the man push her I ran...and I ran…

I woke up with my heart pounding like thunder, and the smell of food sent me scrambling for the toilet again. This time I made it to the one in the room. I had never felt so ill, and the sickening waves of nausea took a long time to go away.

"Are you all right, Clarissa?" I walked out slowly, steeling myself for the smells again. But they weren't that bad now.

"I'm fine." I knew I looked terrible.

"Do you think you're pregnant?" he asked.

I just froze. What a question. "I...I don't remember the last..." I had to stop as tears filled my eyes. He grinned and waved me over to the bed.

"Sit down," he said. I did, but couldn't help remembering what happened the last time this had come up. I think that was written clearly all over my face. With his good arm Jim pulled me close. "I don't want to upset you. It would be a good thing. Is there any better way to show how much we love each other than to have a baby?"

I relaxed against him and wrapped my arms around him gently. "I don't want to be disappointed again," I said into his chest. "Let's wait for the blood tests before we talk about this." He was fighting another huge smile when he gently pulled my chin up to look him in the eye.

"Okay. But if it's a boy, we're going to name him Lionel."

I couldn't help it. A dam burst from somewhere inside me and I cried as if I hadn't all day. I cried until I fell asleep, safely wrapped in Jim's body, and I did not dream.

Muted evening light spilled through the drawn hospital drapes. I was still in Jim's bed, but he was not. I stood and walked cautiously around the curtain that separated the beds. Jim and Detectives Saunders, Ren, and Edwards were seated in a loose circle around Joy's bed.

"We were trying not to wake you." Jim smiled tightly.

"It's good that you're awake now, though," said Detective Ren. Jim frowned at him and I knew immediately that something was wrong.

"We're about to watch the video, Clarissa. The one I told you about," Joy said, biting her lip.

"Do you know what's on that video, Jim?" I asked.

He hung his head. "I know a little bit. I know my mother attacked you this afternoon in the restroom." His eyes were heavy under a frown as he looked back up at me. "I know that she's been having an affair with Richard Dane for a long time, and I know that this video is incriminating. So, yeah. I'd say I do."

I walked around his chair while the Detectives set up the laptop to connect to the hospital television. I squeezed his shoulder. I didn't know what to say, but I could support him just by being there. One of the Detectives moved a chair next to Jim's for me, and I sat. He reached for my hand without looking as the video began. I held it in both of mine as Brenda Rothschild tip-toed to kiss Richard Dane on the television screen.

"That man was in the hospital when your dad was sick," I whispered.

Jim never flinched. "I know," he said softly. I squeezed his hand as the real-life characters on screen casually talked about Patrick Devlin wanting Creed out of the way, how they'd make it look like a suicide.

Dicky zipped Brenda's dress as they got ready, discussing what the suicide note would say. They had wanted Lionel to sign the Will that they forged, and had tricked him into signing it anyways despite his initial refusal. They were obviously very proud of themselves in recounting their success. The forged Will, birth certificate, and other papers that Joy had seen in the brief case at the Regency Hotel were all now in Brenda's possession. There was no mention of the DNA, so it was possible they didn't know the test existed.

"Rosemary told me she wouldn't let us get to Violet or Clarissa," Brenda said. She laughed as she told described Rosemary's accident, and how Patrick had helped Creed cover up her death. "Patrick would have killed her either way for her betrayal," she finished. "She was dead anyway."

Tears stung Clarissa's eyes, and she knew she hated this woman.

"Lionel will have to die. I'll let Creed do that; he's wanted to for a long time. His precious Violet loves Lionel instead, so it will be a simple matter." Dane laughed at the revelation. "The Will makes Patrick and Rosemary Devlin Clarissa's guardians until she turns twenty-five. Patrick will designate you as his beneficiary, as part of the agreement." They suddenly looked like a pair of demons in disguise. "The newspapers will love the headlines." He brandished his hands across an imaginary screen. "It'll be a nice flaming car crash for Patrick and Clarissa."

Brenda fiddled with her hair "I never did like that girl. I don't know how they ever found her as Clara."

Dicky helped her with her coat, then placed his hand on the small of her back as they left the apartment.

Jim cleared his throat. "Lionel Watts was a good man who loved his daughter very much. He was nobody's fool. He had a safety deposit box in his best friend's name. That's Andrew Cuomo, the Governor of New York." He gave a pointed glance to each Detective before continuing. "The real Will is in that box, and all the other original documents. They were created to stand on their own in court, in case something like this happened. Mr. Cuomo and I will swear to it as witnesses." The Detectives didn't say anything. There was a harsh note of finality to Jim's words, as though they had no say in what happened next. His voice softened when he looked at me. "There's also a letter in that box for you." Jim looked just as tired as his weakened voice sounded. "He only wanted the best for you."

I had to suddenly remove all the attention from myself. "You need to rest, Jim. The doctor said you need a lot of rest after losing all that blood." He looked at me without smiling, and struggled to his feet with a hand on the chair. Detective Ren took his arm and assisted me in getting him to bed. Jim cringed in pain as I helped him lay back, but I saw the tears in his eyes. That didn't have anything to do with the pain, and it sent a white hot rage through me. He was asleep as soon as his head hit the pillow.

Joy was staring wide-eyed at the blank television, looking a little more than tired.

"Maybe we should talk outside," I told the Detectives. The way it came out wasn't a suggestion, and while they glanced at me in surprise, they followed me out of the hospital room without question.

I looked into three serious faces. Competent, professional law enforcement, but I still did not feel safe. "What now?" I asked.

"We've already issued an arrest for Brenda Rothschild and Richard Dane, but we're having some trouble digging them out of the dirt."

It occurred to me then that my mother was missing too. I'd been so occupied and sick all day that I hadn't even noticed her leaving. "Have any of you seen or heard from my mother?" They gave me blank looks and shook their heads.

287

I rolled my eyes and dug in my pocket for my cell phone. Maybe she'd answer her phone for once. There was one missed call on the screen and a message from an unknown number. So I played the message.

"Ms. Clarissa Banks...this is Richard Dane." I immediately punched the speaker button. "I have your mother here with me. I want *you* in trade, then I will release her. If you don't come, I will kill her. I'll call you back." The line went dead and Clarissa fainted.

Detective Saunders caught her with little difficulty and Edwards held the door while he carried her to the cot. Detective Ren went called for a nurse, and dialing his cell with rapid, purposeful intent. The three Detectives were eventually joined by two more and they waited impatiently for Clarissa to regain consciousness.

Dr. Wells was making his rounds and returned to the hospital room. The Detectives grumbled to each other as he added Clarissa to the room's examinees. "She's pregnant," he said softly, "and I haven't given her the results of her blood-work yet. But this is too much stress and tension for her right now. She needs to rest. Don't let any other visitors in, and I'll have a nurse bring up a mild sedative for her. I think we should keep her excitement to a minimum tonight, hmm?" He peered over his glasses at the detectives.

Detective Adams and Roughney would replace Saunders and the extra uniformed officer for the night. Detective Ren gave strict orders not to leave their posts. No one knew where Dane was, and the cell phone he used to leave Clarissa the voicemail had been turned off.

There weren't any more visitors, but four hours into the new Detective guard shift a male nurse entered. He went first to Clarissa's cot to take her blood pressure and record the results on a clipboard. The Detectives watched with the tired expressions formed in routine. He moved to do the same with both Jim and Joy, who also slept through the process, and bid the officers a good night before leaving. Shortly after, another nurse showed up with a broad grin and her own notepad, explaining she was on her rounds to collect vitals.

Detectives Adams and Roughney exchanged nervous glances. "A male nurse was here about twenty minutes ago to check on them," Adams said. "Do you think you got your schedule confused?"

"We don't have a male nurse on this floor," the woman said. Her name tag read Crystal.

"Please go get the charge nurse now," Roughney said, and with wide eyes Crystal rushed off. Once the charge nurse appeared to confirm that Crystal was the actual nurse on rounds on this floor, and that the man who had entered earlier was not a hospital employee, everyone burst into action. Crystal was sent for the patient charts, the charge nurse called Security and handed the phone to Detective Adams, and then returned to the room to ensure that the patients were still all right.

Detective Roughney made a quick call to Edwards again, who was almost at the hospital by the time Crystal returned with the patient charts. Jim, Joy and Clarissa were roused from sleep for an update. Clarissa was groggy and could not fully comprehend what was patiently and repeatedly explained to her. Roughney filled Jim in on the phone call from Dane, and that an unexpected visitor had secretly come and gone. Clarissa was unsteady on her feet and Crystal helped her to the bathroom. The unmistakable sounds of retching echoed behind the closed door. Jim managed to overhear the charge nurse's orders for Clarissa's sedative, and a confirmative ultrasound when she was feeling better.

CWC – The Concierge

Detective Edwards finally arrived, and I heard Jim talking to him in quiet tones. Joy had drifted off and was sleeping soundly. I felt so weak I could barely move, and I realized that everything I'd eaten today had come back up. Jim put his arm around me as the nurse removed a gloved hand and what looked like a needle. He got on his knees and looked into my eyes. I tried to smile but my mouth wouldn't work right.

"Clarissa, can you understand me?" I just nodded, and closed my eyes after the room spun. "We're going to have a baby," he whispered in my ear. I opened my eyes and found happy tears in his. I tried to hug him but didn't have the strength.

"I love you," I told him, and fought to keep my eyes open.

As he bent to kiss her Jim, he slipped his arm partway under the pillow in an attempt to give her a hug in her sleep. His hand slid across a piece of paper, and he stopped. Slowly, he removed an envelope from under the pillow, stared at it, and called to the Detectives waiting outside. When he knew he had their attention, he opened the envelope and pulled out the single sheet of paper. He read aloud to the Detectives, who frowned and told him they'd need to take the whole thing in to check for prints.

Dearest Clarissa,

I hope one day you can forgive me. I am so proud of the young woman you have become.

I had been inconveniently shoved into the trunk of a car when I heard Dane leave that lovely voicemail for you. I had no doubt that you would try to help me, and that he would kill us both.

It was no little convenience that I managed to secret away the pistol from under the delicate Investigator noses this

290

morning, and it was a great comfort to me to have when I pretended to be unconscious. I listened to Brenda, Dane, and the Watts plan, in graphic detail, how they planned to murder both of us.

Please tell Jim that I am ever so sorry. His mother's body can be found with Dane at the Thrift Store, alongside Lord and Lady Watts. Everyone who ever sought to do you harm is gone now, my dear. It's all over.

I turned myself in to the Castle Hill Sanatorium about the time I paid that nice young man to deliver this to you. It is high time I focused on making some much needed changes in my life, and I don't know when I may be able to see you again.

My dearest Lionel and I, we may not have been the best parents, but we both loved you, Clarissa. In the end, we did what we had to do to protect you and keep you safe. Now you are.

Violet

Jim stared at the letter, then handed it to Adams. The charge nurse was at Clarissa's side again, checking her vitals and whispering in a soothing voice. Clarissa gave a tired cry that sounded more like relief than fear. He went to her.

I had heard Jim when he told me, but hearing the nurse's congratulations had hit the information home. I was still pregnant. Jim knelt beside my bed and I looked at him. I cracked a real smile, and glanced up at the ceiling in relief and understanding. I thought I had really been sick.

"I love you too," he whispered. His face said it better than his words when he placed his hand gently on my belly. "Both of you."

COLLABORATION

By Virginia Carraway Stark

Where did you go
And what are you doing there?
It's a puzzle
It's a riddle
It's a pile of yarn
With loose ends flying
It's not for the faint of heart
Be brave, be bold
But most of all be clever and true
When the baton is passed to you.
All that is asked
Is that you rise to the challenge and do your best
Grab the story with both hands
And tell the truth
Of what *you* think
Happens next.

www.ingramcontent.com/pod-product-compliance
Lightning Source LLC
Chambersburg PA
CBHW070313260626
47160CB00003B/823